I0710138

THE CY-SOLDIER FROM EARTH

A citizen of the planet Earth

Parts of this document were translated from the written "Standard Galactic" language, the official language of the Interstellar Condominium of Planets and Empires, (ICOPE); and also from the standard Reptiloid oral, written, and telepathic languages and published in the reader's native language. The memoirs of many Imperial Magi were also used by special permission of the Caretaker of the Eternal Archives of the Imperial Seers; which is buried deep under the surface of Empire Prime, the Capital Planet of the ICOPE!

(As per standard Empire notation, telepathic conversation by either Humanoids or Reptiloids is also translated into the reader's native language and is indicated by italics inside pound signs.)

JOHN R. CARDEN

Copyright © 2024 by John R. Carden

Paperback: 978-1-963883-64-0
eBook: 978-1-963883-65-7
Library of Congress Control Number: 2024907007

All rights reserved. No part of this publication may be reproduced, distributed, or transmitted in any form or by any electronic or mechanical means, without the prior written permission of the publisher, except in the case of brief quotations embodied in critical reviews and certain other noncommercial uses permitted by copyright law.

Copyright granted by the Emperor 513,348 AF (After Founding of ICOPE). Cautions against copying this document and also against slurring members of the Royal Line are stated in a section at the end of this document.

This Book is a work of fiction. Names, characters, places, and incidents either are the product of the author's imagination or are used fictitiously. Any resemblance to actual persons, living or dead, events, or locales is entirely coincidental.

Ordering Information:

Prime Seven Media
518 Landmann St.
Tomah City, WI 54660

Printed in the United States of America

This book is respectfully dedicated to the millions of military veterans and those men and women presently serving in the Armed Forces of the United States of America! It is especially dedicated to one very special United States Air Force veteran who faithfully served our nation during 'Nam: Larry Snyder of Huntsville, Texas; (the "Secretary of the Air Force" in one of my books; <u>Samson Blair the Time Marshal!</u>) Since our Country's founding; without the valor and total commitment to Duty by the men and women serving in our Army, Navy, Air Force, Marines, Coast Guard, and our other "Armed Forces"; during peace time; the "Cold War"; and the wars necessary to literally protect the whole world; our very blessed Country; our basic freedoms; and the customs and traditions that we take for granted; would have long ago ceased to exist; being replaced by tyranny!

TABLE OF CONTENTS

PROLOGUE

One of the most technically advanced planetary empires, populated mostly by one of the "Hunan" subspecies of the "Reptiloid" race of sentient beings; is situated in the Cletorian System; (which has been give various nicknames such as "The R System"; the "Worlds of Continuous Thunder"; or "Thunder Alley")! Its population is situated mainly on three large and unique planets; Reptilon, Reptilee, and Reptilus; (the last planet being named after the wise and powerful Reptiloid being who ultimately united the system under one government. These three planets are officially called the "Thunder Worlds"; for good reason! The entire surfaces of all three planets are crisscrossed almost daily with violent thunder storms; which produce extremely intense cloud-to-ground lightning, so-called "Red Sprites"; and cloud-to-space bolts called "Blue Jets"! Every so often there are strange ground-to-cloud emerald-colored lightning flashes called "Green Bolts"; and ground-to-ground brown-colored bolts called "Brown Bolts" because of their unique color! All these electric bolts literally crashing up; sideways; down; and around the environment of the Thunder Worlds; makes the surfaces of the planets very dangerous to beings that are not resistant to lightning strikes; as all of the "Reptiloid Species" of beings native to the planets have to be; or their entire species would have long since been totally destroyed!

But in addition; the "Blue Jets" darting upward through the atmosphere of each of the Thunder Worlds are very dangerous to unprotected spacecraft entering or leaving the planet and satellites in low orbit!

About a thousand years ago; a system-wide civil war culminated in the total, and extremely difficult, unification of all the planets in the solar system; with the huge Reptiloid named "Reptilus" being the first of a line of many competent reptile rulers to be crowned absolute monarch of the solar system! When Reptilus died during a traditional "Succession Duel"; after a very successful wise reign of several hundred years; he was buried with full military honors by literally the entire population of the United Planets of the Thunder Worlds in attendance or watching or listening by electronic media! Then by full agreement of the King's Counsel of Advisers and the permission of the entire "Egg Line Family" of Reptilus, the huge center claw on his primary, right top limb was ceremonially removed at his funeral; hermetically sealed in a layer of extremely hard "Eternium Plastic"; and used thereafter by each Reptiloid planetary ruler who was legally crowned Ruler of the System; as a visible symbol atop the Royal Scepter of the king's absolute power! But, as the oral; telepathic; and the written histories from many races of beings throughout the Time Span of the Cosmic All have frequently recorded; it is a fact that any tool; weapon; and/or any religious or political "symbol" can be used or manipulated for both "Good" and for "Bad"; and as such; what became known as the "Claw of Reptilus" proved to be no exception to that wise bit of wisdom! It was a perfect example of the common saying on at least several hundred thousand planets in the ICOPE and its Sphere of Influence: **Power tends to corrupt; and absolute power corrupts absolutely!"**

Thus; as the Annals of the Imperial Magi have recorded many times through the over five hundred thousand years of the Empire; when a planetary or multi-planet or interstellar government gains absolute power over a world or a federation or an interstellar confederation; it usually tends to slowly become totally corrupt; then over decades or centuries or millennia; the totalitarian regime slowly starts to disintegrate; which causes the government's society to gradually slide into anarchy and total chaos! The Thunder Worlds were no exception to this maxim about the ultimate downward "spiral of power" for any planetary, interplanetary, galactic, or intergalactic government!

But could anything save the "Thunder Worlds" from anarchy when one fateful day another rival planetary confederation stole their precious political symbol? Only the "Winds of Destiny" knew if there were enough reptile patriots living on the troubled planets who had enough Backbone; or in the case of the Reptiloids; **cartilage**; to organize a sufficient force to rise up in time; and know what to do; in order to save their home worlds from being taken over and probably destroyed by their enemies! Because of their unique powers; the legendary and controversial Winds of Destiny; (See Appendix II); knew the <u>probable</u> outcome of the future civil conflict on the Thunder Worlds; but they very rarely communicate or interfere in the affairs of any solid sentient being living on any planet in the Cosmic All! (An exception to their rule is documented in both sections of the Imperial document **Two Time Winners** – "Ryan Nelson Bax-ter Jones" and "Blow"; and also in the Imperial Document **Cleonardo the Trecian Witch!**; one or both of which should available at your local Imperial library; online store; or local bookstore.)

And so; with the ultimate fate of the Thunder Worlds in jeopardy; and the fabled and very controversial Winds of Destiny watching; several seemingly unimportant players; each of which were somehow also involved in their own personal Ultimate Destiny; slowly moved into position on the Main Galactic Time Line! These sentient beings; who were to soon play major parts on the so-called "Galactic Checkerboard of Power"; were as yet unaware of their importance and how their moves on their own Life Path would ultimately determine their own . . . . **Ultimate Fate!**

CHAPTER 1

It seemed to be a typical day at the imposing subterranean Imperial Seers headquarters of the ICOPE, (Interstellar Condominium of Planets and Empires), on the Capital Planet called "Empire Prime", which is situated in the First Quadrant of the Official Original Mapping of the Cosmic All; produced by the Empire's first FTL robot mapping endeavor several hundred thousand years ago. Working in the deep basement of the heavily shielded and physically protected building, a mid-range seniority Seer with the formal public Magi name of "Rondoe Kanne" was checking messages that had been received on the Imperial FTL exclusive com channel reserved for the Imperial Mages to send messages; when he noticed an alert broadcast by an Imperial Seer named "Kancor Crokan", who was stationed in a far off quadrant of the galaxy! In the last few hours the Mage had sent several reports electronically; (all of which would be saved in the "Annals of the Imperial Seers" for all of Eternity!) They had been automatically printed out on archaic paper, sent telepathically, and also sound recorded, by the far off Magi; to alert the rest of his "Scout Team" at Imperial Seer Headquarters to the fact that his mindar senses had detected a particularly strong belt of the fabled, and controversial; "Winds of Destiny" blowing into his present position! Kancor Crokan reported that; after precise research using FTL communications lines to tap into Imperial data banks on Empire Prime and use astronomical information compiled over the entire history of the Empire; and originally transmitted by robot scouts; he had found that the vector's only possible source was a small insignificant solar system a few million light years away from the Capital Planet.

Because of the alert given in this communication, Rondoe Kanne; at this time the only Seer on duty in the Magi's secret headquarters which is deep underground on Empire Prime; followed standard protocol and investigated the possible source in the region by using his mentally controlled computer to follow up the example of the reporting Seer and tap into the Royal Astronomers' enormous database of suns, comets, and solar systems; which had been mapped out by the ships of ICOPE'S Royal Survey ships and also by robot space probes over the long millennia of the Empire's existence; in order to double-check Seer Kancor Crokan's information before sending it to the other Imperial Magi. Adding to the information given by the other Seer by checking other sources on Empire Prime; he found the small planetary system where the Winds of Destiny were supposedly blowing from, only contained eight planets; and one "dwarf planet"; of which; only one planet was heavily inhabited by a Humanoid-type species of beings known as "Humans". The rest of the planets were either "gas giants"; composed mostly of methane and other gases; and barren; rocky globes; a few of which had only scientific outposts sparsely inhabited by the Humanoids using pressurized settlements and supplied by crude chemical rockets.

The area around the small solar system also had a very large "Oort Cloud" far outside the system which contained billions upon billions of large and small pieces of so-called "space debris". Also a little further in toward the system's sun was a large "Kuiper Belt" containing icy planetoids and comets; most of which orbited in and out of the orbits of the eight planets and one dwarf planet; sometimes colliding with the planets with disastrous results; and forming "rings" around a gas giant the Humanoids call "Saturn"!

Also the Imperial probes found that farther out from the Kuiper Belt there orbited an extremely large planet which was undetected by the Humanoids inhabiting the solar system. Over the last fifty years, the astronomical literature of the single inhabited planet hinted that there seemed to be a very large object orbiting extremely far out from the sun; but its true orbit was unknown; and it would not be found until the technically backward Humanoids were able to produce more advanced spacecraft and space sensors in several hundred years.

The seemingly unimportant and unimpressive solar system also had a very large asteroid belt; containing literally trillions of objects, in the middle of the orbits of the major planets; where perhaps, in the distant past, a medium to large planet broke up for some reason; (such as a prehistoric atomic war or a collision with a large asteroid, a comet, or some other huge object orbiting in from the solar system's previously mentioned Oort cloud and/or Kuiper Belt).

The mentally-skilled Magi all around the Cosmic All who were following what was going on immediately wondered how such an insignificant; tiny group of planets in such an out-of-the-way place could somehow produce or contain such a rare event that would suddenly become so important that the eerie Winds of Destiny would somehow take notice of its importance as a pivotal local "Anchor Event"; or even perhaps a "Galactic Anchor Event"''; and begin to rise to gale force so that it could be detected so far away from the Happening!!

Bringing up the protocol for investigating such an Event on his very large holographic compu-screen; the experienced young Seer Rondoe Kanne; with five hundred years of Magi mental experience; familiarized himself with the procedures to research such an important extremely rare event and began to use his mental powers to visualize the Galactic Time Stream in order to try to research the unknown possible present "Happening"; future "Happening"; or quite possibly even an extremely rare "Galactic Anchor Event"; which had been indicated by the unusual outpouring of the Winds of Destiny from such an insignificant place!

But even as Rondoe Kanne; closely following the strict protocols taught him during his Magi training in the Imperial Seer Headquarters which; as documented before; was buried at a secret location several hundred Imperial miles deep under the surface of Empire Prime; started to use his extremely rare cerebral powers to attempt to mentally sense the Galactic Time Stream and also try to cerebrally reach across millions of light years to investigate the important happening from far across the Cosmos; **something suddenly changed**! Instead of obtaining different facts from the two different sources like he expected, the Magi was astounded when an extremely rare event happened! The two totally different visual and mental information sources matched--exactly! At the lowest levels of his mental being the Seer suddenly sensed the information that he seeking; with his mental visualization powers; from the tiny solar system's far off Time Stream; **totally matched and backed up the information that he obtained from his visualization of the Main Galactic Time Stream!** Both data sources revealed the same amazing fact that at such an insignificant; unimportant; and "out-of-the-way" place as the small solar system, (whose only inhabitants were weak Humanoids possessing few mental talents; and having an extremely low technological base); incredibly against all the odds and for one of the few times in all of the detailed Galactic History, (faithfully recorded by the Emperor's Advisory Council, called the Imperial Magi); a so-called "**Galactic Anchor Event**" was actually, (and impossibly); about to happen!

Immediately Seer Rondoe Kanne again followed standard protocol and used the Magi FTL emergency com system to send an alert about his sensing to all the Seers who were the closest to the general area where the Winds of Destiny were being produced. Almost instantly Rondoe received several answers to his message on his floating holographic computer screen. One by one most of the Seers in the area reported that, as yet; they had not yet detected the Winds of Destiny with their mental powers because their location was not in the vector of the flow of the Winds! They reported that they would immediately try to investigate the location of the possible "Galactic Anchor Event" and report back to him if they could visualize any other important information different from what he had just transmitted to them.

As the Seer read their replies on the holographic screen, he wondered if the very important projected "Galactic Anchor Event" would be so powerful and so important that it would somehow affect him on Empire Prime; and even possibly affect the entire Cosmic All by changing the path of the Intergalactic Time Stream! To find out the answer to this important question, Rondoe immediately mentally transposed to a sound-proof and sensor-proof room in his apartment in order to mentally focus on the important event which was about to happen! The Seer relaxed in the darkened room and began to attempt to "tune in" and use his extremely rare mental powers in order to try to visualize the unique Cosmic Event that was unfolding so far across the Universe in the small solar system; that, according to the unprecedented magnitude of the outpouring of the Winds of Destiny; perhaps would affect him and possibly virtually every sentient being in the Cosmic All!

As subsequent events on the Main Galactic Time Line that were affected by "The Anchor Event of the Millennia" were studied as they happened by the Imperial Seers at that particular position on the Galactic Time Stream; and also by every Seer investigating "The Event of the Millennia" for the next million years would prove; most of the answers to Rondoe Kanne's important mental question that they could visualize were "**YES**"; but not all!!! So because of this fact; all the Seers could state before the Happening occurred; was that the Event **PROBABLY** would eventually affect Empire Prime-but they could not **KNOW FOR SURE;** until the **EVENT** got much closer to actually happening; was in the process of happening; or had finished!!

The Seer's prediction was correct; but not in the way Magi Rondoe Kanne could ever have imagined; or at the present time on the Main Galactic Time Stream; have been able to visualize! As yet, as the ultra-important event had not yet unfolded; even the Winds of Destiny could not visualize just what would happen; and how it would affect literally every sentient being in the Cosmic All! Because it had not happened yet; one small facet of The Happening could suddenly and unexpectedly change and literally erase the Event from ever occurring; or work to create an entirely different "Anchor Event"! Ergo, all the Magi and the Winds of Destiny could do was . . . . . . **WAIT!**

CHAPTER 2

As previously mentioned in the Official Imperial Document above, it came to pass that at a particular instant on the Main Time Stream; far, far across the Cosmic All; at a position extremely distant from where he was situated on the enormously important Capital Planet of Empire Prime; Seer Rondoe Kanne was investigating with his mental powers a very small solar system that apparently was the source of the very rare surges of the fabled and famed Winds of Destiny from such an unimportant place. He checked the available Imperial robot survey records and found that the solar system in question had a very small sun and only one planet inhabited by one of the literally hundreds of Humanoid species of beings that live on planets in the ICOPE sphere of influence, or in sections of space mapped by Imperial FTL robot probes throughout the centuries. So apparently, the cause of the surge was somewhere on a very small; seemingly unimportant planet! Rondoe thought that perhaps one of the Humanoids had somehow invented a unique destructive device that would somehow affect a very large area; or perhaps the planet was about to explode and cause the gas giants in the small solar system to ignite and create two new suns; or explode and the expanding cloud created by the explosion would somehow; someday; or some millennia; the resulting radioactive cloud would somehow affect a large area; thus affecting the entire Cosmic All! But the missing answer to an important question was **HOW** such a small and insignificant planet could cause such an outpouring of the Winds of Destiny? The Seer knew that he had to find out the reason and the only way was to use his trained mental talents, even though he only had five hundred years of experience! So hour after hour and day after day the Magi tried to extract more information from the Main Galactic Time line and its branches using his rare mental abilities; with perhaps the future of his home planet; or even the fate of the Empire; both at stake!

As he worked, Magi Rondoe Kanne suddenly got an idea that perhaps learning more physical information about the suddenly important planet would help in his very vital quest. Further research produced the fact that the small orb's sentient inhabitants were Humanoid beings who called themselves "Human Men and Women". The very small planet was covered mainly with the rare substance known as H_2O, called liquid "water"; instead of the much more common liquid deuterium, or "heavy water"; which is the liquid that is vital to the metabolism of most Humanoid beings throughout the Cosmic All. Since most of the surface of the planet being examined was covered with the regular water; this left only a very small portion of the planet's surface to be solid ground on which its inhabitants could live and build their living structures.

But other than those few physical facts obtained from the automaton probes, there was no new information to help Rondoe Kanne solve the riddle! Perhaps he could obtain reports written by "Proxies", or Imperial Citizens living on the planet, whose job was to provide information about the planet. But even as he looked for such reports, the Seer did not think that such a small and insignificant planet would not have anything reported about it. To his amazement, he found that for some unknown reason, Proxies had been stationed on the planet literally for centuries and had filed regular reports! But he wondered why would such a small, insignificant planet have Proxies stationed there for so long? Did the Imperial officials in charge of stationing Proxies on alien planets know ultra-secret information that was not in the intelligence reports or the data banks about the planet? He did not know and probably could not find out through "regular channels"; so he would have to use unorthodox sources of information! (One reason for "Proxies" being stationed on Earth is given in **One Time Winner!** and also see Appendix III of this document.)

Patiently, hour after hour; day after day; as Seer Rondoe Kanne used intensive visual and mental probing to investigate into the matter, he found no other sources that could help his quest for important information! So because the Magi could not obtain what he was seeking; he became more and more convinced that further facts about the planet, and the "Galactic Anchor Event" that was happening or about happen; would have to be wait for further examination on or near the planet by Imperial "proxies"; or by personally interviewing the Empire's representatives! But if the so-called "Galactic Anchor Event" lasted long enough, information could possibly be obtained by Magi taken close to the planet by units of the Imperial Navy. The closer the Seers were to the event or events that they were trying to visualize; the stronger and more accurate their visions would become.

But eventually; when all the pertinent facts had been discovered and the single reason for the Winds of Destiny almost continuously surging was eventually discovered; the underlying cause was amazing; unique; and literally almost "mind-blowing" to the Seers who were given the assignment to travel to Earth to find the answer to the perplexing riddle of what was causing the Winds to blow so heavily over so long a record distance!! The incredible cause that all of their visions indicated was the source of the surging of the Winds was only caused by what was seemingly the benign actions of <u>a single Humanoid being</u>; <u>living on the very low-tech planet with no FTL spaceship technology</u>!!

Before this Unique Event; to list only a few examples; Galactic History recorded that such an immense outpouring of the Winds had previously only been caused by such "universe shaking events" as an impending barbarian invasion of Empire Prime; large escape migrations of sentient beings caused by multiple supernovas in the same general area of a nearby galaxy; an invasion of the Empire sphere-of-influence by a member of the ultra-powerful "First Citizen race"; and the invention of the first FTL drive by one of the first Imperial scientists in the first planetary government based on Empire Prime! **But during the over five hundred thousand year history of the Imperial Seers, such an outpouring had never been caused by the actions of such a single unimportant small object; by a single event; or by the benign; harmless actions of one mentally and physically weak sentient** being who was simply "minding his own business"; while roaming around his small planet without causing any uproars; riots; or disturbances!

And so it came to pass that several Imperial Magi; aided by the "proxies" or Imperial citizens who had been assigned to live on the planet for intelligence purposes; covertly transposed to the planet's surface by the very famous HMS "Sargon". Operating separately, they each had tried to visualize and understand who or what was causing the Winds to blow so much; since it could not be just one Humanoid! But as each Seer, stationed at different positions on the planet, pondered their daily visions to find out the cause of the rare surge, they never dreamed what their Magi powers would ultimately reveal! Amazingly when all the Proxy Magi signaled that they were ready to assemble for a conference, for the first time in the history of the Cosmic All, when the Magi convened in a secret meeting to compare their findings, each of their separate visualizations of the Galactic Anchor Event as it was unfolding, produced the same Galactic Time Stream visions that indicated all the Past, Present, and Future possibilities of the very important Galactic Anchor Event!!! Their extremely rare mental powers indicated that incredibly, it had been/it was/it would be, **caused by the same Humanoid "Man" simply moving about the planet**; without, (at that moment); causing any harm to any other being! If their visions had indicated that a powerful Reptiloid leading a planetary war that would spill out into the galaxy was causing the Winds to cascade, maybe they could have believed; but for the surge to be caused by a single weak Humanoid traveling alone on the surface of the orb, never bothering any other Humanoid, and very rarely talking to anyone?!?! **NO WAY!** But there had to be an unknown reason for such harmless actions to cause the Winds to accelerate; and all the Magi had to do was find it! If the harmless Humanoid was not presently doing something to cause the Winds of Destiny to rise to gale force; perhaps the Winds were simply indicating that he had done something in the "Past" or would do something in the "Future" on his personal Life Path that had been, or would be Extremely Important!?!

But, after they had positively identified the single Humanoid who was causing all the ruckus by the Winds, and whose actions perhaps sometime in the coming days, weeks, or years would literally change the course of the Main Galactic Time Stream, all the Seers could legally do was covertly watch, and secretly wait to see what would eventually transpire; they could not intervene using their mental powers to change what they had found out!! Under the strict Imperial Laws concerning the use of their mental powers and the actions which were possible and legal to be done by the Seers after they had obtained information using their visions; and those actions which were possible and yet illegal by the Seers; the Magi could not interfere or even mentally, or using any other form of communication, contact the "Anchor Event Person" or any being on the planet Earth with information about what had happened, what was happening, or what would happen, which they had visualized using their mental powers! The Imperial laws concerning the use of the mental powers of Magi were very strict; in order to prevent permanent damage to the Main Galactic Time Line! Stipulations of the Imperial laws stated that even if the actions of a <u>single Seer</u> would save the life of one being; or save one planet, one solar system, or one whole galaxy from destruction; **THE SINGLE MAGI BY THEMSELVES**

COULD NOT LEGALLY ACT BY CONTACTING, BY ANY METHOD, AT ANY "TIME" IN THE PAST; THE PRESENT; OR THE FUTURE; THE ANCHOR EVENT PERSON OR PERSONS IN THEIR VISIONS, OR ANY BEING WHO MIGHT MAKE CONTACT WITH THE "PIVOTAL PERSON(S)"; AT ANY "PRESENT"; "PAST"; OR "FUTURE" POSITON ON THE MAIN GALACTIC TIME LINE! ALL ANY SINGLE SEER BY THEMSELVES COULD DO WAS WATCH, WAIT, AND DOCUMENT THE EVENT AS BEST THEY COULD! Then they world record their visual findings on their eternal records which would still exist deep under the surface of the Capital Planet when the last sun of the billions upon billions of suns in the Cosmic All ceased to shine, and all radioactive substances had transmuted to lead!

But there was an important exception to this important rule! If the Magi visualizing the important event thought the event was of sufficient importance to somehow act to change it; they could then give the information about their vision to a committee of Senior Imperial Seers and let them decide if the Magi should intervene on the Main Galactic Time Line in order to keep stability on the Time Line and prevent chaos! (There have only been a relatively few times in Galactic History when this happened; and their effect on the Main Galactic Time Line is still being studied!)

All the important documentation about the Event was available to any Seer for mental or visual reading, but any information which they obtained and visually or mentally read could not be told to any other living being, except covertly to another Seer; who also could not reveal any of the information at any time in the "Past"; the "Present", or the "Future" positions on the Main Galactic Time Line! Although at first glance these laws seem harsh and senseless, they have been; and are actually very wise; since they were all designed to prevent the creation of "Alternate Timelines", "Alternate Realities", "Time Paradoxes", and damage to the Main Galactic Time line; if at any time during their long existence the Imperial Seers had been allowed to "dabble" with other Time Lines in order to prevent some terrible disaster like all the population of a planet being killed when its radioactive core exploded, or even to save the lives of billions or trillions of sentient beings!

But again and again, incredibly; as each of the unbelieving Magi reinvestigated; each and every one of their separate visions again impossibly found that; instead of being caused by something catastrophic like the historic Hunan invasion force headed for Empire Prime several hundred thousand years ago, or a Super Nova whose radiation would strike Empire Prime or other important inhabited planets; for some unknown reason, the source of "The Gale Force" cascade of The Winds was actually just **ONE** seemingly unimportant young male Humanoid life form living on the small planet's surface; doing nothing to warrant the Winds of Destiny rising to gale force!

The Imperial Seers could not believe this fact; so they kept up their mental investigations!! Day after day, the Magi visualized that he was riding alone; not causing any trouble or conversing with anyone else for days on end! He was simply riding what in their mental pictures seemed like an extremely primitive and very crude, internal combustion-powered; two-wheeled vehicle, (which he had named "Daisy

Mae" after his mother); down relatively smooth petroleum-surfaced roads on the only densely settled planet in the small solar system!

Incredibly; against all logic and against all the experience of the Magi during the half-million years of their existence; all their visions showed that it was apparently just the seemingly insignificant act of one small Humanoid being; riding an obsolete vehicle down a primitive tar-covered road; that was causing the Winds of Destiny to rise to gale force! Since the Humanoid male was not interacting with any other being, it had to be that the Winds of Destiny knew of a "Pivotal Event" that he would be involved in; sometime in the very near Future; which caused them to surge at the present time! But how far in the "Future"? Unfortunately, at that instant on the Galactic Time Line, the visions of the Imperial Magi did not extend that far!

So all the Magi could do was to 28 hours a day and 8 days an Imperial week; try to visualize what was happening/what was about to happen/and/or what was going to happen in the "Future" on the Main Galactic Time Line to the "Lone Humanoid", as he came to be nicknamed! The extremely delicate mental research by the Imperial Seers produced some other very intriguing information about the Humanoid; which is documented in the following pages!

CHAPTER 3

The visualizations of the "Lone Humanoid"; i.e., the single sentient being, who was apparently causing the surge of the Winds; enabled the Imperial Magi to find out vital information about the "Man"; including the unique, descriptive name usually given to every Humanoid male being in that solar system. They found out by translating various signs and printed pages in their visions that he was known, by various members of the Military and Civilian segments of the Humanoid society on the continent on which he was born, by the name of "Samuel Eliot Steele". (For a short time the Magi visualized another young man they finally identified as rookie patrolman "Barney Drum" and at first thought that he was the ultra-important Humanoid causing the Winds of Destiny to surge; but subsequent visualizations corrected that notion. Drum was only a good friend to the Humanoid man causing the "ruckus"!)

Samuel Steele could be described using the military jargon of any civilized planet in the Empire as a "blooded warrior"; "a very experienced combatant"; and "a being to have at your back when the going got tough in combat"! Using more common civilian terms used on the small planet, it could be said that the young Humanoid, (who was called a "Man" on that particular planet; instead of the terms "Klip", "Xenor", or "Quan"; which are used to describe or name, Humanoid males on other planets in the Empire); at the present time was a so-called "military combat veteran". The young male, also called "Slate" by his close friends; specialized in covert operations involving dangerous secret missions. He could literally fly anything with or without wings, (such as a lifting-body fighter, a propeller plane, or a very crude spacecraft barely able to reach 18,000 mph and unable to travel outside the orb's solar system)! The Man was also very expert in to-the-death hand-to-hand combat anywhere on or off the world!

The Magi also found that several of the planet's years ago, Humanoid Slate had been "honorably discharged" from serving in one of his country's military branches, after being highly-decorated for his long, dedicated and committed covert service on literally all seven continents of the Earth; and under most of its seas and oceans! He had also incredibly survived several extremely dangerous missions on the Earth's moon, and had successfully completed several ultra-secret missions on the planet, in the small solar system, called "Mars"! But sadly for Imperial Historians researching Earth's history, those covert; extremely secret missions, described by the planet's military forces as "Above Top Secret Operations"; will probably be buried in bureaucratic secrecy for at least several hundred years!

During that "Time Interval before the Anchor Event", if you ever happened to meet him, the young "Man", (as

Imperial Cartographers and Being Species Researchers finally have officially labeled the particular branch of the Humanoid species that live on the small planet Earth), outwardly appeared to be a normal, ordinary Humanoid bipedal being, four Earth "inches" over six Earth "feet" tall, of medium build, with short, blond hair, usually cut to "military specifications", i.e., very short, and having piercing brown eyes which made many people uncomfortable when he looked into their "eyes"; as the vision organs of the Earthian Humanoids are called.

Throughout his early life Samuel Steele was known by various "handles". The man was known to his hometown friends when he was a Cleburne High School "Yellowjacket" as "Speedy"; which described his blazing foot speed! He also starred as the star "quarterback" on the "Football Team", (an archaic local physical game), in his hometown of Cleburne, Texas; and was a close friend to Barney Drum, the Humanoid male that was at first thought to be the one that was causing the Winds to blow so hard. When Samuel Steele graduated from High School and joined the U.S. Marines, to his closest military buddies, for some unknown reason, he was given the nickname "Slate". As he rose in military rank, to his military "acquaintances" he was known as Major Steele; and to his old Marine DI Larry "Sarge" Snyder, who he loved like his own Daddy back in his hometown; in private he was called affectionately "Son" or "Boy"; and in public, just Major Steele. He was also known to his closest military comrades and loyal friends on all the bases around the world where he served his country as simply **"THE MAN"**; a soldier to have with you in a "fire fight" because when the going got **TOUGH,** he would never flee; he would ALWAYS protect a comrade's back instead of retreating; and his body bore many scars to prove it!

In order to have any chance of meeting the Humanoid usually called Slate, after he retired from his planet's military and started roving; you would have to be traveling on the continent called "North America"; virtually anywhere on one of the antiquated country two-lane highways; from the Arctic northern part of the continent, to the warm south. The combat veteran never traveled around the crowded parts of the continent on many of the new extremely wide automated 16-lane auto-pave and steel lines designed for unmanned transportation rail, monorail, and "park and ride" vehicle systems. The man called Slate would always be seen wandering alone on the old-fashioned highways of the states or countries called "Alaska", the "United States", "Canada", and "Mexico", on a vehicle that looked and sounded like what the Earthians called an obsolete, two-wheeled, gasoline or diesel-powered "motorcycle".

But outward visual appearances can be deceiving because internally, the 2-wheeled vehicle was actually a highly modified in-line electric motorcycle; which used heavy-duty, high-capacity; deep cycle "Trankor-brand" Tri-Lithium batteries continuously recharged by a deuterium-powered generator; with solar power used to lengthen its range by during daylight helping to continuously produce electric power and thus decreasing the consumption of its deuterium fuel. The design of the vehicle had several other hidden; and very advanced "features"; such as solar cells, disguised as fancy buttons on the leather fringe all over the top and the sides of the motorcycle, to add extra range to the two-wheeled electric-powered vehicle; and various infrared, sonic, and microwave sensors to provide nighttime protection while Slate was sleeping.

Whenever any passerby traveling in another vehicle observed the young man, he was always traveling aimlessly alone; camping on the eastern seaboard in a sturdy one-man tent to have protection from the rain of a "Nor'easter" one week; then the next week, literally freezing up in Adak, Alaska, wearing warm clothing for a few days! He would then next be seen visiting the cool Canadian Rockies for a few days in faded long-sleeved shirts; and a few days later wading barefooted on the warm Gulf Coast sandy beaches in a bathing suit with a "U.S. Marines" emblem on it, compliments of his very decorated Marine veteran dad; (to whom he could never show most of his military decorations, most of whom were labeled "Ultra-Top Secret"!).

After a circular route of travel lasting several months to a year, following a certain routine of touring moving literally from the top to the bottom of the so-called "North American Continent"; his cycle of travel would start all over again, using different roads; and ultimately covering most of the dirt backroads and two-lane highways of the entire continent every few years. Slate always wanted to use different routes; guided by the small but effective LED computer screen situated below his cycle's handle bars, which showed the output of a GPS navigation system which was a smaller and more advanced descendant of the installation that had been put on the good old F-111 "Aardvark"! Slate liked to use the system so that every year he could go to different places to see the sights, make new friends, eat new exotic foods, and always trying to have a good time; **in order to try to forget certain painful facts.**

But wherever he was, the young man was always constantly looking around and alertly observing everything around his immediate vicinity with "his head on a swivel", as if he were still on an authorized combat mission in enemy territory. But contrary to other retired military veterans, Slate was not "ultra-alert" because he was dangerous to anyone and suffering from "combat fatigue", "post-traumatic stress fatigue syndrome", or some other combat-caused condition. His idiosyncrasy to be so watchful at all times was simply the fact that, since early childhood, he just liked to be alert to everything that was going on around his position. His loving parents had also taught him the "Golden Rule"-"**Do unto others as you would have them do unto you**". Because of this alertness, as he roved far and wide, whenever he saw anyone in trouble or needing help, the young man would always stop and render aid, such as helping to change a tire, "jumping" a stalled car off with his portable "Atomic Jump-Off Battery" that he always kept charged in his saddlebags, or while eating at a fast food restaurant even giving CPR or the "Heimlich Maneuver" to anyone in distress! He would also provide all the assistance he could to any homeless person that he saw walking along the highway he was traveling. Following the Golden Rule, he would give out blankets, food, and/or warm coats in the wintertime; fold-up umbrellas to hikers any time it was raining, or even monetary help; to be used to buy food, to anyone he saw in need! After several years of roaming and doing good deeds, Slate had earned a very good reputation all along his usual routes of travel, and the local people in each of the towns that he regularly visited began to look forward to his consistent stops; and always invited him to come back in a few years!

Whenever Slate happened to meet one of the people he had helped in the past, the person usually remembered what he had done, and would attempt to "return the favor" by trying to pay for a meal. Most of the time the young Marine veteran agreed to have a meal with the grateful person but would always manage to covertly slip money to the waiter to pay for the food; then have the waiter tell the person that someone else in the restaurant paid for the meal! This would always add to his "lucky" reputation that good things seemed to happen around the young military veteran! After always shaking hands with the person that he had the meal with, Slate would leave the restaurant and continue on what was literally his "journey to nowhere"; in search of the elusive goal of "peace in his heart" that would somehow calm the fierce storm in his Soul!

The hidden real reason for his seemingly aimless travel was to somehow mentally cover and try to forget something very traumatic—something very personal; painful; and heart-wrenching that had happened in the past! The man traveled frugally; spending very little except for new energy packs for "Daisy Mae", his Andorse Servo-Electric Motorcycle, every six months or so when the Tri-Lithium batteries; which were continuously being recharged by a deuterium-powered generator; wore out from such hard, almost 24-7 use. The young Humanoid male very rarely stayed at any of the cheap motels on the antiquated highways on which he always traveled; preferring to quietly camp out alone with the wild animals in the open countryside. Slate was a "loner" and loved to be out on the prairie by himself; listening to the prairie dogs barking; the crickets chirping; the wolf packs and the coyotes howling, the mountain lions roaring, the wind blowing across the grass all around him; and camping in the open under the stars in any field by a seldom-traveled dirt country road or obsolete two lane concrete highway which usually paralleled the wide main highway. But no matter where he slept, sensitive electronic sonic; infrared; and microwave "sentry devices" on his cycle always kept watch for anything that came near during the night and would softly sound an alert from the small amulet he always wore around his neck if any wildlife or Humanoid predators came near.

Lately as he roamed the lonely highways, Slate had become very 'hot-natured', which he thought was caused by having a high metabolism caused by his constant daily exercise. At night he frequently sweated profusely; even during the very rare times he stayed in an air conditioned motel room or slept on a snowy Alaskan field far off the highway. Because of this frequent high body temperature, he only had to use a light blanket during the wintertime, even while camping amid thick blankets of snow on the ground; and almost always preparing and eating food bought at highway grocery stores that he cooked over an old-fashioned open campfire or using a portable Sterno pack to heat his meal. Following his Boy Scout training, each morning early before he left each primitive campsite, Slate always thoroughly cleaned up the lonely and Spartan camp site so well that it would have taken sensitive scientific instruments to ever detect that anyone had ever been around.

As he traveled around, the young former combat veteran always wore loose-fitting very comfortable clothes that usually looked worn but were very clean; and if not cooking for himself in the woods among the wildlife; he usually ate at the cheapest fast food restaurants on the edge of towns and cities on the highway; eateries such as "Hamburg's Hamburger

Haven", "Uncle Fred's Chicken", "Tuti's Famous Tacos", and "Ho Chi's Sushi". Slate carefully kept his clean clothes in one of his cycle's very large saddle bags and the clothes he had worn in another. When any of his comfortable shirts or pants wore out, he always replaced them at several military surplus stores at the edge of small Texas and New Mexico towns that he loved to visit; especially during holiday seasons when local celebrations, such as the famous "Pig Beauty Pageant" celebrated during "Pig Week" in the small town of "Tarzan", Texas; the very popular "Donut Day Festival", with a thousand different kinds of donuts to be sampled free, held near Carlsbad Caverns, New Mexico, (and the winner of the donut tasting contest voted on by the crowd); and "Veterans Appreciation Week" held in the historic town of "Cut and Shoot" in the "Heart of Texas"; northeast of Houston, Texas. Other celebrations that he loved to frequent were the famous Sagamore Hill "Soapbox Derby Finals" in Fort Worth, Texas; the "Texas Pistol and Rifle Contest Week" held in the town of "Dime Box"; and many other annual celebrations which were held in dozens of small towns in the "Lone Star State", the "Land of Enchantment", the "Sooner State", and many other rural parts of the country! Whenever Slate went through a small town, he would always buy a local area newspaper and make new friends at the local "mom and pop store"; so that he could keep track of all the celebrations, festivals, and county fairs, by putting the dates in his electronic calendar on his cycle's handlebars. (These get-togethers gave him things to look forward to and helped him divert his thoughts in order to try to forget one important happening and quit seeing one very troubling picture!)

When necessary, every week or two, Slate washed his dirty clothes at self-service laundries at the edge of small towns off the highways he frequented; every morning always putting on clean clothes when privately dressing, far off the highway; deep in a wooded section; or in the bathroom of a gasoline station at the edge of a town. To any observer observing his old worn clothing and his frugal spending at small town restaurants and the tiny "mom and pop" grocery stores that he frequented, the young veteran seemed to be just a very poor wandering homeless person; but actually, he could have afforded to stay every night at the best motels or hotels in any large city in the country, and dine three times every day at extremely expensive eating places! His military retirement check was always electronically deposited in his national bank account promptly on the first day of every month; and any amount was available for him to withdraw 24/7 at virtually every ATM in the country without any service charge. But with all this money accumulating and available for Slate 24/7 to use anytime to cover his food, clothing and miscellaneous expenses; every month the young man never spent anywhere near what was regularly deposited by the United States government which was very grateful for his previous beyond-the-call-of-duty service, which had caused terrible injuries during a very fateful foray in the Middle East!

In addition, all of the veteran's medical and dental bills were also covered by his military retirement account. Any time he needed medical or dental help he could avail himself of the services of literally thousands of walk-in country hospitals, doctors, and dentists 24/7; and pay 100% of any hospital, doctor, or dentist bill with his military medical card; in literally any "wide place in the road"; any town; or any city in the country!

But for some obscure reason, despite having more than enough money to do so, Slate chose not to wear expensive hunting clothes and eat at famous restaurants in large cities; preferring to dress casually and to eat and sleep at obscure, out of the way places; travel and sleep deep in the native woods all across the country; ride a motorcycle instead of driving and expensive sports car; and keep a low profile; as if he were avoiding something very painful, (which he was).

The effects of what the Imperial Seers call his own personal "Anchor Event" that happened in the past; which literally changed his "Life Path" forever; and the young veteran was continuously trying to forget; would eventually affect what would happen in the future to many sentient beings all across the Cosmic All! It was literally so important to the so-called "Fate" or "Karma" of his immediate surroundings; the minor planet on which he traveled; and ultimately so important to the greater part of the known Universe; that, even as he quietly traveled on the small back roads and trails of Earth, the fabled, and very controversial invisible Winds of Destiny, constantly swirled about him and also at another certain position on the Time Line! Added to what some Magi were beginning to call the "Mystery of the Lone Humanoid", was the fact that suddenly, for one of the times in their existence, for some reason the Winds of Destiny blocked the mental vision channels which allowed sentient beings with sufficient mental talents to tap into the Galactic Time Stream in the immediate area around them! (Another is recorded in the Imperial document about <u>Cleonardo Zantrick Watson</u>, the Trecian Witch; available for viewing by any Magi, deep down in the Imperial Seer Headquarters under the surface of Empire Prime!)

Since Slate started his roaming, the Winds of Destiny were always blowing undetectably at light to moderate force around him, and ultimately the "energy vector" they were producing because of Slate; was eventually picked up by Magi Kancor Crokan in a far off quadrant of the galaxy and ultimately by Seer Rondoe Kanne on Empire Prime! The Winds gradually increased their velocity as a certain "Pivotal Event" approached on the Main Galactic Timeline; which would cause a permanent change in its direction!! If Slate had possessed the mental facilities to sense the Winds, he would have had to constantly keep his strongest mental shields up all the time in order to avoid being uncomfortable, or even to keep from having his "mental circuits" fried on the occasions that the Winds surged higher! (But since the retired soldier's ordinary Humanoid brain did not have the mental capability to be able to sense the Winds, such a defense was not necessary!)

Far away in the Cosmic All on Empire Prime, the Capital Planet of the Empire, if the Imperial Seers had been able to visualize his presence in their mental "visions" when the Winds first started blowing, they would have realized that this unusual 28/8 manifestation of the Winds indicated that the present; past; and future Karma of the seemingly insignificant Humanoid was of extreme importance to his planet and even probably to the entire Universe! (The Capital Planet of the Interstellar Condominium of Planets and Empires, Empire Prime, because of its rotation has a 28-hour day and by Imperial Law, 8 days in each week on the Official Empire Calendar.) However when they first started trying to visualize the cause of the Winds surging, the nearest Imperial Seer was too far away from the ultimate cause of the manifestation of the Winds; to be able to "sense" the Man known as Slate in his visualization of the local "Time Stream". The reason the Seer was not able to visualize the reason for the surge was because even a "moderate" force of the Winds of Destiny could only be "visualized" or "felt" by the Magi from a few hundred thousand light years away only if their location was located in the "Vector" of the stream of the Winds. Back on Empire Prime, because the Seers could not visualize what was happening, Seer Rondoe Kanne had requested that a ship of the Imperial Navy convey members of the Royal Magi close enough to the suspected Anchor Event to be able to visualize what "Important Event" was happening; even though he felt that the position was so far away that the Happening would probably be over by the time the Seer was close enough to use his mental powers to analyze the situation.

But the young man so far across the Cosmic All who was causing the surge would not have cared about the Winds; even if his heightened regular Humanoid senses could have detected them! (If that would have been possible, he would have kept up his protective mental shields and totally ignored them!) The answer to what was so important about one insignificant Humanoid that the famous and controversial Winds of Destiny were involved, lay back along Earth's Main Time Line and it was also imbedded deep in the Past segments of the "Main Galactic Time Stream", (or if you prefer, in the "Time Cloud"! Both terms can be proven to be equally correct in describing the flow of that mysterious commodity known as "Time"!)

Another component of the answer to the enigma of the young man incredibly involved a "Time Nexus", i.e., a sudden meeting, interconnection, and meshing of the "Destiny Lines" of several important beings; coming together to cause one very important "Galactic Anchor Event"! This unlikely "Time Event" on the Main Galactic Time Line was caused by several peculiar single minor events; each happening to different sentient beings; and each originating up to several million light years away from each other! Among the many different unusual "variables" or "facets" of the "Time Nexus" was the fact that it incredibly involved the interaction of Humanoid and Reptiloid alien beings! These reptile beings look like something like walking intelligent "dinosaurs"; which were very large reptile creatures which existed in the early prehistoric era of Earth's past.

But with such a stirring of the Winds of Destiny caused by one solitary "Humanoid", not hurting or harming anything, riding around on one tiny planet far, far away from Empire Prime; how could this supposedly peaceful travel affect the Capital Planet or even one of the member planets of the Empire closest to the insignificant planet Earth? But just when the Magi had been close to visualizing the totality of the Anchor Happening, for one of the few times in the history of the Cosmic All, the Winds of Destiny somehow cut off their visions; causing all of the possible "vision tracks" to be either totally dark or totally blank! Since they could not visualize what was to happen to the Humanoid, the Magi could not investigate any further the unique being who was apparently causing the blackout!

But more importantly, how would the Main Time Lines of the Empire's galaxies be affected by such a strong force of the Winds, whose subatomic energy flow was known by the Imperial Seers, after several hundred thousand years of research and studies, to have lasting effects on the entire Cosmos? After their visions were shut off, the Imperial Seers could not find out the answer to this important trans-galactic question--**YET!!**

If such an important question had been asked to the elite society of the Imperial Seers when the Event concerning the young Humanoid known as "Steele" was happening, not even the eldest and most powerful of that unique group of mental adepts could answer that fateful question! Because the Empire's Magi, while they were so far away on the Capital Planet, could not totally visualize the situation before the Very Important Event totally unfolded, and so they could not possibly have answered that important question! Even the group of Seers taken closer to the "Anchor Happening" could not totally comprehend or visualize its final ending after careful study of the event for many months, before, during, and after its supposed final end; when their visions were somehow turned back on!

As previously documented above, the Seers ultimately were able to visualize the single Humanoid who was causing the Winds of Destiny to surge, but just as important as identifying the cause of the surge, they could not even grasp the effect it would have on virtually all the sentient beings in the Cosmic All, until all of the effects of the important happening causing the surge of the Winds of Destiny were totally complete; which would ultimately take many, many Earthian years and Imperial centuries!

With their careful research after the pivotal Anchor Event was over, the Magi discovered that "The Event" was unique! It was unique because it was not a single happening; it was how several other so-called "Anchor Events" combined to affect the entire life of one single; solitary Humanoid sentient being! Then it was the effect the life of that one sentient being had on the rest of the Cosmic All that would last until the last sun burned out at the start of Eternity!

But at that point on the Time Line, since the Seers could not interfere in the Event, they realized that the strain such an ultra-important Anchor Event caused on the Time Lines would have to self-adjust with no outside interference as the Anchor Event or Events affecting this Anchor Person ultimately played themselves out and were totally finished on all the planets and points on the Time Line strewn all across the canopy of the Cosmic All! Legally and morally, all they could do was wait, watch for the Main Galactic Time Line to again be able to be visualized; then record, and debate the effects among themselves for at least several hundred thousand years into the "Future"! By Imperial Laws several hundred thousand years old, and strictly enforced, that was literally all the Seers could legally do! They could not interfere before, during, or after an Anchor Event or Events were happening; unless they were given special permission by the Emperor or Empress in order to prevent an "Ultimate Calamity"!

So at this important time in the History of the Empire, all they could do was to continue to try to attempt to visualize all of the now invisible "Life Lines" being affected by this one, solitary weak Humanoid! Also, they tried to figure just what "Life Line", "Planetary Time Stream", or "Main Galactic Time Stream", was being affected by this unimportant being to cause such a unique and unprecedented effect on the Winds of Destiny to both surge and then cut off their visions! Following standard procedure, each of the Seers or any number of the Magi working together in conference on their assigned "Event", before the visions came back online, could write their conclusions on the imperishable pages of the Annals of the Imperial Seers. Then these conclusions could be discussed and debated, before, during, and after the effects of the "Anchor Event" had run their course in changing the Main Galactic Time Stream. By an ancient Magi custom, all of these speeches, debates, and opinions would be recorded on the eternal pages of the Seers and used as a learning tool to teach beginning Magi about how they should operate before, during, and after they visualized the Time Stream. The notes and observations could also be used by any veteran Seer, with the proper service time or rank, in order to obtain all the information they could about the Winds of Destiny.

So now, beginning or veteran Seer, or Citizen of the Empire legally authorized to see the pages of this Magi document, (which has been translated and copied from the eternal pages of the Annals of the Imperial Seers in order to give information to the Emperor and Empress and advise them about certain happenings), read the following document and be prepared to ponder its meaning! At some point in the Future, adhering to an important Imperial Law several hundred thousand year old, you will be visited by an Imperial Seer; who will show you the proper picture Imperial Seer identification, and a document signed by the present Emperor of the Empire; in order for you to be able to tell the authorized Magi about the illuminations, clarifications, and insights about the Event that you received; as you pondered the meaning of the following pages!

CHAPTER 4

The complicated reason for the enigmatic man's lonely quest, over the back roads and almost abandoned highways of the entire North American continent, involved a series of related events that started a little over 5 Earthian years before. Samuel Eliot Steele was at a top-secret location in the Middle East; in order to carry out a so-called "Black Covert Ops" with a secret combat and Intel team from one of the United States military branches. Because of several acts of bravery and strength Samuel Steele had used to support the other men in his team during their initial training, the man quickly became known to his combat buddies during their first mission as "Slate" Steele. Unfortunately, a few months later, the young man was on night patrol in the desert and was severely injured when he stepped near a proximity fused plastic-cased land mine in Afghanistan which had been planted by a terrorist. The resulting explosion severely injured the young man and was the signal for the terrorists to start a firefight with the remaining troops unaffected by the explosion! As the battle raged, his buddies risked their lives to rescue Slate while experiencing heavy machine gun and mortar fire! After the brave soldiers had successfully retrieved his heavily-injured body, with the permission of their commanding officer several of them left the battle scene and immediately rushed the severely injured young man to the nearest "MASH", or "Mobile Army Surgical Hospital". After the local MASH doctors had done their best with the relatively limited medical equipment they possessed to stabilize Slate's serious condition, he was immediately picked up in the desert and flown by a hypersonic stealth VTOL, (nicknamed the "U-4" since the "U-3" handle had already been given to the methane-powered stealth hypersonic spy plane called the "Aurora", and the "U-2" to the original "Dragon Lady" which has been improved and in constant service since the 1960's), to the very famous Lexington military hospital, a United States Armed Forces hospital in Germany; which serves extremely critical patients for every branch of the United States military. It is an installation which even today is among only a handful of military medical facilities which specialize in using the latest "cutting edge" standard medical operations to save the lives of our combat soldiers, who are risking their lives for us in literally every continent on the face of the Earth, and several places off our planet! (Those familiar with the ultra-advanced techniques used by the military hospital say "off the record" that the medical procedures remind them of a certain television extremely popular program in the 1970's about a doctor known for using his very advanced and "on the frontiers of medical knowledge" operations to save the life of his patients).

When Slate was quickly transported from the U-4 into the Lexington Military Hospital installation in Germany, he was immediately examined by a team of skilled surgeons headed by the eminent surgeon Dr. Martha Wagstaff. The doctors examined all the X-rays and cat scans that had quickly been performed when the young man had been brought in and formulated a plan to help him survive! Both of his arms and both of his legs were so heavily damaged and full of infection that, to save his life, the team of doctors had to amputate all four of them! Sadly, they also had to remove one of his arms and one of his legs extremely close to his body. Slate's head was so severely burned from the bomb that exploded very near to his body that the preliminary medical reports written on the battlefield reported that the young man's head wounds were so acute that he would be almost totally blind even with corneal transplants and the most advanced inner eye surgery! Added to these terrible injuries; because of tremendous damage to his ear canals caused by the bomb explosion, he would probably be totally deaf the rest of his life; even after complex inner ear surgery.

Dr. Wagstaff and her team of skilled doctors quickly ascertained that not even the advanced 21st century medical procedures available at that cutting-edge facility could help the severely injured patient! The scale and literally the depth of his injuries were beyond what their medical teams could heal or repair with even their advanced techniques! Because the facility could not help him, a decision was made by a committee of veteran doctors to immediately stabilize the patient using ultra-advanced cryogenic techniques to keep his internal organs from shutting down from shock and also to prepare his heavily-damaged body for a trip to allow even further advanced cutting-edge medical operations at an ultra-secret location that were only used only as an absolutely "last resort"! The techniques used on Slate would be literally "last ditch" radical surgery in order to try to first save his life, and perhaps enable him to walk again; or have at least give him some "quality of life"! Dr. Wagstaff and her staff sent a report to their commanding general of their hospital organization telling him that they could not help the young man with even their advanced medical techniques, and the use of another medical hospital was needed.

After reading the gloomy report and the recommendation, Brigadier General Ron Cleere, the commander of the Lexington Hospital installation, made the final decision and the severely injured young soldier, after being thoroughly sedated, examined, and stabilized, (using cryogenic techniques developed from studying frogs and other small creatures and insects that in cold weather deliberately allow themselves to freeze in order to survive the harsh winters where they live); was quickly sent on his way to a secret location in order to get the very best care available on the planet to try to save his life and tremendously improve his "quality of life"! The General had hoped that the advanced medical research available in Germany was up to the tremendous task of giving the young man his life back; but now he was going to secretly send him to another medical facility that was also "off the record" and used the results of "black programs"; so that ultra-advanced techniques could somehow help him! So again, an ultra-secret U-4 was utilized to transport Slate to what hopefully would be his last stop for reconstructive surgery to somehow rebuild his arms, legs, and eyesight! (If they could not help Slate, then he would literally be a "vegetable" the rest of his life; living 24/7 in a V.A. hospital bed until he died of "old age"!)

Several years before; while the ultra-secret U-4 "lifting body" spy craft was being designed and built using CAD programs and ultra-strong and extremely light, 3-dimentional printing of its Titanium parts; several of the attack craft were constructed differently by adding a small interior cabin constructed into the aft fuselage. This section was normally used to house missiles for ultra-covert recon or precision bunker busting of terrorist nuclear installations extremely deep underground. On the special aircraft that would be used literally as flying hospital ambulances, this section had been designed to allow severely wounded patients to be very quickly transported for treatment in comfort to any military or civilian hospital in the world.

To allow critically injured patents to be air-lifted without pain, the hospital transport airplane contained a top-secret auxiliary propulsion apparatus whose operating principle was accidently discovered by a talented research physicist Doctor Townley Green in the late 1950's. The source and foundation of this astounding scientific advance began a little over twenty years ago during totally unrelated electrical research on several types of capacitors. Originally Dr. Green had been an ordinary research physicist working in a government laboratory trying to increase the voltage capacity of an advanced type of electrical capacitor. He was weighing the capacitors as he was charging them up to their full capacity, in order to determine if his modifications had improved their storage ability, when suddenly he noticed a startling fact! During one of the tests, Dr. Green happened to move one of the small electrical devices and he noticed that, when the capacitor was charged up to almost its total amperage and voltage, and it was tilted at a certain angle, the very precise scales on which it was resting indicated that

IT HAD SUDDENLY LOST WEIGHT! It lost only a few thousandths of a gram of its weight, but it did lose a small bit of weight that was measurable! In every test when the capacitor was discharged, or it was tilted at another angle; its weight returned to normal! That amazing fact gave Dr. Green a startling new avenue of research that ultimately took him beyond the frontiers of present-day knowledge of physics and science to literally uncharted territory! That new secret military research program was the start of what ultimately became the United States Air Force's ultra-secret antigravity program; (which used technology different from the antigravity units developed from those reverse engineered from the "Roswell crash" artifacts!!

After several years of intense research and development after his first chance discovery, using the basic principle discovered, Dr. Green used his first crude systems to propel several small saucer-shaped aircraft in the wide expanse of large, closely-guarded military buildings! The models were attached to a tall pole by an electric wire that powered the device and propelled the flying model round and round in a circle around the tall shaft at a speed of around 50 mph; using only Dr. Green's first prototype of an antigravity propulsion system! After much research and development of the amazing discovery, in a series of tests spread over more than a decade, larger and larger self-powered models were flown without wires using internal power sources in tests around the large area around the heavily-guarded secret base known as "Area 51". Eventually, after much hard work and research, Dr. Green's more advanced anti-gravity systems allowed the saucers to exhibit physically impossible ninety degree turns at supersonic speeds; by literally canceling out "inertia in the aircraft"! (This was the source of the large number of UFOs seen above Area 51 doing 90° turns! So interested reader; if you are ever at that famous military testing field at night and see a point of light doing ninety degree turns; the craft you see is not of alien manufacture; it has been designed and flown by the U.S. Air Force!)

Since that time, a very much-improved direct descendent of that first crude system, that had the amazing capability to overcome some of the gravity and partially shield the contents of that saucer-shaped craft from inertia, had been greatly modified and improved have the capability to dampen almost 100% of the inertia in what was supposedly just an advanced "scramjet" aircraft, ("supersonic ramjet")! It also allowed very fast VTOL takeoffs and landings by repelling gravity; which greatly increased the efficiency of its auxiliary jet engines!

While Slate was on the way to the next hospital, an auxiliary internal gravity shield was employed in the back cabin to ease the pressure on the severely injured young man, who was kept in a medically induced coma; while his body temperature was kept near freezing as the ultra-advanced craft's ultra-secret devices literally deflected gravity and rose silently by pushing against the Earth's gravity in order to travel vertically out of the secret base! Once at a sufficient altitude; held aloft by its antigravity system, the lifting body-shaped craft slowly accelerated with its turbo-scramjet while climbing to its operating altitude of over 250,000 feet! Since the craft's weight was almost negligible due to its antigravity systems, the scramjet, was very, very efficient; compared to any other operational jet, scramjet, or rocket plane in the world!

When the ultra-advanced aircraft reached the proper altitude; guided by a navigation system that used the stars to plot the preset course, (since an inertial navigation system would not have worked in the antigravity field!); it headed west and accelerated to over Mach 8; with the pilots and the patients in the interior never feeling any discomfort or G forces to toss them around when the craft accelerated and maneuvered at such high speeds! Under orders given by Brigadier General Ron Cleere, the young man would be taken to the top-secret Bomar Research Hospital hidden under the desert sands of Nevada, (and nicknamed Area 51½), by the advanced inertia-less craft in order to continue the efforts to save his life; then improve his "quality of life", using reconstructive surgery techniques that were medically far beyond what had been done before; (except in the exciting fiction science fiction stories where the aliens could change a person's Double Helix and Triple Helix in each of their cells in order to regrow limbs, eyes, and brain neurons!)

While the U-4 was in transit, the best surgical medical facilities on the planet were preparing for Slate's arrival. Following the surgical plan developed for the severely wounded soldier, several crack medical teams quickly went into action when the VTOL landed on what appeared to be a flat dusty surface on top of a barren deserted hillside in Nevada, literally hundreds of miles from the nearest settlement. The landing was timed to be between the regular orbits of unfriendly spy satellites and because the moon had yet to rise in the daytime sky, to inhibit observation from the moon bases of the Asian Alliance. After the lifting body landed, the areas over and around the ultra-advanced craft were quickly covered by radar, visible light, and infrared-proof netting; rising up from the sides of the flat surface, as a protection against any possible undetected stealth enemy satellite that could suddenly change its orbit in response to covert reports of activity at the base. Next, the craft was shuttled down into the earth by a high-speed elevator; while above, the radar, visible light, and infrared protective cover still shielded all around the opening to protect the craft from prying enemy satellite sensors and any possible ground observers. Seconds later another flat dusty covering of the elevator shaft reappeared, the radar, visible light, and infrared protective covers retracted out of sight until the next time they were needed, and the barren hillside again appeared to be deserted. When the craft carrying the unconscious young man finally stopped over a thousand feet below the surface of the desert, the moving platform and the plane was in a brightly-lit area surrounded by uniformed medical personnel and armed military guards. Orderlies quickly took Slate's gurney into the surgical area with a minimum of delay; with all the medical team being briefed beforehand. Immediately the scheduled multiple delicate surgeries were started; all under the direction and control of Doctor Antonio K. Gillespie, the very famous surgeon who specialized in very extreme physical reconstruction cases. The heavily wounded man, who had survived radical surgery in Germany to remove his heavily-damaged arms and legs, was slowly unthawed and kept under heavy anesthesia; while during the next thirty-six hours, cutting-edge medical procedures were to be attempted, that only a few years previously would have been classified as "science fiction" taken out of imaginary scientific "Science-fiction" episodes of the "Stranger Zone" or its rival program on another com-network, the "Future Zone"; tremendously popular sci-fi television programs! (See Appendix IV) These programs could be received in High-Def, 3-D, or holographic imaging, depending on the capabilities of the viewer's receiving system.

The repairs were very extensive, but the young man was constantly kept comfortable with advanced anesthetics to keep him asleep, and then he would be given carefully measured regular pain killers to ease his discomfort when he would eventually be gradually brought to consciousness; after the advanced surgical procedures being planned had been completed to Dr. Gillespie's satisfaction. All of the complex and very detailed medical plans for Slate were designed to be carried out so that he would never feel any severe pain, and only mild discomfort when he was conscious. The ultimate goal was that his body would literally be repaired so carefully that anyone seeing him could not tell that he had ever been severely injured!

But would the extensive medical repairs be totally successful to repair his hearing and his eyes; and replace his arms and legs; or would Slate be a cripple or a total vegetable for the rest of his life? Only the end results of the skill of the surgeons, and passage of "Time" on the "Main Galactic Time Stream"; would reveal the answer to that difficult question the Imperial Seers! But the ultimate answer to the unknown medical riddle of how well Slate's extensive wounds could be repaired, and how his "quality of life" would be improved by all the radical surgeries; (as indicated by the unique actions of the Winds of Destiny), would literally deflect and change the direction of the Galactic Time Stream and influence future events, either for the "Good", or for the "Bad"!

For many hours the groundbreaking surgeries went on; with several surgical teams working on different parts of Slate's body at the same time, in order to literally repair his wrecked body! Working according to a very meticulous surgery plan, as each team finished their assigned surgical job; taking as much time as they needed to do the job, the next team began their delegated assignment to repair another limb, eye, or ear! Using ultra-advanced technology, life-like limbs made of plastic, steel, and microscopic electronics were seamlessly attached to the ends of the living bone and sinew in Slate's short arm and leg stubs! Each newly replaced arm and leg mimicked the missing limb, being the same length and having the same scars as the old appendage; along with always having the same body temperature as the surface it was attached to! The replaced limbs could also be cut, and they would bleed in order to heal themselves, just like the real thing! Advanced electronics were inserted in Slate's eye sockets to replace his corneas to attempt to allow him to see again; and other electronics were placed in both his auditory canals to hopefully allow the young man to hear again! But how well each new part would function could only be determined when Slate woke up; and his new limbs, his new eyes, and his new ears were literally electronically brought online; so that he could tell the surgeons just how good the "repair job" had been!

Finally, when the meticulous surgical plan was totally completed; each replacement limb was checked; his two new eyes were meticulously tested; each new substitute ear was examined; and all the life-like plastic skin and skin grafts which were used to replace flesh destroyed by the ravages of war were scrutinized and certified as being "combat ready"! As the soldier known officially on his admitting papers as "Samuel Eliot Steele" was slowly allowed to finally be slowly thawed; his body temperature brought up to normal; and become completely awake after his long journey of surgeries, there was one big problem had to be solved to allow the young soldier to successfully regain consciousness and cooperate fully with the physical therapists! The difficulty was that in the mind and thoughts of the young veteran, he was still on the battlefield in the MASH unit, since he had had been unconscious during the entire time he had been injured until the present time after his latest ultra-advanced surgery! Because of this fact, the young soldier would probably wake up thrashing about, shouting orders, and tearing out his new surgical sutures! But the facility's veteran Chief Nurse, Major Brenda Hill, during her long and distinguished medical career, had developed a remedy for that problem, which she told to the person in charge of Slate's recovery procedure!

After the very extensive ground-breaking surgery was completely finished on the young man, groups of skilled doctors, dedicated caring nurses, and veteran military physiatrists; headed by the renowned surgeon and psychologist, Dr. Terry Sinclair, and helped by Head Nurse Major Brenda Hill, put into operation a plan to bring Slate mentally completely back to normal! Unselfishly giving of their time off and days off; the doctors, nurses, surgeons, and hospital office help and orderlies; all worked together as a team to very, very slowly bring the young man back to normal consciousness and ultimately be able to live a normal life.

Since the power to hear is the first sense to come back "on line" when a person emerges from a coma, by design; hour upon hour; day after day; the volunteers sat beside Slate's bed and calmly read to him, so that before he became totally conscious and able to talk, he would hear a calm, steady voice telling him about the weather, reciting a poem, or reading a travel brochure. Hopefully, this would allow the young soldier's psyche to gradually "come back online" and allow him to slowly come back into the "real world" from the unconscious state in which he had been for so long!

For safety, Slate's electronic eyes and ears were turned on; but his cyborg arms and legs were left inert, and he was tied down in his bed so that, as he regained consciousness, he would not hurt himself by trying unsuccessfully to use them. Also, the plan covered the possibility of Slate slowly regaining consciousness; then unexpectedly, he suddenly awakened and was totally conscious and able to talk. To cover that possibility, veteran military counselors were on duty 24/7 in his room in order to explain to him just what was going on; so that he would not be confused and somehow hurt himself trying to get out of his bed.

When he was mentally stable and aware of his surroundings and he knew that the people around his bed were trying to help him after his extensive injuries were repaired, the coordinated teams would very, very, gently orientate him as to where he was, and what had happened to him; hopefully without literally damaging and destroying his psyche forever!

A lot of important questions had to be answered in the coming days! Would Dr. Gillespie and his team of doctors be totally successful in attaching cyborg arms and legs to Slate's body, or would his body reject one or all of the cyborg limbs? Would his eye and ear devices fail to work? At the instant that Slate started regaining consciousness, the Imperial Magi did not know and could not find out, since the Main Galactic Time Line was still not cooperating! As the Galactic Anchor Event was about to happen, and the necessary events were coming together to create it in its entirety, for one of the few times in the recorded history of the Imperial Seers, virtually all the questing Magi on Empire Prime still could not visualize any of the future timelines of the ICOPE and their home planets; **AND THERE WAS NOT A THING THAT COULD BE DONE ABOUT IT--EXCEPT WAIT!**

After careful research over the millennia since that ultra-important Main Galactic Time Stream Anchor Event completely unfolded and the Time Lines of the Universe settled down; it was also found that at that instant, virtually all sentient beings with Magi-like or similar powers anywhere in the Cosmic All suddenly could not use their powers to visualize any Time Line! Incredibly every facet of the Main Galactic Time Line was suddenly darkened, which apparently meant a very, very special "Galactic Anchor Event" was in the process of happening, which apparently would affect every sentient being in the entire Cosmic All! But was it an event whose outcome would destroy the entire Universe? There was nothing in their recorded history, or any vision evident to their powers, that could tell the Imperial Seers the answer to that terrible question! But all the Magi could do was-------**WAIT!**--—Wait for the occurrence of what would one day be called the "Event of the Ages", and strenuously argued about, for over the next million years of Galactic History!

But the <u>cause</u> of the darkening was eventually found out; after the fact, and after virtually all the Time Lines had stabilized; and the cause could not be argued about! It was found that the shutdown of the Magi powers to visualize the Time Lines was eventually caused by the Winds of Destiny rising to record levels; apparently their maximum velocity; and just because of this, their record speed affected the Main Universal Time Line; effectively stopping, and making virtually every Time Line invisible to the mental talents of the Imperial Seers or the mental adepts of several nearby empires; including the Mambanian solar system!

But fortunately for the safety of the Universe, as "The Event" was about to end, the Winds of Destiny slowly decreased in velocity and the powers of the Seers and every sentient being with similar powers also slowly returned! The Imperial Magi all immediately tried to visualize the Future and could visualize several possible future happenings for the "Pivotal Humanoid" known as Steele. But some of these projected events the Seers visualized could or would happen only after the Anchor Person known as Samuel Eliot Steele regained consciousness and could work his new "hardware"! But would the actual vision happenings be "good" or "bad" for the direction of the Galactic Time Stream? With literally dozens of possible avenues possible to their visions, the Magi did not, and could not KNOW--**YET**! So just like the previous time-span in which their visions were totally dark; again, all they could do was **WAIT;** which was, and is; something they do not do well!

CHAPTER 5

The first thing that Slate remembered when he was slowly regaining consciousness was someone softly talking to him in a smooth, calm, low woman's voice about the weather and how much the area need rain. This made him wonder deep in his subconscious mind just exactly what was going on, and who was talking; because he did not recognize their voice! (His subconscious knew that the gently-sounding woman couldn't possibly be talking about rain in the Middle East, which was where he was the last time he was conscious!) But even as he wondered about who was talking, he slipped back under the effect of the anesthetic.

It was decided by the psychologists assigned to his case that Slate would first slowly be brought back to consciousness for a short time to be able to judge his "mental state"; then he would be allowed to remain conscious for longer and longer periods to allow him to gradually become more and more aware of his surroundings and to slowly adjust to his surroundings and become cognizant of just what was going on.

But each time he regained partial consciousness, Slate would hear something for a very short time, and because of the uneven effects of the anesthetic as it was being slowly decreased to gradually bring him back to full consciousness permanently, he would lose consciousness again for anywhere from a few minutes to an hour; (in his unconscious state, neither his subconscious or his conscious mind was aware of the passage of time); then he would gradually regain consciousness and faintly hear another calm voice reading a poem to him or a child's bedtime story; always in a smooth, calm voice. But each time he regained consciousness, he stayed awake for a longer period of time because of the lower and lower dosages of the anesthetic that he was given. The dedicated nurses, hospital office workers, orderlies, and doctors would read literally anything soothing in his presence to help him want to come out of his medically-induced coma and be able to face reality again. The medical personnel were to continue to read to him 24/7 until he regained full consciousness, because again, a patient's hearing is the first sense to come back online when a person comes out of a coma or the effects of an anesthetic. Hearing a soothing voice helps to calm a severely injured patient before they completely regain consciousness and are able to focus their eyes and observe their surroundings. When a patient in a shallow coma or coming out of anesthetic hears someone speaking in a calm voice; even if they can't yet understand what the reader is saying, they know that they are not alone and someone is around; and they know that they are in a safe location, since the person whose voice they hear seems very calm and is talking softly.

When Slate first slowly opened his eyelids and was able to focus his eyes the first thing he happened to see, before he lost consciousness again, was the blurry image of a person dressed in white attending his IVs. He immediately thought it was an angel, and he was not far wrong! The groups of dedicated nurses that day and night, ceaselessly attended to Slate's every physical and medical need, truly worked like angels! It was their tender care and the efforts of the military doctors and physiatrists that slowly brought Slate back to reality and literally performed medical and psychiatric miracles on the young man, who; without the fantastic surgery to repaired his heavily damaged body and their strenuous efforts afterwards; would have been a blind vegetable without arms, legs, hearing, and his sight the rest of his very short life! Ultimately, it was the <u>total dedication</u> of the doctors and nurses and physiatrists and the day-and-night readers; who saved Slate's life and gradually brought him back to reality, and able to function in the "real world"! It took the highly skilled; highly coordinated <u>team effort</u> of literally every medical professional person working on the case; that allowed the successful body reconstruction and rehabilitation of the mental facilities of their unique; and very important patient!

Day and night the very involved plan of care formulated for the severely-injured young man was carried out literally to letter and to the specified second! A health care professional to constantly check Slate's condition, and a counselor in case he suddenly awakened; were always in his room 24/7. In addition, someone was still reading in a relaxed, tranquil voice next to his bed while he was being treated by dedicated medical personnel. Shots were always given on time; IVs were constantly checked; cleaned; and replaced like clockwork. The surface of Slate's body was constantly inspected by the nurses, and aloe or an antibiotic salve was immediately applied to any spot of dry skin or infection that they found. The young soldier was regularly turned in his bed to prevent "bed sores". His room was kept spotless to prevent the spread of germs, viruses, and bacteria. In the secret underground hospital, there were literally no day and night shifts for the caregivers and physical therapists worked continuously to improve the quality of life for Slate and the other patients under their care; often going beyond their assigned work schedule "off the record", and doing more than what was asked of them to heal their patients and help bring Slate back to full consciousness and health!

After days of fading in and out of consciousness, the anesthetic was finally low enough to permit the young soldier to become cognizant and aware of his surroundings for a short time before he faded out once more. The next time Slate became aware of where he was, he could finally understand what the nurse was explaining to him, when she saw that he was finally awake. Nurse Brown, the health professional on duty, first explained to him that he was tied down to prevent him from hurting himself. She also told him that as soon as he regained consciousness for the period of time established by Dr. Gillespie, the physician assigned to his case, the straps would be removed. The combat veteran slowly nodded and went back to sleep; while the readers patiently kept on reading.

But the important question that still needed to be answered was could he actually hear the nurse with his cyborg ears and see her clearly, or was he just nodding at her? A simple test would answer those two questions. The next time Slate awakened the nurse asked him how many fingers she was holding up. Slate slowly raised his head, looked at her hand, and correctly said "four", and then gradually went back to sleep! The nurse, who had faithfully cared for Slate for many days, started crying tears of joy because the young man could see using his cyborg eyes and hear with the electronic implants! When she could control her emotions and had dried her face, she reported the wonderful news to her charge nurse in the ward's office; who also started crying tears of joy. Then the charge nurse dried her tears; and using her cell phone and sending emails from the medical computer in her office; she spread the wonderful news to the rest of the extremely dedicating and caring medical team!

The periods of wakefulness became longer and longer as the young man was gradually brought back to full consciousness so that he would completely understand what was going on; so that he could start his physical therapy to allow him to successfully be in complete control of his new limbs, his new eyes, and his new ears! The days passed quickly for Slate and gradually his periods of being totally awake equaled; then were longer that his sleep time. Dr. Gillespie then ordered his physical and mental therapies to start. His limbs were gradually turned on using the low power setting, which exactly matched the strength of his normal limbs that were heavily damaged and had to be removed. After this procedure was judged to be successful, the young man was slowly wheeled to the physical therapy room to start his very intricate training that would allow him to totally control his electronic titanium limbs.

Slate also had several sessions scheduled each day with psychiatrists and counselors; who simply had short talks with him about nothing in particular; to help him adjust to his new surroundings and his new strong body parts. Gradually as they got to know the young man, and he got to know and trust them; he opened up to the doctors and started to talk about the things that were troubling him. But because Slate had come from a very stable family environment, he quickly adjusted to his new capabilities, and after a few weeks, the counselors and psychiatrists voted unanimously to report to Dr. Gillespie and the military authorities that Slate was mentally stable and could be completely trusted with his super strong cyborg limbs!

Because Slate had been a superb athlete in very good physical condition before the explosion, he was able to quickly gain partial control of his limbs so that he could walk unsteadily around the physical therapy room without help, and shakily pick up plastic cups without completely crushing them; then move on to practicing with glass cups when his control was steady enough. Dr. Gillespie had written out a list of physical goals for him to reach before he would start the next level of his training of his "attached equipment", with their power levels permanently set on high. His final work to attain mastery of his new body parts would take place at another location; where his final training in their use would occur and he would learn (almost) everything about the electronic miracles which had been placed the stubs of his arms and legs, the craters of what had been his eyes, and in his repaired ear canals.

Throughout all Slate's preliminary orientation and first training in the use of his new limbs, all the counselors were amazed at his patience and the quickness with which he was able to realize just what had happened when he had first awakened, and thus he was able to listen with his new ears and cooperate fully with the nurses and the physical therapists who were trying to help him. After several weeks, when Slate had reached the required physical goals, a conference was called and literally all the healthcare professionals who had been assisting Slate voted to allow him to go to the next phase of his training in the full use of his cyborg body, and further counseling.

But even though the Humanoid causing the cascade of the Winds of Destiny was well on the way to full recovery, the Imperial Seers were still baffled about what was going on in the Cosmic All! The problem was the fact that on Empire Prime, and elsewhere in the Empire, the mental visualizations of the "Future" portions of the Main Galactic Time Stream were still either dark or empty! For one of the few times in the five hundred thousand year history of the Interstellar Condominium of Planets and Empires, amazingly the Imperial Magi still could not visualize any of the Galactic Time Stream branches which concerned the well-being of their empire! Which meant that even though they knew **WHO** was to cause the galaxy-shaking event, apparently the ultra-important event had not happened-------**YET**-----and the only thing they could still do was **WAIT!!!**

But even more important than the coming Event was the fact that each of them could also not visualize anything important, or dangerous that was about to happen to their planet, their empire or confederation of planets, or the entire Cosmic All!

For the first time in many millennia, the entire Cosmic All was literally defenseless and at the mercy of "Fate"; without the help of the visions of the Imperial Magi, and similar organizations across the Cosmos; to help their planets and empires literally "see" into what could be the future and deter disaster! And the Imperial Magi and the mental adepts on other planets could not fathom just how long this very dangerous condition would continue! All they could do was . . . . **WAIT!!**

CHAPTER 6

Only a relatively few months after the long operation to replace his limbs and restore his hearing and his eyes, and the gradual restoration of his psyche by the psychiatrists and counselors, were completed, Slate was released from the ultra-secret subterranean hospital's critical care unit and taken to another military hospital on the surface to receive further treatment and training in the use of his new body parts.

The day he left the hospital facility where the medical staff had worked so long and so hard to literally reconstruct his body and his mind, behind the scenes in the medical lounges many a nurse and therapist shed tears of joy when the television monitor showed the young man being wheeled out the door! Then they observed Slate asking the orderly to stop the wheelchair so that he could wave goodbye at them to thank them for their tremendous service to bring him back to reality! (In the nurses' lounge it was said that even hard old Doctor Gillespie was observed to be dabbing at his eyes when he noticed the exit of Slate out the front door and his stopping in order to wave at them! The veteran surgeon remarked to all the nurses and doctors around him that it was simply a reaction to the cold air hitting his eyes from the conditioning!) When Slate could write, he asked for a list of all the medical people who had worked to bring him back; then he laboriously wrote a personal "thank you" note to all of them; with each note different and specifically thanking the recipient for the exact care that the healthcare professional gave to him! His writing was not very good and was barely legible; and he could have used a word processor or had someone else write them; but every recipient of his notes did not care; they knew what he meant, and they knew that Slate remembered what they had done and appreciated their work! Most of the thank you notes were framed and placed in prominent positions in each person's apartment or house. (They would not be able to explain just what the note meant, and who wrote it; to any member of their family for many years!)

All the healthcare professions who had taken care of Slate knew what terrible injuries the combat veteran had been through; but to a casual observer in the underground hospital "not in the loop", he just seemed to be an ordinary hospital patient who had been given normal operations to repair the usual combat injuries, with his arms, legs, and head apparently completely healed as he was taken by an ordinary ambulance from the subterranean installation up a long circular highway curving upward to reach the surface inside a heavily-guarded military warehouse. From what appeared to be an ordinary military supply warehouse, complete with the road winding through tall, stacked pallets of military uniforms, K-rations, and similar equipment designed to cover the installation below; the ambulance took him outside heavily guarded gates; and down a state highway to a nearby regular military hospital. When Slate arrived and was taken to a private room, supposedly for physical therapy, to the regular hospital orderlies and nurses not cleared for top secret information, he actually looked like he had never been injured; just apparently like other similar patients; being clumsy after apparently not being able to walk for many months after radical surgery to repair combat injuries!

After a thorough physical examination and a total X-ray scan of his restored body, Slate was transferred to the hospital's physical and psychological rehabilitation floor; where he would literally have to learn to walk and run again with his new legs without being clumsy, bumping into things, and move about without any indication that his legs had been replaced with super-strong cyborg limbs! He also needed to learn to smoothly control his strong new ordinary-looking arms and hands without jerking and starting and stopping, and without crushing everything he picked up. His new mechanical arms and legs somehow looked and felt and were warm; like they were his own flesh! Somehow; some way, using a secret formula and a very intricate design; the designers also added what looked like hair on his new arms and legs; which could actually grow!

When Slate first awakened from his extensive surgery and tried to use his new arms and legs, it was exactly like a baby first learning to control and synchronize its arms, legs, and fingers. Much later when his cyborg parts were turned to full power, the young man had to learn again how to pick up a glass with his powerful new motorized hands without smashing it; how to walk using his new mechanical legs without losing his balance or jumping ten feet in the air or slamming into the nearest wall; how to covertly use the extra senses given to him by modern technology; and just how to live normally with his new abilities without literally acting like a "bull in a china shop"! His new limbs were powered by atomic deuterium batteries which obtained their fuel from the blood veins and arteries which were extended from his stubs and routed into and back out of each limb and connected back to the correct vein or artery to which was connected in his original arm! The tiny powerful motors in each limb also used "Roswell technology"; which had been reverse engineered from artifacts found at that location; to give Slate his tremendous strength! The scientific principle that enabled his cyborg limbs to grow hair was; and is; a very secret process that even today is very closely guarded!

Even after all this time, the young man had not been told exactly what had been done to him, and WHY; although he could tell just what had been replaced by simply feeling each substituted part. Slate had no memories from the exact instant the bomb went off to the instant he first regained consciousness at the hospital! He could actually feel the touch when he tapped any point on his new limbs; but the sensation of that touch was somehow "different". The total extent of the repairs on his body, and his new powers, would gradually be disclosed to him by daily talks with the physiatrists, the counselors, and the doctors with whom he visited to enable him to successfully fit back into military life as he continued to recover mentally and physically from his terrible injuries caused by the terrorist bomb. Several weeks later when he started his final daily periods of physical therapy exercises and his other military training sessions, Slate was able to walk by himself, with a cane for support and balance, as he traveled to his assigned appointments and Intel classes which were held at a separate building on the hospital grounds. To the sharp eyes of the alert sentries always on patrol 24/7 around the fenced hospital installation and the nearby classroom building; who would never know just what had happened to Slate; he still appeared to be a normal young man apparently recovering from some type of surgery that was just slightly clumsy because of long term incapacitation. After a few months of successful physical therapy that would completely restore his balance and his ability to walk and run exactly like he could before his terrible injury, Slate would be sent to a top secret base nearby to continue his training of his new physical capabilities in both indoor and outdoor settings; carrying substantial packs, heavy firearms, and trekking extremely long marches in the extremely hot Nevada desert.

Finally, when the young man progressed with his mental and physical recovery so that he could walk and run well enough without a cane, he was transferred a series of other bases and began intense training at secret ground-level and subterranean bases deeper in the deserts of Nevada; close to the Lexington medical facility that had originally saved his life, in order to train him to use the full extent of his new abilities made possible with ultra-modern technology. "Off the record", one of his old DI instructors even showed up to help him master his new limbs and his other "extra equipment!!

When Slate had finally mastered his new body attachments, he trained with several other young men and women with similar cyborg equipment; although none of them had such extensive radical surgery as Slate, with literally all their limbs and their eyes and ears replaced! Some had an arm replaced; because of combat injuries some had one or two of their legs replaced with mechanical legs; and one soldier had just an eye restored using fiber optics and life-like lenses for the cornea. The trainees nicknamed their group "The Area 102 Team". Throughout their training each of the trainees wondered and dreamed about what missions they would be sent to complete using their special abilities. Slate, during the past few years before the bomb blast, had successfully completed intensive training which enabled him to fly helicopters, cargo planes, jet fighters, and, according to his old DI, Sarge Snyder, "anything with or without wings"; ("without wings" referred to top-secret lifting bodies, able to fly from any airport looking like an advanced airplane, but capable of low Earth orbit, and lunar missions with help from a "Titan 16" rocket booster!) The young soldier had also successfully completed several "black opts" missions on the moon and on Mars before he had been injured!

Yet with all his experience at that time Slate was not able to fathom just what was in store for him in the Future! When the mental powers of the Imperial Seers partially came back "online", they could not visualize the specific "Future" Life Path of Slate beyond their present position! Because at that point on the Main Galactic Time Line, not even the most powerful Imperial Seers could use their mental powers to visualize what lay in store for the young man! Far under the surface of Empire Prime when they tried to visualize and comprehend the possible Life Paths of one Slate Steele, a unique phenomenon; never before seen by any Imperial Magi; presented itself! In each of their visions; literally hundreds of auxiliary time lines paralleling Slate's Present Primary Time Position were visible to each and every Magi who attempted to visualize his Future Path! But only one of these possible Life Path would come to pass; but which one?

Another problem was the fact that because each of these possible Future Happenings had not happened yet; they were all of equal brightness; indicating that each of them had the same percentage chance of happening! So the Imperial Seers could not fathom or prick out which ONE of Slate's Life Paths would happen; one that would ultimately change the course of the Galactic Time line!

So, all they could do again was WAIT-- and USE THEIR MENTAL POWERS TO ATTEMPT TO WATCH THE POSSIBLE LIFE PATHS OF THE SENTIENT BEING THAT, AT THAT INSTANT ON THE MAIN GALACTIC TIME LINE, WAS THE SINGLE MOST IMPORTANT BEING IN THE COSMIC ALL; WITH THE FATE OF ALL THE KNOWN GALACTIC PLANETS AND CIVILIZATIONS AT STAKE!

CHAPTER 7

After almost a year of training in the use of each of his new physical capabilities and vision capabilities, the completely physically restored young man was given a month of leave and used it to go see his parents and Dixie Davis, his faithful high school girlfriend in his old hometown, Cleburne, Texas. He had constantly written to her when he could from all over the world when he was on missions; and also, when he was recovering, using the attending nurses to write the letters for him and mail them. After his leave was over, Slate was to report to a secret military base in the western United States for his first assignment after his recuperation from his severe injuries.

But alas, his good fortune did not last! The first few days of the young man's leave were very relaxing, and he had a good time staying with his parents, Daisy Mae and Hank Steele; in their new home that they had just built on Buffalo Creek in the southwestern part of the town. He also liked catching up on the local Cleburne news, eating in the local restaurants, looking up old high school friends, and cruising around town on his motorcycle observing how much the small town had grown and changed since he had been gone. He also spent some time with Dixie; who he hoped to ultimately marry when he retired from the military or when he could transfer to a desk job and not be bound by regulations that prevented him from marrying because of his extremely dangerous top-secret duties, which he had been briefed would be both on and off the planet!

The hands of Time moved very quickly and too soon it was time for Slate to leave his hometown so that he would be back on time for his deployment to his new assignment. But just before he had left his hometown to go back on duty, **he disobeyed some very serious strict orders that he had been given**; strict orders that if he disobeyed, and the military found out; would put him in a military prison for the rest of his life! The very last day of his leave he left the home of his parents, went back to his old neighborhood, and once more searched out Dixie so that he could find out what she wanted to do and make final his future plans, (which hopefully would include the beautiful young woman). One last time, Slate and Dixie held hands and slowly walked to the shady, fenced backyard behind her parents' house for their final talk before he had to leave. It was there that Slate disobeyed his orders not to tell anyone about his new capabilities and told what he hoped was his bride-to-be about his severe combat injuries; the amazing new technologies that had been used to save his live and give him new abilities; and what exactly had to be done to his body in order to get them! He wanted to be absolutely honest with the young woman that he wanted to marry, and against his orders, he told her everything so that there would literally be no "surprises" after they were married! When she heard Slate's explanation of his severe injuries caused by the terrorist's bomb, the young woman was extremely horrified! She covered her eyes with her hands and started quietly crying! To try to calm her down, he continued his explanation by telling her and showing her the full extent of his new physical capabilities, by bending a crowbar and jumping to the nearby house roof and back to the ground! But unfortunately, his honesty and his showing of his new physical capabilities did not help the situation, it made it much worse! Incredibly, after his honest explanation and visual demonstration, Dixie started bawling louder, and between sobs she told him to get lost; she did not want to see him ever again in her life; without explaining the reason why!

But as he started to leave, between sobs, Dixie explained: "About a year ago, I heard over the nearby base's 'scuttle-butt grape vine' that you had been severely injured by a roadside bomb in Afghanistan and at the same time, you stopped writing to me! Since that terrible moment I have waited for any scrap of news that I could get over the regular news channels on Hi-Def television and the "gossip circuit"; but then your letters suddenly started coming again; each letter was written in a different and unfamiliar handwriting, which meant you were severely injured and had to get someone else to write them! You never told me in any of your letters the reason that someone else had to write to you and you acted in your notes to me as if nothing had happened! But now you show up here in person on leave, seemingly as good as new, without giving me any explanation! But I remained calm and waited for you to tell me what had happened to cause someone else to have to write your letters! After almost a week of ruining my hairstyles riding around with you on your motorcycle; and talking to you about trivial matters; you never told me about your almost fatal injury, and you acted like nothing was wrong! But at the very last minute before you had to go back, you suddenly tell me this incredible story about how your extensive combat injuries were somehow healed with advanced medical techniques using mechanical arms and legs! I am very glad that you have somehow been healed like the science fiction 'semi-robotic person' of the 1970's on the television show called the 'Rebuilt Man'; but I cannot, and I will not; be a wife to a. . . . a machine; in science fiction literature what is called a cyborg! Since I was a very young girl, in my dreams I have always wanted to marry the one man on Earth that I would come to love, like my mother loves my father, but I have to draw the line when it comes to self-preservation! I want a man for a life-mate who can caress and take me in his arms to kiss me without me having to worry about being accidently crushed to death; or violently strangled at night if you have a bad dream, like I have heard some military wives whose ordinary husbands are assigned covert ops have described at our weekly bridge game at the base! Several of the wives have related that sometimes they wake up in the middle of the night and their husbands are having violent dreams caused by their experiences in secret combat missions! The only problem is that in their husband's dream, their wives are the enemy, and this causes them to attack them!! When the wives wake up, they discover that they are being strangled by their husbands, who are having very violent nightmares! Some night if you did that to me with your superior cyborg strength, I would have no chance! I would be dead with my back, or my neck broken!! No, thank you! I want a 'normal' husband, with 'normal' strength and abilities; to cherish and grow old with! I don't want to live with a . . . a semi . . . robot and have to constantly worry about being crushed to death in my sleep when you have a nightmare!!!"

Slate was totally devastated; as all his hopes and dreams for a stable married life with the girl of his dreams were totally destroyed! He could not understand why Dixie felt that way! He loved her with all of this heart and he could not understand why she could not reciprocate! Even if he had been given new electronic eyes and mechanical arms and legs, he was still the same old Slate inside that graduated with her from Cleburne High School!! He believed in his heart that he would never hurt her; either while conscious or asleep! He was not like the evil cyborgs in the popular science fiction movie series, the latest of which was titled "Cy-Man", were playing all over the country; which he thought probably had influenced Dixie's outburst! He knew that he was not like that fictional very violent half-man-half-machine, and he could never be so evil! But as he thought and pondered about the terrible situation, he came to the final conclusion that Dixie's decision was heavily influenced by the theme of that popular make-believe movie genre; combined with the gossip she was always hearing from the wives of servicemen playing bridge every week.

Slate was perplexed, as his thought processes literally hit a brick wall!! What could he do to make her change her mind? He pondered the situation and finally came to a conclusion. Maybe he could leave her alone for a few months; not call her and not write to her; and his beloved would settle down and realize that deep down, below the "machinery", he was a normal human being who just happened to have needed his limbs replaced because of an accident sustained in combat; not like in the movie and act like an evil scientist wanted to conquer the world!

After the unfortunate cutting remarks from Dixie, Slate left her house after giving her his new Omni-phone number, looking into her blue eyes, and lightly giving her a final tender hug; even as she was still sobbing! He noticed that she did not look up after the hug or as he was going to his motorcycle! Wishing circumstances had been different; the tall handsome young man left her neighborhood very, very quickly; without looking back to wave! He then went across town to his parent's house to visit one final time with them and tell them goodbye before he left the area for what would probably be a very long time. He talked to his parents for over an hour as if nothing had happened and told them he would write when he could. With tears in his eyes as he carefully hugged them and told them how much he loved them; Slate again told them that he would write as often as he could; then he quickly left town; without telling them of his new powers; why so many other people wrote letters for him; or any of his future plans.

As they waved to his departing vehicle as it roared away along Buffalo Creek and curved out of sight, Slate's dad turned to his mother and said something very, very strange: "Daisy Mae, in the long years that we were raising our son who was born here in Cleburne; just after we arrived on Earth and assumed normal identities among the Earthlings; do you think we should have told Samuel about his true heritage? Should we have told him about being the son of Humanoids who covertly settled on Earth from the eerie planet Marvana; which is situated beyond all the nearby stars? Our particular species of Humanoids has peacefully coexisted with the so-called 'Wer-Men' and 'Wer-Women';

'Haf-Cott beings'; 'Trankor Beings'; and the famous 'Trecian Witches' and 'Warlocks'; for millennia on that planet; which because of the many different types of beings living serenely together has been nicknamed the "Halloween Planet"! Our son acted normal during his visit, and it doesn't seem like he has made 'The Change' yet! I hope we can see him again before it happens and tell him about his amazing legacy of being related to the Old West Marshal Samson Blair; who is my great uncle many times removed! You know, Sam is still alive and living peacefully somewhere in Nevada! He doesn't look a day over 25 in the picture that he emailed me a few weeks ago! He actually looked like Deputy Marshal Wyatt Earp did pictured in one of my old history books! Sam once told me that he had met himself dressed like a descendant of Wyatt Earp, when he had first been transferred to our time from the 1880's by what he called "The Comet of Omens"! (As documented in **Seth and Samson Blair!**) My wife, since you and I are Humanoid beings that have 'shape changers' in our past; this is why our son also will eventually have the power to instantly change his shape when he physically matures! I wish we had told Slate before his metabolism changes like I told you it would! 'The Change' has to happen sometime soon!"

"I hope so too, dear! I felt of him when he hugged me and he did not seem too hot, which is the first indication that his body is changing because the small gland in his brain that allows him to literally change his body shape is finally maturing! He has always been 'hot natured', but when I hugged and embraced him, he did not seem hot enough for 'The Change' to be taking place! We can only hope and pray we will see him before that happens, so that we can tell and show him a few things as soon as we can to help him adjust, and be able to control his powers! He has been so busy the last few weeks that I did not have any opportunity to tell him; and all during his life here in Cleburne every time you or I wanted to tell him, something intervened!" Slate's mother returned.

As his parents were discussing his past; Slate was thinking about something else-his lonely future without Dixie! As he left his home town very fast on "Daisy Mae", his motorcycle; the young man tried unsuccessfully to leave the cutting remarks of his beloved Dixie behind and not keep thinking about what she had said! But unfortunately he could not forget the rejection of his Loved One! He could not forget the look in Dixie's blue eyes as she looked into his brown eyes and firmly refused to accept him the way he was; even though before he had been injured, she had previously agreed to ultimately marry him when his military enlistment was up and he was able to get a local job, or when he could be assigned a permanent desk job! A nightmare picture of those beautiful blue eyes he looked into when he was leaving had literally burned into his psyche and he knew that unless something drastic happened, he would see them in his dreams for the rest of his days!! But unknown to him, in her own Soul, Dixie also retained a picture of his piercing brown eyes, which she knew would appear in her dreams the rest of her life!

After traveling several days, Slate arrived back at his assigned secret base of operations located somewhere in the desert lands of the western United States and checked in; having a warm reunion with some of his old buddies from previous combat assignments. The young man quickly resumed his secret duties, covert intelligence ops and other "needed combat missions" which he always performed quickly, quietly, and seemingly to even the new soldiers he met; and to his close combat veteran buddies who on combat missions in the past had somehow acquired nicknames such as Snuffy, Curly, (who was bald), Greenie, and Binko; Slate did each mission or job assigned to him, almost "mindlessly". To his closer-than-a-brother comrades, since the young man had joined their unit several years before, Slate always had a "faraway" look in his eyes and moved almost "mechanically" to accomplish his ordered objectives. But when he came back from leave, Slate seemed even more aloft to everyone he was around. Totally immersing himself in his job, for as long as he served his country, he had little or no social life except on the weekends to go out a few times with his buddies in one of the local steak houses or hamburger joints. He apparently only lived totally to carry out his assigned missions in all the seven continents of the globe; (with even several Ultra-Top Secret missions on the far side of the moon and, incredibly to even the surface of Mars!) With his total concentration on his covert and very dangerous duties which he was able to perform quite well with his advanced hardware, the required years of his military service to his country passed by very quickly, (and very slowly to Dixie back in Cleburne and ultimately in New York City when she moved to also try to forget those two large brown eyes!)

Day after day; month after month; as he neared his "Anchor Moment" which could affect the entire region of the Cosmic All around Earth and all the way to Empire Prime; Slate could not feel the Winds of Destiny constantly flowing around him as he traveled along his Path of Destiny! He also unknowingly faced what his mother had covertly called "The Change", which would somehow affect his body in an unknown way!

Until finally one "Day of Destiny", against the normal Laws of Chance, several Life Paths of other veteran warriors came close and merged with Slate's; the effects of which would affect and hasten the Anchor Moment he was destined to live through! But would this "merging" affect his Moment of Destiny for the good, or for the bad! At that position on the Galactic Time Stream, only the Winds of Destiny knew, and the Imperial Seers would ultimately be able to visualize and record permanently, (until the end of Eternity), "after the fact"; when the Galactic Time Stream's branches concerning Slate "came back online" and they could use their mental powers again to visualize what could; or what would eventually happen! So as the seconds slowly ticked by; finally becoming days; then spanning month after month; then finally achieving several years; the Moment of Destiny for the Cosmic All gradually came closer on the Galactic Time Line. . . . . **AND THEN . . . .!**

CHAPTER 8

So after being enlisted for the required number of years in the military after outstanding meritorious service, Slate handed in his resignation and began the arduous process of going through the very involved standard procedure that allowed combat veterans to go back to civilian life. After successfully passing all the required physical and psychological exit tests, Slate was honorably discharged from his black ops duties, having sworn verbally, and on his discharge documents; to never reveal his true powers to anyone, or tell any details of any of the literally hundreds of missions that he had successfully, or unsuccessfully carried out, on pain of immediate arrest and an immediate court martial and imprisonment! Each day of his enlistment he would not have been surprised if Dixie had "spilled the beans" about the classified information he had told her and, because of that, he had suddenly been arrested, charged with disobeying orders, and imprisoned for life! But Dixie kept mum about what he had told her, and the authorities never learned about his telling her about his ultra-secret cyborg body parts; (although several decades later when the Imperial Seers were researching his Time Line when he became an Imperial Officer, they discovered his secret, but by that time, the illegal event was "moot" and unimportant!

His discharge papers stated that one day every one to two years when electronically contacted, he would be required to visit Bomar's "outpatient clinic", so that his ultra-secret computer implants and their software programs could be updated and/or replaced. A signal sent from a military satellite to a tiny transceiver in his right arm would remind him of his appointment to get his cyborg parts checked and repaired or replaced back at his old military base. Computer programs in his right arm's electronics also automatically kept track of the condition of all of his atomic-powered cyborg parts; and were programmed to send daily reports, via a coded satellite connection to the secret base in Nevada, about the condition of each of his subsystems. This allowed the military authorities to keep track of Slate, classified as "B-RED", "Benign; but Retired, Extremely Dangerous", 24/7, and 365 ¼ days a year! Officially this tracking allowed them to contact him in case there was a national emergency and his services were needed once more! (Another important reason was to allow the military authorities to track and catch him if he went "rogue")!

His retirement check each month would always be electronically direct-deposited into his checking account which had been established with the base's American Military National Bank, which allowed him to obtain all the funds he required for his lonely travels from any of the literally hundreds of thousands of ATMs nationwide, free since no bank fees were accessed on retired military personnel.

Slate's military medical card would cover virtually all his medical and dental bills. He had served long enough so that the modern version of the famous "GI Bill" would pay for any college courses he would want to take—possibly all the way through getting a PHD and beyond in any subject or discipline that he wished; and at any college or university that he wished to attend.

Slate was also given a 24/7 emergency line by his original psychologist Dr. Terry Sinclair, who signed in triplicate his final release papers. Dr. Sinclair also told Slate that he could call Dr. Wagstaff or him, anytime he felt that needed help, or even if he just wanted to talk, for any reason; day or night; rain or shine; 24/7-365 ¼ days a year. That fact was so important that the psychologist emphasized several times that whenever the young military veteran felt he needed to talk or vent, or even needed a place to live. In which case, Slate could communicate with either him or Dr. Martha Wagstaff, the doctor who had taken such good care of him when he first came in, and was kept in a coma as his case was being studied at the Lexington Military Hospital; and permanent or temporary living accommodations for him would be immediately set up.

The course of his future was literally up to him; with many open doors for him to choose from; but at that time in his life, with all the tools available for him to be able to succeed at literally anything he wished. But with all the resources available to Slate to help him build a bright future, at that instant on the Time Line, all he wanted to do was roam mindlessly and have a good time; trying to forget; **TRYING TO FORGET . . . . THOSE. . . . !** Trying to erase the memory of that one last glimpse of those beautiful, beautiful blue eyes!!! But now; even as it was in the past, as year, after year, after year went by; despite trying as hard as he could, **he could. . . .not. . . . . . forget. . . . THOSE EYES . . THOSE EYES . . THOSE EYES!!! THOSE BEAUTIFUL BLUE EYES WOULD ALWAYS BE BURNED INTO HIS MEMORY! (And elsewhere in New York City, for a short time; and then back in Cleburne, neither could Dixie forget his piercing brown eyes; spending many sleepless nights after waking up because of seeing those brown orbs of the man she loved in her dreams!)**

So with no money worries, for long; lonely months the physically healed; but still mentally-wounded; young combat veteran wandered all over the entire North American continent; up into Canada; then traveling the entire coastline of Alaska on his faithful two-wheeled vehicle "Daisy Mae"; trying to outrun his haunting nightmare of those two beautiful blue eyes! He felt that the reoccurring dream was so deeply personal that he did not want to discuss the nightly nightmare with his parents, or Dr. Wagstaff, or Dr. Sinclair! Perhaps in a few decades; but not now!

Along his useless journey-to-forget, the military veteran made many "roadside friends" at the highway cafes and gasoline stations that he frequented; visiting each favorite stop many times as he continuously roamed, always striving with no success; trying to forget those two blue eyes almost always appearing in his dreams!! He was traveling aimlessly "as if in a fog"; trying to forget the almost nightly visions of the hauntingly beautiful blue eyes and blond hair of what he believed in his Soul was his One True Love, which he knew, would be an instant forever frozen in time; and forever etched in his mind until the instant that he died!

But even though Slate tried without success to flee from his dark vision and his Future, no matter how far he roamed, his "Karma" or Fated Destiny would not be denied! "Cross-related" events were about to happen, and all the sentient beings which would be required to ultimately rendezvous with the Important Person so that he could fulfill his Kismet, were slowly moving into place on the Main Galactic Time Line/Time Cloud; the result was the Galactic Time Stream twisting and turning serendipitously to create a very rare Time Nexus! Like the large solid holographic pieces created on the Emperor's Imperial Chess board and moved during an important tournament on Empire Prime; like mere puppets; important and powerful beings all over the Cosmic All were unknowingly performing their regular assigned duties; while at the same time, unknowingly moving into their necessary place for "The Event of the Ages"! But these "regular duties", in turn, were causing important seemingly unrelated events to happen; and all these "pieces" on the Time Line were moving faster and faster on several planets millions of light years away from Earth! These were far off beings and seemingly unimportant events that would soon affect the young man's Destiny! Some possibly for the better; and some possibly for the worst! The effect of each would depend on Slate and what he did in response to unfolding events. Even the Winds of Destiny could not know if the effects of each event would be "good" or "bad" since these actions hadn't happened yet' and the happening of one small incident could change or totally erase the whole important coming Event! Ultimately, how they would affect him and his Karma was literally up to him and what he would do at each important "Anchor Moment" that would literally produce a very rare "Galactic Anchor Event", when his important actions would literally change the direction of the Main Galactic Time Line, probably until the so-called "End of Time"; an infinite distance down the Main Galactic Road of Time!

The Future Time Stream direction and the Ultimate Life Quality of one "Samuel Eliot 'Slate' Steele" would depend on how his used his strong new physical skills and his reasoning when confronted with several "Anchor Moments" to act, which he would experience in the near Future! For each of these so-called "Anchor Moments", (the description given by the Imperial Magi on Empire Prime to certain important happenings in the Cosmic All on which all Future Events on that particular section of the Time Stream "would depend upon or spin about"); Slate would have a split-second with which to make a decision! At each of the coming pivotal points would he: watch and listen, when confronted run or fight to protect himself; take the easy way out of a problem or choose the hard path; tell the truth about something or opt to lie for the "Common Good"? What Slate opted to do was important; with the young man not knowing that, sometime in the "Future", literally billions and ultimately trillions and quadrillions of sentient beings would live or die according to what he chose to do; **OR NOT TO DO!** But all of these future events were just that, in the future further along the Time Stream, (or if you prefer, Time Cloud); and as such, could not yet be accurately visualized by the Imperial Seers or even the Winds of Destiny----**YET!!**

So day after day; year after Earthian year as the History Changing Moment or Moments came nearer on the Time Line, the young man continued to ride alone down archaic highways, back alleys, and dirt roads; always burdened down with his painful memories and his nightly agonizing visions of those two lovely blue eyes! As he traveled, Slate made many acquaintances, but no close friends, at the dozens and dozens of mom-and-pop grocery stores; hardware stores, gasoline stations, dry goods stores, and fast, and "slow" food restaurants he frequented on the narrow state highways and dirt roads that he always used. But as he traveled mile after weary mile, he was unknowingly speeding down his Life Pathway toward an existence somewhere between his Final Doom . . . and Paradise-—i.e., a life between Death......or a completely Fulfilled Life; and the odds were that his mental and physical burdens after such important happenings would probably be greater than what he was carrying now!

So year after year; seemingly carrying the entire world on his shoulders; Slate traveled aimlessly up and down the dilapidated highways of the North American Continent; **UNTIL. . . . . the first of Slate's "Moments of Destiny" arrived!!**

CHAPTER 9

Late one hot summer night after the extremely bright "Hunter's" moon had gone down, as a result of his totally random roaming all across the North American continent, Slate was camping on a dark; lonely hillside in Zion National Park, Utah; after traveling many miles off Interstate 9. He was camping at that spot because of what he privately called his "7th combat sense"; something that seemed beyond the so-called normal Humanoid "5 senses" and abnormal "ESP". About a week ago he had been traveling up in Maine along the coast when he had a very eerie feeling. For the first time in his relatively short life, Slate suddenly got the eerie feeling deep down in his soul that he should be traveling west! The impression was similar to a sensation that he sometimes felt, when he was on a combat mission; that he should walk in a certain direction. He always obeyed his feeling and, just about every time, enemy sniper fire or artillery came down where he would have been if he had not changed his course! (For some reason, his 7th sense had not worked to protect him from the terrorist bomb!) So because of his past military experiences with obeying similar "feelings", the combat vet "went with the flow" and instinctively obeyed his instincts and feelings, which he explicitly trusted because of the safe outcomes of most of his previous combat experiences when he obeyed his inner urge to suddenly do something unexpected!

So day after day, accepting what was happening; when he settled in for the night before he tried to sleep, Slate relaxed his mind and allowed his thoughts to wander; and immediately he would get an instinct of which direction he should go the next morning. So as result of his obeying all of the strange feelings to travel in a certain direction; he was successful in achieving what Fate had decreed-- that at a specific point on the Time Line he would be in the one spot in the physical Cosmic All which would allow him to achieve his Ultimate Destiny! Amazingly, Slate's "Spot of Destiny" was on a dark; lonely hillside in Utah; many miles from the nearest city and town. While following his instincts to travel, Slate stopped on the side of the highway many miles from the nearest small town and carefully guided Daisy Mae off the deserted road for several hundred yards to pitch his camp on the rocky ground. After a cold supper, he stretched out on a flat piece of ground with only a light blanket against the desert chill which was caused by the extremely dry desert air cooling down very quickly when the sun went down.

As the Winds of Destiny silently watched from their subatomic homes, Slate had been tossing and turning on the rocky bare ground; unable to sleep; when he suddenly opened his eyes; glanced up into the still night sky; and noticed what appeared to be a shooting star, a meteor, or a fireball, coming down to the west of his location. The point of light, with what looked like a trail of sparks and smoke trailing out behind it, was coming down at very steep trajectory! An instant later, it finally disappeared behind a tall mesa a few miles from his present location into a rugged mountainous area filled with treacherous rock-strewn slopes; vertical cliffs; and loose shale and rocks; all of which made any travel across the terrain very hazardous! As he watched the spectacle, Slate instinctively waited for the sound of a crash or a flash of light indicating that the luminous fiery object had hit the ground, but he saw or heard nothing!

Curious, the young man dressed and put his hiking shoes back on to investigate on foot what he thought was a meteor falling in the desolate and lonely country far away from civilization landing behind the tall mesa; which masked the sound and the light flash when it hit. After carefully traveling several miles over level dry sandy ground, the terrain became literally covered with rocks and large boulders; and gradually sloped upward as he neared the tall mesa where he had seen the fireball vanish. Being very patient to avoid an injury, he slowly wound his way among the scattered rocks and boulders using his infrared night vision and his natural tracking instincts to try to reach a position where he could see where the strange object had supposedly smashed into the ground. Another hour's trek found him walking in almost total darkness at the base of the large mesa; with a gentle breeze blowing from behind him toward his objective; with only extremely faint star light and his cyborg infrared eyesight to guide his journey. Finally, he climbed over a final barrier of large loose rocks and reached the edge of the tall flat mesa. After the very long hike he was finally close enough to be able to observe a pale column of yellow light that was being emitted from what looked like the interior section of the tall, rocky mesa. The location of the light appeared to be on another flat surface twenty or thirty feet higher that the outer rim of the rocky formation. The laser-like light was pointed upward as if signaling to something high in the sky and shielded by rocks so as not to be visible from the ground unless reflected by smoke or mist and the observer was very close. As he moved forward, two things start to happen simultaneously: he suddenly developed a very severe headache, and unseen and unfelt by his ordinary; nonexistent ESP senses, the Winds of Destiny slowly started to grow from moderate, to gale force; indicating that something was about to happen that would forever change his Personal Destiny along with the Time Line direction of the Destiny of Earth; its Galaxy; and perhaps even the far off Empire of Empires!!!!

Trained to withstand battle injuries, the former soldier, who had also earned the nickname of "Steel" because of his extremely high pain tolerance after being slightly wounded several times and refusing to get medical care until the mission was over; ignored the intense throbbing in the back part of his head, and continued to move forward to sate his curiosity; and in the process, literally moving to meet his Karma head on, and thereby change it-for better or for worse!

Carefully climbing over small stones and boulders at the edge of the sides of the high mesa, and being as quiet as he could, after much searching, the cyborg found the only possible way to the top without using wings. Slate came upon what looked like a water trough from the top of the mesa; apparently made by extremely rare rainfall draining down over a long period of time. He slowly made his way up a narrow; almost vertical chimney-like chute, by simultaneously grasping the sides and pushing up with his feet in order to force his way up. With his infrared vision he had observed that the etchings that apparently had been made in the hard stone trough over thousands of years by infrequent deluges of running water, seemed to indicate that the worn rocky chute offered a way to the top of the mesa, and he hoped that the stone shaft would not widen as he got to the top. If that happened, he would have to painfully inch his way back down to the ground and look for another way up. Slate was in luck; for the chute eventually gently curved forward to allow him to safely exit to the rubble-covered top; strew with literally hundreds of boulders of every size and shape making travel over; under; and around them; very dangerous!

After several minutes of careful climbing up and over the dangerous terrain, he again used his infrared night vision to observe what was happening far across the surface of the mesa. His night vision revealed what appeared to his military-trained eyes to a large building atop the mesa. The size of the building indicated to his military training that it apparently covered a very large underground installation. From behind large boulders he watched as what appeared to be equipment and supplies were unloaded from some sort of aircraft by shadowy figures and stashed next to the building. It also looked like the aircraft was being worked on; since what appeared to be side panels had been taken off and dark shapes looked to be repairing something in its interior. As Slate continued to watch, he saw a sliding door suddenly open in the side of the building; revealing what looked like a brightly-lit interior of a freight elevator. Immediately the dark shapes started loading what had come off the aircraft into the elevator's cavernous depths. The dark figures worked fast, and it only took them a few minutes for what probably was equipment and supplies to be stashed inside the elevator.

A few seconds after the last indistinct form came out of the opening, the door closed and what was in the elevator was probably transported down into what; in all probability his training told him; was a covert base to allow military operations of an unknown nature by an unidentified force!

Perhaps this covert base was being run by a domestic military force such as the Central Intelligence Agency, or even a secret foreign spy base, run by the KGB, MARAN, or the supposedly friendly international spy organization nicknamed "AUNTIE"! None of his ultra-secret military briefings had mentioned such a hidden enemy military base on American soil; so perhaps, hopefully, it was being run by forces friendly to the United States! Slate did not know and could not tell from his present position, but he felt that for the safety of the country, he had to determine just what military force was running a secret base in the desert; so further investigation was necessary! His cell phone had no service in this remote area; so he would have to reconnoiter by moving much closer to the unknown activity in order to find out just what was going on; then he would move back to an area with phone service to get help if this hidden base was enemy territory! Continuing to scan with his telescopic and his infrared vision of the jumbled mass of shadows as Slate slowly moved forward, the surface of the mesa revealed an incredible fact about the unknown base! As he slowly got closer to get a better view and patiently watched, the door of what had looked like an elevator again opened. He was now close enough to observe that the beings working to load and unload supplies, instead of being Humanoids; appeared to be a group of nightmare creatures created out of the vivid imaginations of the writers of the popular "Stranger Zone" science fiction television show!! They looked like extremely tall scaled alligators; with small tails dragging behind; and walking upright around in the shadows of the mesa! In the dim light it seemed like they each had six appendages in front; four small paws or arms tipped with large claws or talons, and two larger appendages shaped like arms and having what seemed like Humanoid-type hands! As he continued to secretly watch, he observed that several of the fearsome reptilian-looking beings not unloading supplies appeared to be huddled around a very large old fashioned campfire; conversing in low guttural tones; as large sparks and embers floated up into the dark sky; borne by the gentle breeze!

But in his quest to find out exactly what was going on, Slate had gotten too close to the aliens and apparently their keen reptilian senses detected him! In unison, as if they were telepathic, every grotesque creature huddled around the fire, and also those working around the elevator, suddenly straightened up; slowly looked around, and stared directly at him! In response to the invader, one tall slim reptile turned around, sprang toward him using long hops; and when close enough, jumped high in the air to apparently attack the unknown Humanoid intruder at the edge of their camp site; without trying to communicate with him to see if he was a friend! Knowing that if he turned his back on the reptile he would be slashed by the being's talons; and believing that "the best defense is a good offense"; Slate returned the favor by turning toward the threat; having to thrust aside a very large log that was in his path as if it were a matchstick, and jumping as high into the air as he could, trying to match the reptile's enormous leap and meet him in the air! He was attempting to fight a being vastly stronger that he was; in addition to going against a foe with large sharp claws while armed with only his bare Humanoid hands!

But incredibly; impossibly breaking the laws of physics, near the top of his enormous leap the reptile creature swiftly touched a button on his thick belt; slowed in midair and successfully landed at a steep angle as Slate had to obey the natural laws of the Universe and continue with his leap! Then incredibly, a split second later, the Humanoid felt that he was somehow slowing in mid-flight, and he somehow managed to safely land a few yards in front of the awaiting fantastic creature! He was immediately surrounded on all sides by a wall of tall menacing reptiles with very large mouths and clawed limbs! They seemed like small dinosaurs out of a nightmare instead of sentient intelligent beings!

Slate did not know what to do! He knew that probably the reptiles could not speak English, so he would have to wait and let them make the first move to communicate with him. Instead of verbal speaking, what seemed to be something other than oral communication from the unknown horrendous creatures was not long in coming!

Giving what apparently was a grin; showing two-inch long fangs, the tall Reptiloid boomed telepathically, *#Welcome to our camp, Earthman! We are called "Reptiloids"! My legal Reptiloid and family name is "Karkanza"; and since you are apparently a warrior, I will tell you that my Battle Pack Warrior Name is "Red Stinger"! That tall warrior over there close behind you to supposedly prevent you from escaping is my second in command, Blue Stinger, and the rest of our band! The combined reptilian senses of my Reptiloid Battle Pack, which you observed around our fire, detected your covert approach to our counsel fire with our sensitive ears and sensitive noses! Suddenly, as we conversed* *about our fire, a strange new odor was added to the scents of the local flora and fauna, which have we constantly smelled since we landed! It was the scent of the skin of a Humanoid, which we all know well, having mingled with many such beings while visiting Empire Prime!#*

The enormous alien being stopped a moment; then continued his explanation. *#When I jumped to investigate you, instead of trying to uselessly flee, you acted like what we call a true "Kif Warrior" and jumped to meet me; instinctively knowing that turning around to flee would have allowed me to use my talons to rip open your back and quickly destroy you! But I do not want to destroy you, I simply want to talk to you as soon as possible about an important matter! So because of this fact, instead of fighting, I used my Imperial defense belt to stop us both in midair and also to try to stop your counter-attack so that we may confer about the important matter I just mentioned, and with your help, the outcome can be mutually beneficial to both of us!#*

The tall Reptiloid stopped telepathically sending for a moment and then continued, *#Now that you are close to my senses and the sensors in my defense belt, I also detect that your extensive wounds on your arms, legs, body, and head; that you sustained sometime in the past, have now fully healed and the surprising technological advances for this backward planet that have been used to compensate for that which your planet's medical technology apparently could not naturally restore with the information stored* *in your Double and Triple Helixes; which are in every one of your Humanoid body cells! All these wounds from past conflicts prove to me that you are truly a Blooded Kif Warrior! Our keen senses also indicate a lack of the usual Humanoid fear pheromones, even though you are surrounded and cannot escape; indicating that your courage would be very great for any of our warriors to face! I can read in your mind the fact that to you, we are like the video science fiction movies shown on your planet that are always unfriendly space monsters! But this time, your hunter's luck is good! We mean you no harm and we will not kill you, even though you have detected our secret base, because we are friendly allies of a gigantic space empire far across the galaxy, which you have probably not heard of, called the Interstellar Condominium of Planets and Empires, or ICOPE! Even though we look like space monsters, we are very friendly to our allies; and we need your help!!#*

#Again, welcome to our camp!!! Relax and stand down! You must eat at our table, where literally every being is an experienced soldier! As a Blooded Warrior; upon my honor as another Blooded Warrior, and Swearing by the First Egg of my Ancestral Line; forget what you have seen on your science-fiction movies! Neither you nor your planet are in any danger of being destroyed by our Reptiloid forces; now, and in the future! Please come dine with us inside! As an experienced Kif warrior you will be an honored guest at our meal; for we appreciate and value the skills of war

that your extensive wounds from the past exhibit! As I said, my tribal combat command name is Red Stinger and I am in charge of our planet's secret operations on your planet! We are on a peaceful scouting mission searching for a specific warrior or warriors that can perform a dangerous mission to help our planet avoid war! Even after researching all the information that the Empire has on the capabilities of your planet, we did not know that you Earthmen had the scientific capabilities to produce the powerful artificial limbs whose capabilities you have exhibited in our presence, Mr. Steele, when you pushed that heavy log out of your way as if it were merely one of your writing instruments I believe that you call a 'pencil'!#

The words telepathically spoken by Red Stinger seemed to explode in his brain in the exact region that he was experiencing the pain in his head! Slate wanted to somehow boldly communicate to the huge aliens and since the reptile was telepathic, he tried to mentally reply to the fearsome Reptiloid by simply thinking the words that he wanted to say; attempting to somehow mentally project them; and hope the Reptiloids could somehow understand him! He was very astonished when the alien reptile's mind seemed to open up to his attempts at communication and the young man communicated as best he could as he projected: *#From the evidence I see in your mind of your previous recon missions, I'm sure you know that the normal Humanoids on this planet are not what we call cyborgs, but after I was severely wounded in combat, I was fortunate that I was given the advantage of the highest Earthian technology* *available that healed the extensive wounds on my arms, legs, and head; while adding to my natural abilities! At the moment, Earth medical technology cannot regrow my limbs! When I saw you jump toward me, I jumped to meet you; like you said, knowing that if I turned my back on you, the battle would have been over very quickly with your sword in my back! Then incredibly I saw you apparently disobey the law of gravity; then when I slowed down also, I thought that my body had learned the trick from you; not knowing that you had used an electronic device to slow both of us down!#* Slate replied; being totally honest because he realized that with total mental communication, subterfuge was impossible.

The huge Reptiloid then projected, *#Actually, Warrior Steele, I too, use ultra-advanced technology my solar system borrowed from the Empire I told you about, called the Interstellar Condominium of Planets and Empires, or "ICOPE", to enhance my fighting ability! Like I previously explained; I stopped my leap using my Imperial defense belt; which allowed me to stop in midair and go to the ground, or jump sideways in the middle of the leap, all under controlled flight! This is an important maneuver to be able to do during fight-to-the-death; claw-to-claw combat! Also like I previously said, when I landed, I used its features to also allow you to land safely!#*

#But enough! We have much to discuss! Come, Warrior Steele! As a blooded veteran soldier by our Blood Warrior Customs several hundred thousand years old, you may enter our Circle of Honor

around our campfire with full voting and speaking privileges! From your extremely unusual full two-way mental communication with me which I have allowed so that you will know that you can trust us, you know that we are what the Empire calls "Reptiloids"; and you also know that we represent no harm to you! From examining my thoughts, you know that you are safe in our presence and a welcome guest at our fire, no matter how fearsome our fangs and our outward appearances! We bring you around our counsel fire because we have something extremely important to discuss with you concerning the wellbeing of our entire Race of Reptiloids! The armed forces of our planetary system called the Thunder Worlds hurriedly used our superior technology to build this secret underground base several months ago to serve as a central point to organize an important search of this part of the galaxy! Before you discovered our scout group, our technicians were in the process of fixing a minor problem with our ship's landing jets; which produced a trail of sparks as the ship was landing. But now our counsel has been debating around our fire, trying to figure out how to solve an extremely difficult problem that is unsolvable for our group because of two peculiarities unique to our culture and our species! We were having no luck getting a solution, but your fortunate visit to our fire may give us one! For weeks we have been searching all the inhabited planets in this part of the galaxy for someone with the required capabilities to help us; with no Hunter's Luck, and absolutely no good luck at all! But now, because of your exhibited leaping power and your apparent great strength, I think you might be the one we require to help save our Home Worlds! We have a need to hire your unique capabilities to perform a very important job that, because of certain mental and physical limitations of our Reptiloid bodies, we cannot accomplish!! But enough! We will talk about such important matters after we partake of food that we hope will be compatible with your body's chemistry! We will bring your supplies and your two-wheeled vehicle up from your other campsite so you will have something to eat if our Yoaka Snake meat is not to your liking! We do not know much about the needs of your Humanoid body; so we will let you check all our food before you eat it! After the meal, if you wish you can go out to your old campsite to sleep or you can sleep undisturbed among other warriors tonight, without having to be bothered with the wolves, wolverines, mountain lions, coyotes and other Earthian predators which inhabit this so-called 'National Park'! We will talk about more important matters in the morning after we all have had a good night's rest!# Red Stinger projected to Slate's newly emerging telepathic senses.

Having mental contact with the alien known as Red Stinger, Slate knew that everything that the alien mentally said was true; so he knew that he would be safe sleeping among the stranger beings that looked like something out of a nightmare, and parley with them in the morning about a dangerous mission that even such strong Reptiloids could not do! As he ate among the towering reptile warriors, his Battle Sense was at ease; so Slate knew he was among friends; even though they looked like the "Martian Sand Reptiles" from his favorite boyhood movie! As he watched and telepathically listened, the relatively small group of large Reptiloid warriors acted exactly like his buddies in his combat group! They ate heartily; they frequently slapped each other's backs with enough force to break his; they joked; and they all told exaggerated tales of their daring exploits in battle; just like Earthian soldiers! The hours passed quickly and, after the meal and fellowship with his unusual new friends, as he lay down with the stars over his head, for some very strange reason that he could not fathom, **for the first time in several years, the young veteran felt at peace within his Heart! He did not have the usual two beautiful blue eyes staring him in the face as he closed his eyes to sleep, like he had almost every night since their breakup!** Perhaps the source of his inner peace was partly because he could not feel the Winds of Destiny cascading around him; while the aroused Battle Sense of some of the more mentally-gifted Reptiloids sleeping around him made the reptiles feel uneasy by the passage of the Winds! But perhaps the real reason Slate felt at ease was because he was back on his Road of Destiny-the path along the Time Stream that he had been born to tread! Because he was so relaxed, among the fearsome Reptiloid warriors the young soldier quickly dropped off to sleep and did not think about his sudden peace! That was something that he would think about in the morning, even as his Road of Destiny was about to meet head on with those of another different race of strong reptile warriors; a very formidable species of Reptiloids; and not from the Thunder World planets of his new reptile friends!

CHAPTER 10

As he suddenly regained consciousness the next morning and looked around without moving as he was trained to do, Slate realized that for some unknown reason, he had slept that night better than he had in years; probably because he had slept without any nightmare of two beautiful blue Humanoid eyes swimming before his vision in his dreams! Perhaps he slept very well because he instinctively knew that he was among friends! But perhaps the main reason was because he sensed deep in his Id that he was perhaps about to perform a feat of daring that all his military experiences and training had prepared him for; and he did not need any distraction to hinder his preparation for the ordeal ahead!

Soon after Slate arose, he prepared and ate a small meal from fixings that he had in his cycle; since the Reptiloid Yoaka Snake meat and the other alien foods that had been offered to him last night were not "compatible with his body's chemistry"! As an expert in "living off the land" by finding plants and animals to prepare for his meals, Slate followed his Battle Sense and only inspected several of the food portions offered him without tasting them, and they all failed his "nose and touch" tests! When he smelled each food, the odors burned the inside of his nose; and literally burned his fingers when he touched them; hence he politely declined to eat them! So instinctively; instead of eating each of the unknown food of his hosts like it was some new dish out of a foreign country whose only citizens were Humanoids with similar stomachs; he had politely declined to partake of the alien cuisine! Out of curiosity, he saved several of the alien foods in a vacuum meal tray and had it tested many months later at a private laboratory in one of the small towns that he had frequently traveled through. It was a good thing that he followed his instincts; because when he read the printed lab report, he found that virtually all of the alien vegetables, fruits, and meats on the lab tests, turned out to be "incompatible with Humanoid digestive tracts"; and contained various poisons, toxins, and nerve-block agents which would instantly cause extreme pain or permanently immobilize any Humanoid if not given some unknown anecdote very quickly! So if he had eaten the alien meal, both Slate's life, and his Road to his Destiny would have quickly ended!

Just after sunup; Slate had an important conference with the strange aliens as the hidden Winds of Destiny swirled unseen and unheard around them! Red Stinger and his military group again met with him around their central campfire, which had been kept burning all night, and started their version of breakfast, which included their food and water; and also if he wanted to eat again, some eatable food for Slate, which the Reptiloids got out of his motorcycle.

Red Stinger began the conference by telepathically saying, *#Earthman; eat up; because we need to have a very serious conference!! We need to hire you for a very important and dangerous mission which, as powerful as we Reptiloid warriors are; we cannot perform without actions of the enemy causing our instant death! Our planetary confederation has been united for many centuries around a much-revered artifact, which was stolen a few days ago by our enemies from a heavily guarded base on our home planet; with the help of several traitors who held trusted positions of authority in our planetary government! They no longer hold any positions of authority on our planet, because we followed the laws of our people and they no longer physically exist! The political icon was stolen by a rival enemy Reptiloid faction and taken to a nearby star system, where our intelligence reports indicate that it will be used in a few days to disrupt and take over our planetary government; without them having to physically battle any of our forces! A designated member of their group will be able to formally announce that they have our cherished icon, and thereby instantly become our supreme ruler without any of our people lifting a claw to oppose him!!#*

Red Stinger paused to drink some water; then projected, *#We can literally do nothing to oppose them because our adversary, which has been plotting and has tried several times over many centuries to take over our government, is very smart and very technically advanced! Several centuries ago, a rival political faction in our tri-planet government tried* *to take over the government by force, instead of at the ballot box! They failed, and were permanently exiled out of our solar system! The exiled group totaled a little over twenty thousand Reptiloids and several hundred ships of various sizes. The group settled in a star system several thousand light years away from the Thunder Worlds and set up their own government on several planets in their star system. Instead of being satisfied with running their own government in their own solar system, the branch of the Reptiloid species called "Hunans"; apparently started plotting to take over our worlds! With the equipment and supplies which they were able to carry from the Thunder Worlds when they were exiled, the traitors quickly used the equipment on their ships over the span of several centuries to build cities and construct a production economy which could produce all the necessary consumer goods, food, clothing, and shelter to support their growing population. They quickly built roads and villages, which over the centuries became cities. Once their settled planets had been moderately "tamed", the Hunans started working on scientific weapons of offense and defense so that they could someday invade our worlds and take over! Their research scientists appear to be very good and their military commanders who led the raid on our world exhibited amazing skill and daring! The Hunans plotted for many years and did the required research very well; apparently using traitors living on the Thunder Worlds to obtain the necessary information to guarantee the success of their mission! Their small invasion force of several extremely fast fighter ships somehow produced the recognition codes that allowed them to approach the planet which housed the Ruling Symbol without being challenged or correctly identified! They also somehow were able to produce the correct daily landing code to allow their ships to land at a remote base with no automatic IFF equipment! The invasion force rapidly disembarked from their ship; used very fast small antigravity ships to quickly and quietly snatch our Emblem of Ruling Power from its place of honor in a government building! Then they swiftly returned to their ships; and successfully escaped from our planet using the proper exit codes so that the theft was not discovered for many hours!#*

#Any attempt to follow the invaders would have been too late to have any chance of success; so our leaders quickly and quietly plotted their own plan to get the Symbol back! But careful investigation turned up several hindrances to getting a safe return of the Claw before it can be used against us! The enemy scientists have produced a detection and force field defense which is being used to shield the entire planet, where the artifact is being stored, from any attempt by our forces to rescue it! Our loyal Reptiloid forces cannot do the vital mission to rescue our revered icon because the enemy is using extremely advanced DNA sensors to prevent any Reptiloid whose DNA has not been recorded in the main computer of their forces from setting foot on the entire planet! Any detection

of reptilian DNA that has not been analyzed and recorded immediately causes the projection of a death field which shuts down all body functions for any Reptiloid being whose blood DNA has not been injected into medical sensors in the defensive system! Our problem is the fact that unless the icon is immediately recovered, chaos will ensue as soon as the enemy faction projects their political message from just outside our solar system and tells us to helplessly surrender!#

The tall reptile again stopped to eat a huge mouthful of food from his plate; then continued, *#To help you in your mission, we must show and tell you certain things! We also need to quickly train you to use our equipment, especially one of our swift one-warrior fighters. Here, Warrior Steele, this is a hologram of our important artifact which was stolen last week from a heavily guarded museum display on our planet! This information has been withheld from the civilian population, but as I just stated, in a few days our enemies will project audio and video shows over our communications network! The Hunans will tell the entire civilian population that they have our beloved artifact on their planet, and that they expect us to surrender to their authority! This will cause a civil war, our government will be overthrown, and because they have the important religious and political icon which has been the symbol of our ruler for thousands of years, they can take over our planet and rule us without too much of a struggle; therefore we must do something quickly!#*

As he looked at the small holographic object hovering in the air in front of him, Slate thought, *#Why, it looks just like the large talons on the ends of each of your four auxiliary arms, and also like an extremely large claw of a predator bird like an earthly Eagle!#*

Red Stinger quickly answered, #You are correct, Earthman! When our Founding Father, Reptilus, who we named our main planet after; united the planetary system, including Reptilon, and Reptilee, he was named the Supreme Ruler of the system, until he was killed in a Duel of Succession, which each Supreme Ruler must undergo periodically, when he is challenged by any Reptiloid, in order to prove his fitness for ruling our People! When Reptilus was laid to rest after he had lost a Duel of Succession, with the permission of his entire Historic Egg Line, his major claw was ceremonially removed and used thereafter as the symbol of office for the Supreme Ruler! Now, enough of our history; after our meal, we will start training you to do the job at hand!#

And with those fateful telepathic words, Red Stinger and Slate Steele started a section of their Life Paths that would indelibly write the name of the two brave warriors and their literally impossible exploits into Imperial History! They would be Life Paths that would still be documented on the pages of the Annals of the Imperial Seers until eons after the last enormous sun in the Cosmic All burned out and became a dark hole; which would be an entrance into the next phase of existence for the mentally powerful Magi! Once a special Imperial Seer council could document that it was the last sun in the Universe, the Supreme Magi would open the so-called

"Doomsday Box" which contained instructions to follow that would allow them to mentally pass to the next level of existence!!

But that would be in the far "Future" on the Main Galactic Time Line; at the present "Time" there were extremely important events about to happen that would affect The Line in the "Here and Now"!

CHAPTER 11

Staying on the mesa and training with the Reptiloids for several days, Slate was given a crash course in how to pilot one of the small ships controlled by an AI computer, which did most of the routine maintenance and navigation work for the Reptiloids. The ship's AI was designed to take commands in the Standard Galactic language which was spoken throughout the Empire of the ICOPE. The only problem was the fact that Slate did not know any language except the one he had always spoken on Earth; so he had to quickly be taught that unfamiliar language so that he could control the small fighter! On Earth that would have taken months or years, but that problem was quickly solved when Red Stinger used one of his race's telepathic teaching machines to directly put the language into the Humanoid's brain synapses; while at the same time also injecting instructions on how to pilot the totally unfamiliar short-range fighter ship! Red Stinger also took valuable time to teach Slate the basic sword and laser fighting techniques of the Reptiloid warriors that he would soon face; so that he would know most of the standard sword moves of his much larger opponents.

After a sufficient length of time to allow his mind neurons to "process" all the new information, Red Stinger showed him the plans of the building where the extremely important claw symbol supposedly was being stored. Intelligence reports stated that the claw was stored in the heavily guarded throne room of the ruler of the planet's public meeting room; in a small drawer hidden in the back of the room's ornate throne chair. Intelligence reports also indicated that in a few days; on a day important to the Hunan society; the important symbol would be taken out of the throne room and used to make a video broadcast to the Thunder Worlds that would either allow the Hunans to take over their home worlds unopposed, or start a system-wide civil war on the Thunder Worlds!

It was a tremendous amount of data and information for one relatively small Humanoid brain to absorb and successfully process so that any part of it could instantly be used when it was needed! When Red Stinger and his associates had given Slate all the necessary information they could, the planet's sun was setting, and plans were put into motion to start the expedition to obtain the claw early the next morning. As to whether the military operation would be successful or not depended on one Slate Steele operating alone on an extremely dangerous mission in enemy territory; (which sounded like the hazardous ultra-secret missions that he had performed with his buddies for years on Earth, the Moon, and Mars; only this time he would do it alone!)

But also this time if he failed, and the broadcast was made to the Thunder Worlds informing them of the fact that the Hunan had their political icon, he would not be the only one to die! Because of their belief in their planet's relic, literally billions of Reptiloid beings would take up arms and blindly follow the Hunans; even though they were the ones who had been the traditional enemies of the Thunder Worlds for centuries! But these new Hunan leaders of the Thunder Worlds would not lead them according to their best interests! They would first probably lead them on raids plundering worlds belonging to the ICOPE; thus starting an interstellar war!

Slate's mission the next day would be a Galactic Anchor Moment; which is why the Winds of Destiny undetectably still swirled around him as he attempted to sleep that night!

CHAPTER 12

A fleet of Reptiloid ships emerged from the depths of their base and used their phantom screens to covertly take off from Earth early the next morning before daybreak. After a journey of about a week, Slate's short range fighter was taken close to the target enemy planet by an extremely large Reptiloid ship; then covertly released behind one of the planet's large moons. An instant later while still behind the target planet's moon, the large ship zipped away from the small ship on its planetary orbit drive; then when far away from the planet's "gravity well", it suddenly vanished into Ultra-Space to escape enemy detection. Operating on its AI systems and protected from detection by the Reptiloid version of the Empire's phantom screens, the small fighter came around the moon; traveling in an unpowered trajectory to enter the planet's atmosphere; with all electrical systems down except the main concealment system to help avoid detection! When the fighter was low enough in the target planet's atmosphere, Slate stayed in an unpowered glide until the fighter was close to the target area; then at the last possible second, kicked in the ship's landing jets to land vertically in a grove of what looked like large plants or trees. The AI controlling the ship allowed Slate to quickly exit to the surface of the planet; then it disappeared to await his return after a success or a failure. It was also programmed to immediately leave the planet and return to the large ship covertly orbiting the planet if its sensors detected that Slate had been killed! Traveling on foot through the shielding plants, Slate moved toward the huge nearby building where Red Stinger's intelligence said the Claw was to be stored until the announcement would be made that would either cause a civil war or a hostile takeover of the three Thunder Worlds of the Reptiloids! Several hundred yards from his object Slate first harmlessly went through a faintly green-tinged shield; which apparently was deadly to Reptiloid DNA, and passed what looked like ordinary water-filled ponds. He safely passed through two more DNA-shielding force fields, and circled to reach the position where the Intel said he could safely scale the wall. Reaching the target building's north cobbled stone wall, with a long rope slung over his shoulders, Slate used his strong arms and legs to jump, pull, and claw his way to the top of the 200 foot tall wall which had flag poles projecting up every ten or fifteen feet. Climbing over the top of the wall, he jumped down to a narrow path between the building and the wall and was able to gain entry to his objective through an open window. He left the rope behind so it could be used later to go down the wall. Using his infrared vision, he secretly crept through darkened corridors following the diagram that Red Stinger showed him to get to the planet's throne room where the Claw was kept; safely evading several tall Reptiloid aliens in the darkened halls before he stood in front of a large locked door! Placing a small box given to him by Red Stinger on top of the door's entry mechanism, Slate activated the electronic device and was rewarded when the door silently swung open. Quietly closing the door behind him without an alarm sounding, he used his infrared sense and slowly crossed a wide expanse in what appeared to be a throne room with a very ornate chair situated at the middle of the back wall. Slate's Intel about the location of the Claw proved to be correct. In a small drawer at the back of the heavily decorated chair, just where Red Stinger told him it would be; he found a small golden box containing the Claw; along with a small broadsword. Putting the box in a small sack and tying it and the sword to his belt, he tried to retrace his steps without any alarm sounding as he opened the door; then he retrieved the box used to open the door, and swiftly traveling down the corridor he had used to get to the room! He tried to remain undetected by the aliens, but apparently a silent alarm had been set off when he opened the drawer, causing an extremely loud siren to sound! Knowing that speed was important, Slate tripled his speed to try to escape back to his hidden ship as further alarms sounded and he heard heavy footsteps coming up behind.

During his escape as he was running down a dark corridor a particle beam fired by an alert guard burned a hole completely through the bag and the box it was carrying; with the ultra-hot beam igniting the box and its contents! Quickly tearing the blazing box open to try to rescue the extremely valuable contents, inside Slate found the strange object that looked like what he was supposed to obtain on his mission, a very large Reptiloid claw! But his heart sank when he saw that the very important Symbolic Claw had become very charred and almost completely destroyed when the box was hit by the energy beam! His mission seemed doomed when the blackened claw crumbled in his gloved hand as he touched it! Thinking quickly on his feet, Slate reached the same conclusion he had when Red Stinger was briefing him: the Symbol of the Reptiloid Empire probably was a primary middle claw taken from its first emperor who united the planets. But now the large original claw was almost totally destroyed and useless as the Symbol of the Reptiloid reigning monarch; therefore, to prevent a civil war among the reptile clans with their treasured relic destroyed, or ultimately the Thunder Worlds invaded by the Hunan, the Symbol of Authority must somehow secretly be replaced without any friendly or enemy reptile knowing the difference! Because of this fact, Slate would have to change his plans! Having come to this conclusion, he stopped behind an intersecting corridor and ambushed two pursuing Reptiloids, one of whom had destroyed the box. He used a relatively low setting to try to only stun the huge reptiles. But the stun setting proved to be too low and, although partially stunned, the very tall Reptiloids kept moving forward! Think on his feet, Slate did the only thing he could; he lunged toward the two partially dazed reptiles to finish the job. With his opponent's reflexes slowed by the low stun setting, Slate was able to dash past the first reptile's swinging sword and land a powerful blow to the enemy's head using the side of the small sword he had taken in the throne room. Like a tall tree falling after its base has been cut, the taller of the two Reptiloids fell to the floor of the corridor totally unconscious! The second smaller Reptiloid also proved vulnerable to a stunning sword blow to the side of his huge head, and he also fell like a giant Sequoia tree being cut down! While the huge lizards were knocked out, Slate used his Earthian hunting knife off his belt to cut off one of the reptile's very large primary middle claw and put it inside the extremely damaged box; while planning to discard the remains of the real claw in a nearby muddy pond. To further cloud his escape, Slate used his energy weapon to char the stub of the Reptiloid's limb to make it look like his claw had been burned off while he pursued the unknown alien! The superior medical technology of the Reptiloids would enable the warrior to quickly regrow his claw! Reaching the window where he had originally entered, Slate exited and jumped down by the wall. He picked up and securely tied the rope he had left on one of the flagpoles sticking out of the top of the wall, and started sliding down the rough stone wall. Swiftly reaching the ground he started out in the direction of his hidden ship; being careful to quickly discard the remains of the charred claw in the first pond he passed before any Hunan warrior spotted him!

Back at the building the intruder alarm had been sounded; all the defensive troops stationed in the area had been deployed in and out of the building; and one by one the building's advanced offensive and defensive systems started going online! One of them was a device that projected a powerful neuronic field which reacted to any tiny mindar electrical fields in any living creature's mind in its field of resolution and automatically tried to set up a reaction electrical field to literally turn off that creature's mind; effectively killing it! The extremely short range device used an enormous amount of power, which was why it was not used until an enemy was known to be in range. Perhaps it was set for Reptiloid minds, but the effect of the neuronic field on Slate's mind was to suddenly make him very weak and very sleepy. But just as he had many times before while in a tense situation in combat; the warrior ignored the numbing effect of the alien device and pressed on as best he could with his failing limbs toward his hidden ship.

As he was struggling on very wobbly legs to reach the area where his ship would appear, the Hunans turned on another of their defense fields; one that slowly melted metal; designed to make any enemy warriors have to drop their swords and metal weapons! As a result, Slate's internal "hardware" immediately began to slowly degrade to liquid metal, and his subatomic electronic devices in his limbs one by one slowly ceased to function! The reinforcing metal inside his repaired parts in his arms, legs, and head; also started to partially melt; degrading his senses and making him almost blind as he literally wobbled through the thick forest of alien plants, with the Hunan in hot pursuit! Thus hindered; with only partial vision and his legs and arms gradually weakening, he still forced himself onward and struggled toward his hidden ship! #*I WILL NOT QUIT! I WILL NOT QUIT!*# Slate kept telling himself!

Finally able to only crawl using his greatly disabled cyborg limbs, Slate was more than half unconscious, and almost totally blind, when he reached the position of his hidden ship only a short distance in front of his pursers, thankfully shielded from their view by the dense screen of undergrowth! The ship automatically transposed around him and Slate found himself again sitting in the small craft's command chair! Although almost totally blind because of the Hunan's metal melting field, he remembered the position of the required controls that he was taught in his piloting lessons! Just by touching each control and remembering its function, Slate immediately set the controls to perform an emergency full-power planetary drive take-off inside the planet's gravity well; with a few seconds delay to allow him to enter and use the ship's medical facilities! Having done all the required actions to save himself, finally Slate gave in to the darkness encroaching on his mind after he literally collapsed into the ship's Medical Cabinet after dropping his important package outside! Almost immediately the automatic systems he had just programmed came on-line and took over the control of the ship; sending it on a predetermined course to take the unmanned ship to safety! Meanwhile back on the surface, the Reptiloid planet's detection system alerted all defensive forces and in response, interplanetary and interstellar fighters rose to chase the intruder and the planet-based long range laser fire immediately scored several minor hits on the intruder!

As the ship ran for cover beyond the solar system; still being controlled by the ship's artificial intelligence computer, Slate's severe injuries sustained during the mission were being treated by an extremely advanced Imperial medical cabinet, which was also controlled by the ship's AI.

Surging up out of the enemy planet's atmosphere, a large cloud of Hunan fighters begin what they thought would be a short chase, since their long range fire had already slightly damaged the interloper's ship! They gradually closed on the invader and were about to destroy Slate's ship when the fleet from the Thunder Worlds intervened; coming between the lone ship and the pursuing fleet of fighters!

While the rest of his fleet engaged the strong force of enemy ships; going against all normal military protocols of his planet for Supreme Commanders, Red Stinger risked the future "Egg Line of his Hive" to leave the safety of the combined defense shields of the Reptiloid massed ships and moved out in front using a larger fighter ship to try to transpose the unconscious Humanoid out of his damaged ship; along with the important package he had brought from the enemy planet; braving Hunan particle beam fire! If the Reptiloid was not successful in his attempt to save the Earthman and was killed; his Egg Line would cease; and his entire Official Family Line Species would probably officially be literally erased, and officially perish; with his Egg Line taken over by other ancestry lines because it no longer had a Senior Heir to defend its heritage! But Red Stinger ignored the consequences of reckless act that he was attempting to accomplish and instead focused on what a successful rescue of his friend would do! It would literally save his people from starting a civil war when the claw was rescued!!

His Battle Sense told the Reptiloid Supreme Commander that he had to hurry or his Earthian friend was doomed because his AI-controlled ship was not trying to evade enemy fire, it had apparently only been programmed to try to escape by going in one direction as fast as it could, which would make it easy for the Hunan pursuers to catch him!

In attempting the rescue, the Reptiloid commander also went against other accepted traditions and Reptiloid military procedures; which said that during combat with any enemy force, every Supreme Fleet Commander was supposed to hang back and let the warriors under his command take the brunt of enemy fire; with his second in command doing all the dangerous work! But to make sure that the rescue mission was successful; because it would literally save the Thunder Worlds from anarchy if it were successful, Red Stinger had ignored tradition and had taken the only possible chance to literally save his Home Worlds! Ignoring several hits on the outside control surfaces of his fighter ship, Red Stinger concentrated on safely securing Slate's image and also the image of important artifact near the medical cabinet in the sensors of the transpose field! When he was sure about the images in the transpose recovery screen, he threw every bit of extra power in his fighter ship to engage the transpose beam to retrieve both the Humanoid who had become his friend, and the very important Symbolic Claw. A split second later, Slate with his precious cargo, was safe in the Reptiloid's ship; and at the same instant behind Red Stinger's ship the Humanoid's fighter suddenly exploded! After retrieving the Claw from the charred box, the Reptiloid eased Slate back into the Medical Cabinet on his ship in order to continue to attempt to save his friend's life! That done; Red Stinger then changed course away from the combat area and continued to safety; hoping to rendezvous with his larger command ship, which was commanded in his absence by Blue Stinger; while the rest of his fleet tried to form a defensive shield behind his speeding ship to stop the enemy fighters from pursuing him! Their defensive efforts were only partially successful as several Hunan ships slipped through their ships and continued to pursue Red Stinger's ship carrying its precious cargo!

The huge Reptiloid's Battle Sense proved correct; since he transposed Slate from his crippled ship only milliseconds before its cold fusion reactor exploded as a result of its safety systems being destroyed by Hunan particle and laser beams! Since he was successful and rescued the Earthian, Red Stinger hoped that his beloved People of the Thunder Worlds would be saved from an invasion or a civil war because the Symbol was rescued! With these thoughts going through his mind; when the proper instant to act arrived, the Reptiloid Supreme Commander acted and maneuvered his ship to continue his escape from the pursuing Hunan fighters!

Swerving to and fro, the Reptiloid commander tried to successfully evade the enemy fighters attempting to attack his vessel; even as they were being attacked by the fighters from the Thunder Worlds! The hull of his fighter made creaking noises as most of the evasive maneuvers put tremendous strains on the supporting structures; even with the ship's inertia-reducing systems on emergency overload! Finally the Supreme Commander reached the edge of the cloud of fighting Hunan and Thunder World ships; but he had to do one more thing to save his friend! By weaving in and out the individual ships making up his fleet of ships from the Thunder Worlds; Red Stinger, aided by a sadio directional beam, sought to find one particular Reptiloid cruiser with an open bay door. At the edge of the taskforce, the skillful pilot finally found the ship he was seeking and piloted his smaller ship into an open port in the side of the ship known as "Tal-a-Kalon", a very large cruiser of the "Tak-Lon" class.

The second that his ship appeared in the empty arms bay of the larger ship, Red Stinger ordered his crew in the cruiser's command center to immediately transport Slate directly to the ship's infirmary; while he personally took a certain charred box on the floor down to be put in his ship captain's locked vault for safekeeping! While he was doing this covert deed to protect his star system from being thrown into a bloody civil war or being conquered by the enemy, neither he nor any of the other warriors on his ship or in his fleet had the mental gift to feel the Winds of Destiny swirling around the ship! Out beyond the range of the Reptiloid's senses, swarms of fighter friendly and enemy fighter ships still fought on; locked in a death struggle! The battle would rank as the toughest and the most important in the long history of the Thunder Worlds, but ultimately Red Stinger's larger and stronger forces were able to triumph over their Hunan enemies! As the cruiser sped on to safety, Slate was unconscious and totally unaware of the dangerous fighter-to-fighter battles erupting behind him; and the gale-force velocity of the Winds of Destiny as they surged through, around, and past the veteran warship known as Tal-a-Kalon!

But would Red Stinger's daring rescue of Slate be in time to save his life?

CHAPTER 13

As Slate slowly woke up and became aware of his location, it was like "Dee-Ja-Voo" all over again! He slowly looked around and observed that apparently his wounds were being treated in a very unusual hospital bed; inside a very large dimly lit room! Although he remembered being severely injured by several enemy laser and kinetic energy weapons; at that instant, he was amazingly free of pain!! It felt like he was floating in water; yet without any pressure on any part of his body! Slate looked around in a daze, and as he was coming back to full consciousness, he tried to figure out just what was going on by observing his surroundings; starting with the very comfortable bed; since the last thing he remembered was literally crawling toward his ship, and about to give in to the immense pain and collapse!

The bed was unusual by Earthian standards because it looked to be about twenty feet long and about ten feet wide; probably because it had been made to hold Reptiloid and not Humanoid patients! Amazingly, the ultra-advanced bed apparently used force fields to literally float the patient above the surface of the mattress in order to help reduce pain from open and healing wounds by lessening pressure on swollen and tender nerve tissues!

As Slate gradually regained full consciousness, he shivered when he again remembered encountering intense pain as he struggled to reach his ship and partially blacking out when his "extra parts" started melting; literally both arms; both legs; and the electronics in his head and his eyes! But he also remembered somehow reaching his ship safely and, while almost blind and deaf, by memory without his sight, he accomplished what was necessary and engaged the AI control system before he completely faded out! As Slate continued to analyze the situation, sound echoes and images continued to float by on the edge of his memory and sight! Faint glimmers of the fang-grinning face of a certain Reptiloid named Red Stinger also faintly came to mind! He also remembered that all his metal replacement parts had been at least partially destroyed by what probably was an enemy defense field, similar to the one that would immediately target the reptile DNA to instantly kill any Reptiloid trying to penetrate it; so as he slowly regained consciousness, he started to evaluate his present condition by following his training and automatically sending out mental impulses to order his very small cyborg main computer in his chest to go through the "checklist" of his cyborg parts. But his attempt to contact the cyborg computer literally "drew a blank"; since he could not mentally contact the electronic marvel that had been implanted in his chest!! Also at that moment as Slate floated above the bed, he could not mentally "feel" his artificial arms and legs for the first time in many months; and as he slowly tried to mentally evaluate all of his previously replaced body parts; he found that impossibly, he could not contact his mechanical arms; legs; eyes; and internal ear mechanisms because **THEY WERE NOT THERE**! Instinctively moving what seemed to be normal arms and hands and fingers, he further investigated the amazing puzzle of the missing cyborg body parts! What he felt in his eye sockets; in his ears; in his arms; in his legs; and everywhere on his body; appeared to be normal, warm, Humanoid flesh, and not ultra-advanced metal medical miracles which had been designed to replace his destroyed arms and legs!!! Yet even stranger still, Slate again reminded himself that most, if not all, of his cyborg parts had been totally destroyed or degraded by some sort of defensive field projected by the Hunans when he was fleeing; so now it appeared that the destroyed parts had been replaced! He remembered this fact; yet now; somehow he had been totally healed of his wounds and he could see normally and move what appeared to be normal arms and legs! Apparently Reptiloid medical science could literally work wonders with Humanoid DNA, RNA, XNA, YNA, and ZNA!

#What a script for "The Stranger Zone"! Nah! Something this far out has to be on the new "Stranger Still Zone"#! Slate thought. Thinking further and touching and feeling all of his arms, legs, and ears, he realized that apparently he could hear with totally natural ears, move ordinary limbs, and see with regular Humanoid eyes without the benefit of artificial means! As impossible as it sounded when the same thoughts went through his thought processes again just now, apparently all of his artificial limbs, eyes, ears; and virtually all his cyborg parts had all been successfully somehow quickly "grown" and replaced by

Reptiloid technology, since all of his original metal cyborg "Earthian replacement parts" had been melted and totally destroyed by the enemy's microwave beams!

Amazingly, even while viewing and feeling the physical evidence of the lack of his metal cyborg parts that he had trained so hard to master; the young man almost refused to think and believe such a wonderful and impossible event had occurred! As confused and muddled thoughts about the situation passed through his thought processes, he again mentally tried to carry out what should have been a thorough check out of all of his cyborg body parts; but again he still could not sense or feel any metal, plastic, or glass parts! **HE HAD TO FACE THE WONDERFUL AND IMPOSSIBLE FACT!!!** Improbably and impossibly, all of his high-tech machinery was gone and he apparently was just an ordinary man again! **But he did not care; since only one thought raced through his mind! He was now apparently just an ordinary man that an ordinary Earthian woman such as Dixie could love without being afraid of being destroyed by a "Cy-Man"!!!**

Again and again the same incredible thoughts sped through his mind! He had to face the impossible-yet-true facts!! Incredibly, somehow, although the facts did not tell him how, as they continued to zip again and again through his mind, and he could not figure out how it was done; he suddenly thought that maybe it was all a dream; he was actually dying back on the Hunan planet; and the whole improbable chain of events, that supposedly culminated in his hardware being replaced with the real thing, was actually just a story line in a science-fiction story on the popular Science Fiction/Fantasy vid program called the "Stranger

Zone", which he tried to see every time he could!! He wanted to believe what he was seeing and feeling---and yet—**WHAT HE WAS SEEING AND FEELING HAD TO BE IMPOSSIBLE—SO THIS WAS APPARENTLY JUST A DREAM; PERHAPS JUST A DREAM THAT HIS MIND WAS CREATING AS HE LAY DYING BACK ON THE ALIEN PLANET!**

As he floated above the surface of the huge bed's mattress, Slate still kept trying to figure the incredible situation out! Logically, the only possible way this medically-impossible "repair" could have happened would be that his extremely grateful Reptiloid friends had used their ultra-advanced medical technology to cause his own DNA, RNA, on the Double Helix and the theoretical XNA, YNA, and ZNA on the newly discovered bottom level Triple Helix existing in each and every Humanoid cell; to somehow regrow his missing body parts! He would have to ask Red Stinger about the miraculous replacement of his cyborg parts when he had the chance!

This parade of confusing thoughts and dreams about the future going through his mind literally took only a few split seconds! Then only a few moments after he had awakened and discovered all the incredible facts of the repair of his body, apparently alerted by medical sensors, Red Stinger came into the darkened room and telepathically boomed information into his mind!

#Well, my friend, the incredible; resourceful; and amazing Earthman, you are finally awake! You have been out over a week, Earth time, while your body was being repaired! It took that long for our ultra-advanced medical computers to finish your 'repairs'; guided by literally all five types of

your 'NA's!! As the Imperial Scientists on Empire Prime have found out after several hundred thousand years of medical research, which as members of the ICOPE we can access, there is a lot of extra information down in your Humanoid Double and Triple Helixes that can be put to very good use when they are all 'turned on'! Your own scientists are just now discovering the wonders embedded in the depths of the Triple Helix which is below the Double Helix in every Humanoid cell, and what amazing things can be done with the literally trillions of bits of information stored there! Now that you are cognizant I can now give you congratulations on a mission well done! Take a long moment to first carefully sit up as you float over the bed; take a deep breath to clear your head; then take stock of your surroundings and your equilibrium! When you can navigate on your own feet, we need to go elsewhere for a conference before I tell you anything else! We need to be shielded from possible enemy sensors and listening devices!#

Slate found that his mind was able to successfully control his replaced arms and legs made of ordinary Humanoid flesh; and after a moment of experimentation, he was able to literally float to the side of the bed in order to get out of his hospital bed and shakily follow the tall Reptiloid out the door! But as he was leaving, the healing of his destroyed limbs was not the only extraordinary happening that he observed! Incredibly, as he was going out the door, Slate noticed that he could somehow read the lettering on the room's inside storage door; even though the lights were turned off and the room was dark! As he walked out of the hospital room, the arms and legs that were now attached to his body almost felt like the "original factory equipment"! Apparently he could successfully control them without a new training period, but they somehow seemed "different"! Later in a soundproof; transpose proof, microwave proof, and mentally-shielded conference room, with a charred box in front of him, his reptile friend was able to explain certain things as he showed a very important object once more to Slate.

#I again must congratulate you on being able to pull off an extremely dangerous mission, one that neither I nor any of my soldiers could have done! Against tremendous odds, you were able to retrieve the Claw of Reptilus; although as I can now closely inspect it, the Claw looks none the worse for wear even though it seems a blaster bolt barely missed you and hit the box that contained it! But wait!! For the first time, as I carefully examine it and mentally compare it with my first-hand observations that I have had of the claw before, I observe that the Claw of Reptilus that you rescued actually now seems a little larger and has a slightly different color than I remember it!# Red Stinger stated and asked while having a covert talk with his Humanoid friend.

Slate was hesitant to tell his Reptiloid friend the truth, but quickly decided to confess what he had to do to literally 'save the day' during his mission when the genuine claw of Reptilus was destroyed!

After hesitating for an instant, Slate projected, *#I must confess, Red Stinger, that the actual Claw of Reptilus was almost totally destroyed by a blaster bolt that bored the blackened hole in the box before* *you, which at the time of my raid was carrying the Claw! Because it was heavily damaged, I had to think very quickly about how I could somehow successfully complete my mission to your Reptiloid race; without leaving the enemy planet a failure, carrying a useless and almost totally destroyed icon! I quickly reasoned that if the original political symbol was destroyed; I had to somehow get a suitable replacement to 'fit the bill', or from what you have told me about the importance of the claw, you would be stuck with a Civil War! My nation had one of those several centuries ago; it was very destructive, and it took many years for our republic to totally recover! So I did what I had to do, and because of this, one of the two unconscious guards I left behind on the planet is missing a primary claw and half his major sword limb; which his combat group will think was apparently shot off and destroyed during a raid on the complex that he was guarding!! His medical techs should be able to quickly grow him another one! I ditched the charred remains of the real Claw of Reptilus in a deep muddy pond outside the palace! As of now, only two beings, you and me, know the difference! I would suggest that after wrapping the new claw in the "Eternium Plastic" which the real one was covered with, you lock it up in another box and let your ruling clan keep it for another thousand years before anyone else sees it! It would also help if you also covertly replace your planet's computer images and solid holographic replicas with new documentation pictures of the substitute claw;*

since the new one looks slightly different! I won't tell anyone if you won't!#

For a moment the Humanoid thought Red Stinger would be mad about his attempted subterfuge, but he was surprised! As he was being told about the substitution, the tall Reptiloid gave his version of a frown; then when Slate's confession about the real Claw of Reptilus being replaced was over, he suddenly opened his extremely large mouth and exhibited two-inch long fangs as he produced his species' version of a hearty laugh! *#My friend, physically you may be a weak; puny Humanoid, but you think like a powerful, experienced, and dedicated Reptiloid Warrior! After having observed you in and out of combat, I can state that as a warrior, or an orator, you are devious; underhanded; tricky, sneaky, and SMOOTH in everything you do; including your thinking!! If it had been the Will of the First Cause to let you be hatched on my world, instead of being born a Humanoid on Earth; with the Id you possess, you would have made an excellent Reptiloid warrior! But even though you don't have a reptile body, you act, think, and behave like one of us incased in a weak; puny Humanoid body; but your superior warrior skills more than make up for it! I watched you on long range view screens during your escape on the planet surface to get away from two Reptiloids which were much faster than you; outweighed you ten-to-one; and outreached you by ten feet! It made no difference to you; you fought hand-to-claw and defeated the largest one of them; then you defeated the second one! Thinking while under severe combat stress, to* *successfully complete your mission, you then took a replacement claw from the larger Reptiloid; and escaped the pursuit of literally hundreds of enemy warriors in spite of their physical advantages! You made it through the 'NA defensive screens, and successfully got to your ship's rendezvous point with only your sword and your lasers; in order to successfully gain a replacement for the Claw of Reptilus; so that you could successfully complete your mission and avert a civil war or an invasion on our planets! Then to top all these combat feats; you successfully escaped even though you were almost totally incapacitated by the metal melting screen! I don't know how you did it! Our medical technicians examined your terribly wounded Humanoid body and found that you were literally almost blind and totally incapacitated; yet you did not quit; you kept on literally crawling over the rough terrain with just the nubs of your limbs that were left; and reached the area where your ship could transpose you to safety! I list all of those fantastic facts about your escape and I state for the record that you are a Kif Warrior Being after my own three reptile hearts and four stomachs!!#*

The tall Reptiloid stopped to take a deep breath and continued, *#It is a very good suggestion that you present to literally save our worlds, Kif Warrior Slate Steele! You are totally correct! I am extremely glad you were able to "think on your feet" and come up with the backup plan B on the spur of the moment when plan A misfired! It was not your fault that the original claw was destroyed because you* *were in deadly combat and you could not control where the enemy Reptiloid's blaster bolt hit! What you have suggested was, and is, literally the only successful scenario open to us! For once, telling the truth would not be the best policy because if the truth about the beloved Claw of Reptilus leaked out to my people, there would be chaos, civil war, and a tremendous upheaval on all Reptiloid planets in our confederation as a civil war would break out to choose a new ruling line!!! Again, I think your wise and crafty suggestion is the best way to avoid such a terrible period of strife on my people! Such a long and bloody Civil War caused by the loss of the Claw would have served no useful purpose! Covertly and by myself, I will do what you suggest, Kif Warrior Steele, because replacing such a fake for the real icon is in the best interests of my People; even though it is theoretically unethical and illegal!!! The substitution will be our secret until we both pass to the next Level of Existence; then it will become one what my species calls the 'Legendary Unknown Secrets of the Cosmic All'!!#*

Red Stinger paused a moment to catch his breath; then continued, *#Again, we thank you Earthman for your service to our humble Reptiloid Empire; which I told you the first time we met, is an ally to the ICOPE, the Empire of Empires! The healing and the energizing of your Humanoid body that we have given you is only a small token of our appreciation! You will never know just what the service you have done means to my people!!!!! You performed an act of heroism and bravery that none of our*

Reptiloid warriors could have accomplished; because we would have all immediately died when we transposed to the surface of the planet of our enemies when we went through the green force field to get to our objective!! Perhaps over the span of a thousand years you can visit our worlds many times as an Honored Guest! You then will be a witness to the important happenings in the Thunder Worlds caused by your brave deeds; and then you will be able to understand the importance of what you have done! (Our manipulation of your Humanoid DNA, RNA, XNA, YNA, and ZNA will allow you to live that long, if you so choose, without taking ICOPE Interferon!) If you had failed in your vital mission, there would not have been enough time to get another warrior from another distant planet able to go through the Reptiloid-killing force fields and train him or her to try to obtain the Claw before their announcement caused chaos on our worlds! Our blood-oath enemies would have triumphed over us and there was literally nothing that we could have done about it! The Ultimate Symbol of the Reptiloid Race that had been stolen from us would have allowed our enemies to land unopposed on our planet and literally take over our government, with either no struggle or with only a little opposition during our civil war! The traditions of the Artifact of Reptilus' Claw are that potent and binding to our Reptiloid people that live on the Thunder Worlds! By the Imperial Mores' of our race, our people blindly follow the one being or organization that controls THE SYMBOL!!!! We owe you a debt that literally cannot be calculated! As a small token of my gratitude, in addition to using the pattern in your body's DNA to regrow your arms; legs; and eyes; as you have already noticed, you have the ability to read in almost total darkness! You also have discerned that we have added a few extras to your RNA in your Double Helix; and your XNA, YNA, and ZNA down in your ultra-deep Triple Helix; to allow your normal-looking arms, legs, and eyes to be at least as strong or have even greater capabilities than your 'old' cyborg parts and to tremendously increase your longevity!#

#While you were healing, back on Earth, technicians at our base on the mesa have modified your two-wheeled vehicle and added offensive and defensive systems, such as a passive kinetic projectile field; a rocket-assist system to allow the vehicle to automatically go over any obstacle that might suddenly appear before you; and an Omni-directional microwave detector to automatically shield you from primitive radar, or even sadar detection! If in the future you need us, you only have to send a telepathic message on the mental band that you have been trained to use and one of our trained communications techs far across the Universe will immediately contact you in order to help you in any possible way they can!! It is a very small token of the tremendous debt that we owe you that <u>we can never repay</u>! Perhaps it can partially be paid back in a few thousand years or so! We also added several permanent corrections

in your ultra-low-level RNA and DNA that, barring accidents, almost makes you and all of your descendants immortal! If and when you wed, our entire combat pack wants to be invited to your wedding! As a further token of our appreciation for what you have done, if you ever marry, I'm sure that Imperial Medical Technology can treat your beloved wife to be able to live as long as you; so you will not be lonely when she dies first!#

Red Stinger stopped projecting for a moment to look around for a moment; then he continued for one last time. *#This is goodbye for now, Earthman! I must leave with the fleet to attend to 'Claw' business on the Thunder Worlds! But somehow I feel, deep down in my Reptiloid version of your Humanoid Soul; that when you leave our ship to live again on your home planet Earth, we will meet again in the future; with our roles somehow reversed!#*

And with the end of these words, the tall Reptiloid extended his enormous right dominant arm to reach down to the much smaller Humanoid and shake his hand, being careful not to crush Slate's hand of soft flesh with his bony and reptile-scaled hand!

Because he was almost in a dream state as a result of the strange and eerie happenings of the past few days, the long trip back to Earth on Red Stinger's ship did not seem very long to Slate as he mingled in the large ship with the Reptiloid warriors and got to know them "warrior to warrior". Even though he was supposedly a much weaker and smaller Humanoid and the Reptiloids were very large and strong, when he communicated with them in the Basic Galactic language that he had learned, Slate again found that they also talked about much the same things that he and his buddies back on Earth did! They communicated among themselves about their deeds in battle; events on their home planet; and bragged about their beautiful wives and their large families!

He talked with a Reptiloid named "Lanstrike" about living on a world that was almost always raining and thundering and lightning! When he describe usual weather conditions on Earth, Lanstrike said he would like to live on a world that was sunny and not forever storming! Slate invited him to visit Earth when he could get permission from his commander, Red Stinger. While traveling back to the base on the tall mesa, Red Stinger had an excuse to throw a celebration with his warriors for the return of "The Claw" and the fleet's safe return to the Three Planets quite a few light years away towards the ICOPE sphere of influence! Following very old Reptiloid warrior traditions, it lasted for several days! Also by reptile custom, the longer it went on, the "softer" the drinks served to the warriors were; until the last few hours only non-alcoholic beverages, similar to Earthian coffee, tea, and colas, were served along with plenty of food to mitigate their hangovers! Slate was treated exactly like a brave Reptiloid warrior coming back from a successful battle; including being seated in the traditional Reptiloid Central Place of Honor during the many hours of feasting! The Earthian man had been knocked down and had a sore shoulder for a few days when he was celebrating with Red Stinger and while under the influence of the Thunder Worlds liquor the Reptiloid forgot who he was reveling with and slapped him on the back! Red Stinger quickly apologized and helped Slate get back off the floor and continue to celebrate!

To Slate it seemed that only a few minutes after the combined ceremony and the rowdy party afterwards with his new Reptiloid friends ended, (who were very careful not to use their reptile strength to smash his shoulders when they got tickled and were laughing uproariously); Red Stinger's cruiser had covertly landed back on the mesa in the covering blackness of night and phantom screens on maximum. After a short sleep under the stars, Slate packed up his sparse belongings and after shaking hands with Red Stinger, Lanstrike, and a few of the other Reptiloids; he left the mesa and was calmly cruising down the highway on his super cycle as if the adventure of a lifetime, eerie enough to be a story on "The Stranger Still Zone", had not just concluded!

Before he left the mesa, Slate was very careful and asked his reptile friends to use their super science to purge the "stimulants" from his system; thus preventing any Earthly Highway Patrol Person from pulling him over and arresting him for "DUI"!! The road seemed ultra-smooth as the device his Reptiloid warrior friends had installed on his vehicle worked to automatically transfer his vehicle over each bump or dip in the road. But again, he did not know how to solve his problem of what to do about his love for Dixie and her refusal to marry him because she was afraid of being assaulted when he had a nightmare! What could he do to convince her that he would never harm her? Who could help him convince her that he would be harmless? His problem was like the legendary "Gordian Knot" which could not be untied; only slashed by Hercules! The more he thought about it, the more that problem seemed insurmountable as mile after mile sped under his motorcycle tires! At the moment he did not feel like talking about the situation with anyone and he had turned off his cellphone and had taken its battery out;

hopefully to prevent anyone from using it to track him. But Slate had already determined his next course of action; he would do something that he had always wanted to do--travel around the country. He thought that perhaps as he traveled around the back roads of his beloved country the solution to his problem would emerge when he could take the time to relax and calmly think through his important problem. But even as one Samuel Eliot Steele sped towards his Anchor Moment, he still could not sense that the Winds of Destiny swirled around him 24/7!

CHAPTER 14

As Slate zipped along the highway; trying to solve his problem, he was slowly finding out about the new replacement powers that his Reptiloid friends had given him! With his own ears, when he concentrated using the same mental pulse to turn his hearing on that he previously did with his cyborg machines; the Humanoid warrior found he could now also detect the sounds and electrical brain impulses of the wildlife and occasionally other Humanoids around the pavement on which he rode! He could somehow also control the level of his hearing so that he could only hear distant traffic sounds in front or behind his speeding motorcycle! When he concentrated and focused his eyes in a certain way, all across the bright sky he could detect several dozen low-level white streaks; probably contrails of civilian airliners. Far above them were thinner white streaks, which to his improved eyesight, appeared to be circling around above him! He figured they were probably military "Scramjets", such as the U-4 which he had ridden in at least ten times as a soldier, and probably twice as a severely injured patient! Although the contrails were very high, he sensed that they were orbiting at one position for several hundred miles around his immediate location; as if they were following him and keeping track of his location! Familiar protocol of his old unit also told him that some of the supposedly civilian sedans, SUVs, and motorcycles; which were all around him on the two-lane highway; were also there to trail him! But there was nothing he could do about the high-flying U-4s, or the trailing units; so he kept on going down the lonely narrow highways; while continuing to act as if he were unaware of the units trailing him on the road; perhaps from orbit; and the planes keeping tabs on him while traveling at Mach 8; from five hundred thousand feet up! Once or twice he thought that perhaps he even sensed that at least one old U-2 "Dragon Lady" was orbiting slowly around him up at merely a hundred thousand feet!

After several hours of traveling, there came a moment when the easy rider settled down to think after a long stretch of lonely; boring highway, and suddenly realized that without thinking where he was going when he left his Reptiloid friends; he instinctively was heading in the direction of his old hometown Cleburne, Texas; probably heading in that direction subconsciously in order to see his kinfolks and literally show his mom and dad the good news—virtually all of his cyborg parts had somehow been replaced with the "original Humanoid factory equipment"! But the young man also realized that he still had to make the decision of whether or not to ultimately go meet Dixie Davis, who was now supposedly working in New York City, and also tell her the good; and top-secret, news about his new totally-rebuilt Human body, which the military did not know about yet!!

But even with his changed new body with 100% Humanoid parts, he still had several problems!

Slate did not know that it would help his problem even if he could show Dixie the now soon-to-be ultra-top-secret that he was now not a cyborg; yet he could do the same things at least as well as before; without the "hardware"!! If she had gone ballistic when he had told her about how his combat injuries had been healed, just what would she do when she learned that he had impossibly been turned back into what appeared to be a normal-bodied man again, although with the same hidden powers? If he was still extremely powerful, why would she want to marry him then? He could not promise her that even with a totally 100% Humanoid body he would never; ever; have a bad dream! But what could he do? Who could he trust? Who, or what, could help him solve his dilemma and advise him on what to do?

But in the middle of trying to figure out the answer to one of his many problems, Slate suddenly remembered another problem that he would soon face! He realized that when he left Earth, this would have caused him to suddenly drop off the detection screen of his military doctors! They would have come looking for him in the last place he was detected, the area around the mesa. They would have kept looking for him near the mesa until he was spotted again on the highway traveling from the area in which he was last detected. But when the searchers on the ground visually spotted him, would they come pick him up or leave him alone until he contacted them? The multiple contrails above him seemed to indicate that they had already located him, probably with an imbedded computer ID chip somewhere inside the trunk of his body or somewhere on his motorcycle! They could find him and then track him day and night using satellite infrared scanners and real-time close-up U-4 telescopic pictures; and were apparently following orders to track him without trying to capture him! He knew; that because of the large group of aerial trackers around him; they had to have some method where the whole group could probably still track his cycle; perhaps using an ultra-small tracer hidden somewhere inside its frame.

Always wanting to be prepared for any eventually, Slate started going over several scenarios of the tactics that the soldiers trailing would use to attempt to capture him, and what he would do if he encountered each tactic! He mentally made plans for frontal attacks, attacks from the back and from each side, and what he would do if confronted with each type of attack. But even as he planned, he realized that if the units that had been trailing him for so many days came at him, the odds were heavily against him, since they could choose the time and the place to attack him they would be able to literally overwhelm him with sheer numbers and take him down from long range with tranquilizing darts! He realized that he would be very lucky to escape any unexpected attack that they would throw at him! But even though the odds were heavily against him, Slate still kept going over each type of attack in his mind and what he would do if faced with each one! He refused to quit planning even when he knew that the odds were against him! The lessons in his military history class about the Battle of Britain, the "Doolittle Raid" and the Battle of Thermopylae; examples of historic "stacked-odds battles" steadied his nerves and gave him comfort! Sir Winston Churchill, Colonel Doolittle, and the 300 Spartans did not quit when facing similar odds; so he too would not quit!

But **WHEN**; (not **IF**, knowing the tenacity of the military organization that he had worked for so many years), the military brass finally decided when they wanted to capture him, what would they eventually do with him? Suppose they found him and captured him, and wanted to medically examine him extensively; i.e.; literally down to the bottom of his cell structure? What would his military doctors think, now that they would not be able to detect his cyborg parts? They would immediately want to know what had happened to him to stop the signals from transmitting from the replaced arms and legs! Slate kept going over and over the basic facts of the very involved situation in his mind! He realized that at that very moment, as he traveled down the highway, if they had lost contact with his embedded sensors, the military authorities would be looking for him, expecting that he had been involved in an accident that destroyed his cyborg transmitter in his arm! When he met them, even though he looked normal, how could he explain how he had become totally Human again?? Literally nothing on Earth could have done it; since replacing damaged limbs by growing new ones using the injured person's DNA was beyond present medical technology; therefore they would know that something "not of this world" had somehow replaced his cyborg parts with totally normal Human ones!! What could he do to escape and live a normal life? He could ditch his bike with its hidden transmitter, obtain another fast cycle; then use his extensive training to radically change his appearance and run from their patrols that would be sent out to find him; trying to hide in crowded cities to escape their clutches! Then he could start a new life under another name, but the military would know he had probably "gone off the radar screen" to elude them and would use they unlimited resources to find him, knowing his traits and habits! In the cities they could use their infrared "facial recognition" scanners 24/7 to hunt him down and capture him!! Just like on the police shows, the military authorities could use facial recognition programs on every public civilian video monitor and every police camera in the country! Probably every broadcast television news program would be scanned for a glimpse of his disguised face!

If they caught him, again, how could he explain the eerie events that had transformed him from a mechanical man back to the real thing!?!?! What could he do about his future path on his own Personal Pathway for His Life!?!? He knew that he could do literally anything that he wanted; but there were certain things that he did not want to do! What would be his ultimate and final decision about the direction he would travel?!?!? Should he covertly seek to further his education and "major in attending college" for a few decades until he decided on a course of action? Should he "come clean", try to reenlist again and ask to be able to volunteer for Black Covert Opts again? He didn't think this would be a good idea!!!!! The surgeons that had saved his life would want to know exactly how his mechanical parts had been somehow replaced, incredibly with no loss in physical efficiency, and in some areas, a very large increase in his powers and several new powers, such as being able to detect mental impulses!!! To do so, they would probably want to do explorative surgery to try to find out the medical secrets that his new body now contained!! But he did not want for them to physically take him apart to try find out the physical secrets that his body now contained; even through it was beyond their capacity to do!!! He just wanted to be a normal soldier serving his county again! But deep down, he realized that this scenario was probably impossible!

Wait a minute! Maybe his only hope was the private "off the record" conference that he had had with Sergeant Snyder before he left his operations base for the last time! The Sarge had looked him in the eyes and stated the fact that any time the young man needed help; all he had to do was call him; 24/7; day or night; rain or shine! Also if he needed it, the old DI said that he would always give him a plug with the "Top Brass", (all of whom the veteran instructor had trained many years ago!), to allow him to do anything he wished!!!

Choices; so many choices! Slate thought as he whizzed down the highway. All supposedly good; but which ONE would be the best for his own personal Pathway of Life? Only the Creator; the Winds of Destiny, and maybe, the medium grade Imperial Seer Rondoe Kanne on Empire Prime in charge of visioning Earth's Main Time Line, all knew his best Pathway of Life! Unknown to Slate, before the present rising of the Winds of Destiny to gale force, Earth's Main Time Line had been a very low priority area; but now; it was in the top bracket!

What to do!! WHAT TO DO!!! the young man thought over and over again as his cycle surged down one of the dirt back roads in the northern United States as the Winds of Destiny swirled around him at record levels, which reached all the way back to Empire Prime!

And then suddenly he knew! HE KNEW! HE KNEW WITHOUT A DOUBT IN HIS HEART EXACTLY WHAT TO DO; AND WHO TO CONTACT TO SOLVE HIS PROBLEM--THE ONE MAN THAT HE WOULD TOTALLY TRUST TO SOLVE HIS IMPOSSIBLE PROBLEM! But how

could he successfully contact him? Then stopping to ponder the problem, Slate changed his mind on what to do! He realized that at the present time, the situation was too dangerous to attempt any communication! He would have to let things cool down first before attempting any contact!

(It was a good thing that Slate did not have the "mental equipment" to sense the Winds of Destiny because he would have suddenly been in terrible pain! At the instant of his Moment of Destiny when Slate realized what was needed, even as the U-4s and the combat teams were literally "englobing him"; the Winds of Destiny set another record on far away Empire Prime!)

CHAPTER 15

On the day that Slate's cyborg signal from his arms disappeared from the top secret military unit's satellite and spy plane receiving devices, at first his former commander thought the young man had somehow gone off planet beyond the range of the signal; or he had had an accident that smashed the chip in his motorcycle or a sensor malfunction in his cyborg parts to account for the signal stoppage which occurred suddenly. Slate's tracer hidden inside the frame of his cycle still worked, but the sensors of ultra-high spy planes reported that its signal was staying in the same location it had been for several weeks without moving; apparently because the young man was supposedly camping in a very desolate region somewhere in the far western United States. His cell phone's global tracker signal, which secretly still operated when the instrument was turned off, for some reason had also stopped working; having stopped at the same time and in the same location as the unit in his arm. But then amazingly, after several months, one of the two signal sources started transmitting and moving again on the unit's long range sensors, which used automatic computer programs to receive signals from at least two or three local cell towers in order to triangulate the exact locations of the transmission. The military cell equipment showed that Slate's phone was not on, but to their dismay, when his unit tried to contact him anyway, he would not or could not answer their call! Following protocol, a radio signal sent out to Slate's arm that should have turned on a secondary beacon did not turn the signal on; and then when they were told of this fact; the "top brass" realized that they had a problem on their hands! They either had a turncoat on their hands, or the young man had been kidnapped by foreign agents and his hardware stripped from his body so that its secrets could be learned by the enemy!

Immediately covert teams were sent out on VTOL hypersonic U-4s in order to secretly track the location of Slate's cycle from a distance with infrared scanners to find out exactly what had happened to their 'super soldier" that his arm was not sending signals and his cell phone was not active and being answered.

Speeding across the country at hypersonic speed to search for Slate and find out just what was going on; the sleek spy planes contained many advanced features. They moved through the air without creating the usual trailing "sonic booms" because the shape of their fuselages caused the shockwaves to travel upwards and dissipate in the upper atmosphere! Their pilots and their passengers also appreciated having inertia-dampening gravity fields produced by ultra-advanced technology obtained from Roswell artifacts that made their long hypersonic trips far easier than piloting and riding in the old "Mach buster" spy airplanes and transports!

The U-4 VTOL transports continuously tracked location of the signal from Slate's cycle and relayed it to the unit's main office. When headquarters had computed his route, General Paxton, the commander of the teams assigned for this mission, gave the circling airplanes orders to drop their combat teams at carefully selected hidden locations. After careful sensor scans, each plane used its VTOL capability and its stealth capabilities to land unseen in desolate areas to drop one of four combat teams, each composed of a man and a woman dressed in normal biker clothing, and their motorcycles out of sight at least ten miles in each direction from their very important quarry: one Samuel Eliot Steele! Their orders were to secretly tail the young man, covertly observe his movements, and decide if he was somehow under the control of another person or outside force; or he was in complete control of himself and traveling aimlessly around the southwest on narrow country roads because he wanted to. Major General Paxton closely observed the location and the movements of Slate and each team on an electronic GPS screen and from telescopic video cameras hidden in each team member's helmet. He could also use the real-time satellite pictures of Slate to see where the young man was going. When it was necessary, over their com radios the general gave every combat team member up to the second descriptions of Slate's movements in order to keep him under surveillance 24/7; rain or shine; hot or cold.

Every day or so the team in back of Slate sped up and passed him; while the team in front of him slowed down to allow him to pass. The team lagging behind then turned around and started tailing him from the rear; after covertly stopping to change their helmets and outer clothing so as to look like different bikers as they again approached him from the back. Using throat mike radios with tiny earpieces completely hidden in their ears, or their helmets if they could not stand an earpiece when traveling fast, each team member was in constant contact with headquarters; with several U-4s rotating over them 24/7; keeping watch over each team and acting as the receptor of their short range signals and boosting them to headquarters. All team members were skilled combat observers; they all reported the same basic facts; and the videos they sent back to base were immediately reviewed in real time by several photo analysts who each reached the same conclusions. The young man Steele riding his cycle alone seemed ordinary in every way, and did not appear to be under the influence of any outside force! He rode with his body relaxed and seemed to be complete control of all of his mental and physical facilities! But the most important questions remained unanswered: **What had happened to the sensors in his cyborg limbs? Had something happened to his metal arms and legs that destroyed the sensors; or had Slate deliberately turned them off?**

But day after day, as the combat teams from the Unit tailed Slate, they gradually found out that everything was not as it seemed; and all that appeared normal; **WAS NOT!** When first used on their "target person", all the short and long range infrared and metal detectors both in the high-altitude U-4 and on all the team motorcycles detected the same startling fact: The man on the cycle was positively identified as Steele; but using extremely low power covert infrared and microwave sensor scans of the young man to allow doctors to assess his physical and medical condition, the impossible fact was discovered that he did not appear to possess any cyborg parts any more, either in his head, his body trunk, or in any of his limbs!! How or why the metallic and ceramic parts could disappear out of his body, and from the ends of the stubs of his arms and his legs; and somehow still allow him to move and still be alive was unknown! Could he be a clone or a robot duplicate of Slate built by an unknown enemy to become a spy in his old military organization? That had to be answer to the virtually impossible situation; since Earthian technology could not successfully transplant or regrow legs, arms, eyes, and hearing glands! Surely the unknown enemy would know that such a clone duplication without the cyborg parts would quickly be detected! But just exactly what was going on; and who did it, was not known! When Major General Paxton briefed this information to all the team members over their com radios, more than one team member muttered that it seemed like an episode out of the new television program called "The Future Zone"!

When this incredible fact about the disappearing cyborg parts became common knowledge by the Covert Operations Department's commanding officer, Lieutenant General Hartford, at CIA headquarters in Connecticut; he immediately transmitted the following orders to all the team members following Slate: **"Follow the person that you are following that looks like Samuel Eliot Steele to the ends of the Earth; keeping him under 24/7 surveillance! Do not allow him to escape your surveillance and do not approach or try to apprehend him until further notice by me! You are not to obey any other orders from any other commanding officer except those sent by me; even the President! The person that looks like Slate Steele** could be a very dangerous enemy agent!! While you are tailing him, we will research and find out just what is going on; then we will keep you informed of any new information that we discover about the situation!"

"Again, take no one else's orders but mine; no matter who they identify themselves as; what they say; or what they order you to do; IGNORE THEM!! If any other general or even the President tries to give you orders over your com, IGNORE THEM TOO! I will use the standard code word for the day that was listed in the written orders you were given at the start of your mission when I order you to do something! Out!"

And so day after day, Slate had rotating teams of heavily armed combat teams tailing him in front; in back of him; and on paralleling state highways or back roads on either side; 24/7, day and night! They were now keeping twenty miles off instead of ten; and keeping track of him with satellite GPS scans of his cell phone and the signals coming from several covert transmitters originally embedded deep in the frame of his cycle when it was constructed! This Intel was supplemented with real-time satellite data and constant infrared scans from the U-4s. The teams were ready at all times to quickly move in if so ordered by General Hartford or if something happened to their quarry's cell phone and the blip on their LED screens which indicated his position vanished. To keep fresh teams following Slate, each of these teams was dropped off and picked up on a regular schedule ever few days by several stealth VTOL U-4s so that Slate hopefully would not notice that he was being followed. Sometimes the teams were two young men; a young man and woman; or a man or woman and supposedly a young boy or girl. Still following standard procedure, each team took multiple changes of outer clothing so they could change into other outfits to help keep Slate from realizing he was being followed day after day by the same teams; 24/7; rain or shine; hot or cold. Using micro radios blended into their helmets; each member of the trailing teams was in constant contact with headquarters so that they could receive up-to-the-second information concerning exactly where Slate was going, the route he was taking, and who he was possibly going to meet. At the same time, several times every hour each team got close enough to Slate so that their hidden telescopic video cameras could send up-to-the-second pictures of Slate to headquarters. Each helmet-mounted camera, hidden behind the right lenses of each rider's goggles, by producing and sending a complete picture every millionth of a second; even on the back of a bouncing motorcycle; could produce a legible telescopic picture; if the front of the device was aimed correctly on level ground; within five miles of Slate! It was the job of each motorcycle's driver to get close enough to Slate on the winding; yet level highway, to allow the covert photos to be able to be sent back to headquarters.

But for about a week all the young veteran did was what he had done for many months: roam far and wide over the whole Southwestern United States; never going into large cities; and camping out at night; even when it was COLD and snowy at higher altitudes; or rainy at lower regions! Some of the team members following Slate had not regularly camped out since boot camp or girl scout or boy scout camp many years before and it took a little time for them to adjust to "roughing it" on the hard; cold ground in Texas; New Mexico; and Arizona; and eating cold cut sandwiches and chips bought quickly at small roadside grocery stores, so that the strange person they were trailing could not suddenly disappear! For some reason, Slate was moving so fast on his cycle that they could not stop long enough at a store to order hot fast food, without him moving out of the range of their sensors; and thus requiring high-flying U-4s to find their quarry again!

But after a few weeks of having to "rough it"; the "tenderfoot" bikers trailing Slate got a break! While the Winds of Destiny swirled constantly and undetectably around him; and at the most critical time in his relative young life while he was traveling in far northern Utah, Samuel Eliot 'Slate' Steele finally reached the conclusion that the situation had calmed down enough for him to finally seek help!! The young man made the most important decision of his life to ask a certain someone for help; (causing the record surge of the Winds of Destiny on Empire Prime)! But at this Anchor Moment on the Main Galactic Time Line, who could possibly help him? At this point on the Main Galactic Time Line, even the movie hero called "Mighty Man" could not help the situation by helping him solve his problems; so what could any lesser mortal do?!? Just who could intervene on behalf of Slate to help him solve his problem and get the teams from the Unit off his back??

It would take ONE TOUGH MAN!

CHAPTER 16

Since he did not want to contact his alien friends for help just yet; and he did not want to possibly put his parents or Dixie in danger from the military by calling or visiting them, he did the very best thing that he could possibly do!! Punching a certain speed dial number on his cell phone that was programed to produce a cryptic coded voice cellphone signal, the former military man, (and maybe "not so former" in the future), Slate waited until his call was answered after the second ring. Then he looked down at the small picture of himself and the person who answered his call; a picture that was made in happier times; that temporarily put a lump in his throat! He looked down at the tiny snapshot that showed the individual he trusted more than any other person on Earth, and loudly exclaimed **"Sarge! SOS! Mayday! I need your help because I have an emergency!!"**

(As he talked, several of the unseen stealth U-4s were using their antigravity units to coast overhead around his location in the thin air at over 450,000 feet. Because of their extreme altitude; their "Electronic Counter-Measures"; and their invisibility to radar; they were visually out of sight and could not be detected from the ground. The advanced craft were intercepting his signal; but they were at first unable to decode his cell phone conversations, which were encrypted! By the time the encrypted cell phone signals had been relayed to the Langley Research Center in Virginia and decoded using ultra-high speed laser-chip enhanced "Crancor Computers", the top military brass had formulated a plan to deal with the possibly rogue agent they were tracking--one Samuel Steele! Unless something unexpected happened, it was a plan that would start to be executed in less than 24 hours!)

The answer from his friend was very quick in coming! "Ok, son; no problem! From your call, it seems that you have not been reading the newspapers or paying attention to the national news lately; and the information that is about me! But that's OK; I will help you; even if I have to stand in the way of a bullet for you; although I don't think that will be necessary!! I see on my cell phone's screen that you are using cryptic messaging; for good reason! Right now, you are hotter than an exploding firecracker on the Fourth of July!! **THAT IS OK; BECAUSE I CONSIDER YOU MY ADOPTED SON AND I DON'T CARE WHAT THE BRASS THINK!** With me, no matter what you have done; everything's in the green; so don't worry, I will help you and defend you in any way I can! I figured you were in a heap of trouble because your former boss, Major General Paxton, called me at 5 A.M. this morning, using my unlisted cell phone number; after he was contacted by Lieutenant General Hartford, the top boss of the CIA and your old outfit! He was ordered by his superior to find you; no ifs; ands; or buts; and he 'point blank' asked me if I knew where you were! I trained him about thirty years ago and he has kept up with where I am; even though he wanted to rise in rank to ultimately become a general, which he did; and I wanted to just train young men to serve their country, and ultimately lead them on covert Mars and moon missions! I told him truthfully that at that moment I did not know anything about your present location and you had not contacted me! General Paxton then supposedly ordered me to let him know if you ever contacted me; even though technically he couldn't command me to do so! I promised I would let him know; but I did not say how soon I would call him after you contacted me! But I won't call him, unless you want me to, after we meet somewhere and confer about the present situation! How about us meeting ASAP at the old bikers' watering hole we love so well in the town in the western United States at the café where that beautiful waitress still works that looks like my daughter, Carol Jane! I am not mentioning the exact place because the spooks at Langley can ultimately crack your homemade encryption in a few hours; probably in just a few minutes; if not already as we are speaking; but it won't do them a bit of good if they don't know exactly where in the western United States! All they can do is track each of us until we get to our meeting place; they can't stop us! I can get to 'our place' about 0900 tomorrow morning! Can you make it, or do you want to meet at the our favorite Cattlemen's Steak House at that small town somewhere in northern Texas or New Mexico; in order that we both can eat a 6-pound steak with all the trimmings; and get the whole she-bang free?"

"Let's see, Sarge! I'm not hungry enough to eat that much of a tough Longhorn steer in order to get it free! Let's see! Can I make it to the café meeting since its only 2100 hours? Sure, Sir; I can be there to meet you at our usual rendezvous place at 0900 in the morning or a little before if I get on the main drag; gun 'Sally Mae' to fly low and use my radar detectors, along with my ECM to evade the 'bears'!" Slate said.

"OK, but be careful, Son! I will keep this call secret since you are using a scrambled signal with a code that we have used before; which my cell phone automatically decoded when it got your signal! That was wise, even though by now the 'geeks' at Langley or an underground C.I.A. intelligence facility have broken your code and the brass are listening in to our conversation, 'real time'! There is also probably a secret 'spook' circuit in your phone which can allow them to track you even when your phone is off and the battery is removed, but you need it so that we can contact each other, so don't turn it off! If they haven't already, I hope by the time the spies decode this conversation at their Langley base we can already have solved your dilemma! Again, be careful and just like my old football coach back in the 1960's at Polytechnic High School in Fort Worth, Texas, so very long ago taught me; **HANG TOUGH, SON! OUT!**" Sarge Snyder said.

Slate immediately turned his cycle around and headed into the sunset, bound from northern Utah to northern New Mexico in order to face his Ultimate Destiny and Karma! As he traveled, he was followed by the unseen Winds of Destiny, which are undetectable to all sentient beings, except the extremely rare; mentally-gifted Imperial Reptiloid, Insectoid, Humanoid, or Snakoid Magi; scattered throughout the Cosmic All of Creation! As Slate had progressed farther and farther along his Main Path of Destiny; when the Royal Seers were finally able to investigate the reason for the surge in the Winds of Destiny along the path from Earth; they examined and researched the Life Path of the Humanoid causing the surge in the Winds and were able to finally visualize several possible paths splitting off from his present one! Each path visualized was apparently created by some action of Slate, Sarge, or the pursing Earthian forces! Some visualizations were very bright, some were very dim, and as the Imperial Seers watched, several dim visions suddenly flashed off like an ordinary electric source of light being turned off! But at this very early position in front of the Anchor Events which would happen on the Time Stream, the Seers could not determine just which vision would ultimately become the Main Path of Destiny; they could only secretly watch and wait; without contacting any of the "players" in their visions, or making any moves to alter the situation; since a cataclysmic event was not indicated! Any one of their visions could ultimately become the Main Path, it was too early to tell, because as the Royal Seers had found out the hard way many times over the last five hundred thousand years: **ALL THE VISIONS THEY WERE WATCHING WERE ACTUALLY ABOUT EVENTS WHICH WOULD, OR <u>COULD</u>, ULTIMATELY HAPPEN ON THE GALACTIC TIME LINE IN THE SO-CALLED "FUTURE"; AND THEREFORE <u>THE EVENTS HAD NOT ACTUALLY HAPPENED YET</u>! HENCE, THE ONE VISION; AMONG ALL THE VISIBLE TIME LINES; THAT WOULD BE THE LAST VISION THAT WOULD ACTUALLY BE THE FINAL PATH ON THE TIME LINE; <u>WAS NOT "SET IN STONE"</u>! IT COULD LITERALLY BE ANY OF THEM, OR ONE THAT COULD LITERALLY POP UP AT ANY INSTANT!**

Any small act by any one of the sentient beings in any of the visions, or even any action by any animal moving around the beings which could be seen in the visions; could instantly delete or brighten any Life Path or vision! So not knowing just which vision was going to actually happen; following the very old, and very strict, Imperial Laws concerning Magi Visualizations of Life Paths and "Future Events"; unless a "Cataclysmic Event" was involved and they got permission from the Emperor; all the Imperial Seers could do was just watch without any interference; and if they so chose to do so, deeming the happening worthy, they could ultimately record what they saw in their visions on the imperishable pages of the Annals of the Imperial Seers; and just. . . . . **WAIT TO SEE WHAT WOULD ACTUALLY HAPPEN THAT WOULD CHANGE THE COURSE OF THE MAIN GALACTIC TIME LINE!**

CHAPTER 17

Slate used his GPS navigation computer situated on his motorcycle's handlebars for guidance, which showed a lighted diagram of the highways in the area; along with a small red dot which indicated his position on the screen. After driving all night always exactly on or just slightly above the posted speed limit, at 7:59 the combat veteran pulled up in front of his destination; noticing Sarge's bulky and scarred "road hog", the "Gena Mae", (named after his old girlfriend in Cleburne that a long, long time ago, refused a proposal of marriage), chained with a Tytano padlock out front to a thick metal post; and probably protected with a few electronic gadgets; like his was. He also noticed what looked like a shiny new "computer tablet" firmly attached in the middle of Gena Mae's worn handlebars; also protected by other electronic devices.

#Now what does Sarge need with a permanently-attached tablet that is always in from of him when he rides? He must use voice entry, since he can't

type while he is riding!# Slate thought to himself as he "cased the place"!

There was also a large black SUV parked at the edge of the café's parking lot; having very dark windshields; antennas and knobs sticking out at all angles; and with several large black numbers permanently printed on the back and front of the car instead of license plates. After observing the SUV for a second, Slate thought that maybe he should leave and contact Sarge on his cellphone to meet somewhere else; but then suddenly, he had one of his "feelings" that "everything was in the green"; so after memorizing the numbers on the SUV, he continued on into the café.

The meeting place was called the "Rusty Bullet Casing", a roadside café apparently converted from an extremely large log cabin situated in northern New Mexico along the circle of roads known as the "Medicine Trail". The cafe was first established by a World War I veteran in the 1920's by renovating a very large log cabin probably built during the Revolutionary War. In the front section of the original title deed, it specified that every time the café was sold, it could only be sold to combat veterans, and only managed by combat veterans. "Pork Chop" Higgins, the present owner, had become a good friend of Sarge when he was training one of his first covert opts group when they frequented the place because they were training nearby for desolate desert regions. Having been a regular customer of the place for as long as he had been in the Service, and knowing that Sarge Snyder was a good friend and army buddy of the proprietor, Slate felt that the café was a safe place to meet for a private conference; since it had many hidden nooks and crannies for covert conferences to take place. When he entered the front door, out of habit, Slate "cased" the room, but there didn't seem to be any "hard cases" around, and the place was almost empty, except for a few men and women dressed in shirts and slacks scattered around the room; casually eating and talking together. At a table near the back of the café there were four men and women dressed in black suits; each apparently working in front of a laptop computer while talking among themselves. Slate continued to look around for any of the restaurant's regulars, but he still could not see any, and he could not see the owner, Carol Jane Jones. Even though it had been over five years since he had been at the popular café; he observed Corinne, the beautiful blond bartender that was always behind the counter when he had been there before, was taking a very large tray of food and drinks to some other customers at the extreme back of the tabled area. Skillfully balancing the heavy tray, when she heard the front door open, Corinne glanced over her shoulder and immediately recognized him. After finishing taking the meals and drinks and meal tickets to several other customers; she slowly walked toward him; looked directly at him and put her pointer finger to her lips indicating he should not say anything. Then the waitress quickly led him to a corner in the back of the café. She quietly motioned for him to step on a large white star painted on what looked like a solid hardwood floor; in front of what looked like the heavily barred back door; with a large oil painting hanging nearby with several of the Founding Fathers portrayed on horseback with drawn sabers pointed forward. When viewed from the side, the metal sabers seemed to rise out of the surface of the old painting like a modern holograph.

When he was slow to move to the indicated spot, she stepped close to him and whispered. **"Please trust me! Stand right here on this star painted on the floor and relax!**

Everything is in the green! Sarge needs to talk with you! He is already here, down below!" she whispered in his ear; "This feature was added during Prohibition to help hide local moonshiners from the Feds! It goes down to a hidden room built probably during the Revolutionary War!"

When Slate stepped on the white symbol Corinne then moved back and pressed George Washington's outstretched sword on the painting. Immediately he felt the floor slowly sinking and he observed that a round piece of the supposedly solid floor was going downward in a narrow tunnel the same size as the circular piece. Looking up as he descended into the basement, he saw that a round piece of flooring swiftly covered the hole above him as soon as he was below the floor level.

The small elevator dropped him to what several hundred years before had been the root cellar of an extremely large log cabin, and during Prohibition had been a hidden room to hide illegal alcoholic beverages from the "G-Men". As he descended into a large room, Slate automatically cased the place to see what he was getting into! He observed that the extremely large well-lit hidden room contained, among other objects, what looked like a metal desk with several different colored telephones; including what looked like a red land-line telephone on it, and a medium-sized oval table with Sarge Snyder sitting beside it; glancing up at him; with a very wide grin on his face, waiting for him. The room also contained a few other chairs, and the ample illumination in the area was provided by indirect lighting. The far wall of the room was lined with tall metal cabinets with what appeared to be locked sliding panels to guard whatever was inside. As he continued to look around, he observed that there appeared to be a small opening in the ceiling with two rails coming out of it and extending down to a small square table by the larger oval table where Sarge was sitting, reading a newspaper and smoking one of his famous cigars. Slate wondered what the strange apparatus coming out of the ceiling was used for, but since he figured it was not important, he decided not to ask the veteran DI; since he knew Sarge would tell him about the rails if he needed to know about them. The experienced observer also saw that on one side the oval table seemed to have a recessed glass-covered computer screen, and touch-key keyboard on its top in front of Sarge. For such an old room, there sure was a lot of electronic equipment! But why would so many telephones and electronic equipment be needed in such an out-of-the-way place as the hidden basement of a run-down restaurant such as the Rusty Bullet Casing?

As he was descending, his trusted friend arose from the table and came to meet him, with a wide grin still on his face, and with his combat-scarred hand extended. "Son, welcome to my own private hideout! This room was first outfitted several hundred years ago during the American Revolution and it has been updated every few years with more modern facilities by all four of the major U.S. military forces! Through the years the Unit has secretly rented the space from the café's military veteran owner! He gave us a 99-year lease for one dollar! What a deal!! During the Cold War high tech communications equipment and computers were added, all of which the management of the café lets us keep updated."

After shaking hands, the two military veterans returned to the table and sat down for an important conference, with the DI sitting in front of the recessed screen and keyboard. (Although neither of them could sense the fact, as they talked, the Winds of Destiny swirled around the table at gale speeds, indicating that this meeting was very important!) As they talked about Slate's "problem", unknown to them, the future destiny of many galactic worlds literally hung in the Balances of Fate; all dependent on a successful "plan of action" that would be formulated at that old, beat-up oval table! It would have to be a plan that used battle-tested tactics and its success hinged on what Slate could accomplish as he was implementing it!!

But also, as they talked, as the Imperial Seers on Empire Prime tried to visualize the Future, for one of the few times in their long history; the Magi could not figure out what was happening! Their powers had finally "come back online" and for a few moments they could visualize the whole Time Line! But then, after a few seconds, the scene changed, as literally dozens of alternate Time Lines on the Main Galactic Time Line started materializing and then blinking out; only to be instantly replaced by other similar visualizations! They did not know that this unusual and unprecedented visual effect on the Main Galactic Time line was happening because far across the Cosmic All an ultra-important meeting was in progress!! The Winds of Destiny rose to gale force as the two military friends; one an extremely experienced soldier with over forty years of command and training experience, and the other having a much shorter career span, but more heavy combat experience; sat down together to talk about what was going on; and for Slate to tell Sarge exactly what he did to merit all the United States Military forces to cooperate in order to find him; maybe **DEAD OR ALIVE! But just how could one former DI help him solve his deadly maze of problems? There were so many facets to the problems that Slate was facing that it would** be almost impossible to solve them all at the same time!

But if it was totally impossible to untie Slate's "Gordian Knot", just why were the Winds of Destiny surging?

CHAPTER 18

Sarge was never one to "beat around the bush" and immediately after they had set down he led out with: "OK, Son, the first thing I have to find out is the answer to several important questions! **What is going on? Exactly what have you done?!?!?!** Even John Dillinger or Al Capone did not rate this much attention from J. Edgar Hoover and the FBI!! But I don't think you would rob a bank; **so what did you do to become so popular all of sudden!!** I just received several printouts about you from my own private "on" and 'off the grid' intelligence sources! You are the first priority on virtually every APB military and civilian list in the nation! Every legal Federal security agency is looking for you, 24/7; and, according to my unofficial 'sources', one or two illegal bounty hunting 'operating groups' are hunting you, wanted **DEAD OR ALIVE**; and all of them hoping for a reward when they catch you! Just what did you do to make you hotter than a firecracker going off on New Year's Eve or the barrel of an M-77 machine gun after firing a full clip of ammo on a firing range or a rice paddy in 'Nam?!? I have heard from around ten federal agencies looking for you and wanting information about your whereabouts!! I even got an APB and an intelligence briefing about you from the Secret Service! For once, there is almost total cooperation among federal agencies; which literally is a miracle! Talk about Murphy's Law! When your old outfit somehow got my number and called me, they apparently shared it with all the other nine! So Son, spill it all out, with no holds barred, and I will do my best, up to, and including being court marshaled and/or impeached to help you by disobeying orders and not immediately contacting General Paxton when you called me! If you can, talk fast, because the posse was probably hot on your tail when you came on the highway and could burst into this room at any time!!" The graying combat veteran DI said to his protégé.

"Well, Sarge, this will take a while! I am hungry and thirsty after flying fast and low with 'Daisy Mae'! Can we please have some food and liquid refreshment before I start?" the young man stated and asked.

"That's a good idea, Slate, because a soldier always thinks and fights better on a full stomach! I'll signal Corinne, and either my sweetie, Carol Jane, or 'Corn'; can send down whatever you want to drink, along with some of your favorite extremely large 'Buffalo Hamburgers', since I feel what you stated is true, this will take a while; probably long enough to get them free!" Sarge declared. "I'll also order your favorite 'Casey's Lemonade' and my usual imported Sada Juice by punching a few coded keys on this keyboard!"

A few minutes later Slate found out what the rails sticking out of the ceiling were used for, as a "dumb waiter" quietly came out of the ceiling gliding on the rails, delivering several bottles of his requested "Casey's Lemonade" in a small ice chest, a very small glass of extremely potent Sada Juice for Sarge, and both of their locally famous 'Buffalo Hamburgers', which each had a beef patty literally a foot across; crammed inside a bun loaded with all the trimmings! The burger was free to any person who could eat the entire meal by themselves; with no help; and with no "to-go box" for leftover food that they could not eat! When she sent the huge burgers down into the room unattended, Corinne always put Sarge and Slate "on their honor" when they came up out of the room to either tell her they had eaten the whole thing, or immediately pay for the meal! In all the years that they had been using the room and ordering the Buffalo Hamburgers, the two soldiers never betrayed her confidence and they each had always paid if they had not totally consumed the literal mountain of meat! Sometimes they could; and sometimes they couldn't; depending on if they had just come back from a tough secret mission or from a week of relaxation!

The instant they started eating Sarge said, "OK, let's try to start your explanation one more time, Son! I know that you have been away from Earth, and haven't kept up with the national news, since you have not read the newspapers for quite a few months! So take it from the top; tell it from the beginning of your apparent escapade as to why the entire United States military and all the 'spy spooks', kooks, military authorities, crack military teams, and freelance bounty hunters are after you! Tell me exactly why your old unit is tailing you; apparently thinking you are a traitor, a robot, a clone, or a rogue agent! I have heard that all the motorcycle teams tailing you 24/7 are under orders to just follow close and keep tabs on you and not to let you get away! Boy, I sure would like for you to tell me the unknown and fantastic reason that I will probably be court marshaled and/ or impeached for helping you!"

Slate did not catch the meaning of two of the sentences that Sarge had said previously over his cellphone, and the one he had just said, about "newspapers"; and just started answering his question by saying, "Well, 'Dad'! The whole thing started like this! I don't think you have heard what happened to me several years ago; the information about which was totally 'off the record'! What I am about to tell you is Above Top Secret; but I don't care! When I was on a very 'black ops' assignment at a certain undisclosed location in the Middle East, after I stepped on a plastic land mine that our sensors could not detect,. . . . ."

The young combat veteran started his story off from the Event which had caused all his trouble! An hour or so later they were ignoring the fact that they had each finished their buffalo burgers; Sarge's cigar had gone out; he was out of Sada juice; and Slate had finished all of the bottles of the newly-famous bottled lemonade. The young soldier had finished the "normal" part of his explanation about being injured; also explaining how all his arms, legs, and eyes were replaced! He left out his breakup with Dixie being the cause of his roaming around the country, but skipped next to the fantastic part of his explanation; i.e.; the "eerie" part of his fantastic narration that still remained to be told!

Sarge took time to relight his cigar as Slate continued the important explanation with: "You are going to think that this sounds like an episode of the new 'Stranger Still Zone', but here goes! The eerie part of my narration that I must tell you started several years ago after I was honorably discharged from The Unit, and I was roaming in the Western United States on my faithful 'Daisy Mae'. Late one hot summer night, after a long, hot day's journey of motorcycling, I was camping on the bare ground on a dark; lonely hillside in Mount Zion National Park. It was after the extremely bright 'Hunter's' moon had gone down, and I had been tossing and turning on the rocky bare ground; unable to sleep; when I noticed what appeared to be a shooting star falling down to the top of a very large mesa a mile or two away! I was curious about the phenomena was, and put my hiking shoes back on to investigate on foot what I thought was a meteor falling in the desolate and lonely country far away from civilization. I slowly wound my way across the extremely rugged terrain among the scattered boulders; using my infrared night vision that Bomar gave me and my tracking instincts that you taught me; what seems like a long time ago in your basic survival training. After carefully walking across the landscape for about an hour in almost total darkness, I was at the base of a large rugged mesa; with only extremely faint star light to guide me. Finally I climbed over a final barrier of large loose rocks at the bottom of the flat mesa where I had observed the light, and found what appeared to be a water chute on the side of the mesa's vertical wall. I decided to use my strength to climb up the chute's vertical sides in order to get to the mesa's flat top; then I would try to exit the chute by pushing off one vertical side and jumping to the relatively flat surface next to the chute without falling and permanently busting my carcass! Being as quiet as I could, I slowly made my way up a narrow almost vertical chimney-like chute, which seemed to go all the way to the top of the mesa; by simultaneously grasping the sides to force my way up, and I was able to successfully exit the chute, just like I planned and turned toward the strange light! Weaving carefully among piles of rocks and boulders I was then able to get close enough to be able to observe from close up the pale yellow light that was being emitted from the interior section of the mesa, which looked like another flat surface twenty or thirty feet higher that the outer rim of the mesa. The laser-like light was pointed upward as if signaling to something high in the sky and shielded by rocks so as not to be visible from the ground unless reflected by smoke or mist. As I moved forward, I suddenly developed a very severe headache, which I ignored!"

"After several minutes of careful climbing up and over the dangerous terrain, I used my infrared night vision and observed what appeared to be the surface equipment and buildings which apparently covered a very large underground installation. From behind large boulders I watched a sliding vertical cover, of what looked like a freight elevator, move back and forth as what looked like equipment and supplies were moved inside by shadowy figures to be send down into what in all probability was a covert base to allow military operations of an unknown nature by an unknown force; perhaps a domestic military force or even a secret foreign spy base! I felt that I had to determine just who was running a secret base in the desert; so further investigation was necessary! Continuing scanning with my telescopic and infrared vision the jumbled mass of shadows on the surface of the mesa finally revealed an incredible fact about the unknown base! As I watched, the beings working to load and unload supplies appeared to be a group of literally nightmare creatures created out of the vivid imaginations of the writers of the popular 'Stranger Zone' science fiction television show; huddled around an old fashioned campfire; conversing in low guttural tones!"

At this point in Slate's incredible narration, Sarge politely interrupted him in order to contact Corinne; typing a request to her using the computer screen on his desk to ask for more lemonade and Sada Juice before the amazing story continued; starting with the instant that he realized that the apparent secret military base was actually run by beings 'not of this Earth'! Many minutes later Slate finished his unbelievable story by saying: "I was heavily wounded by the effects of strange electronic fields that I had to go through to return to my hidden ship. The fields almost totally destroyed my metal cyborg parts, but I retrieved what they wanted and escaped from the surface of the alien planet in the ship they let me use for the mission; with many enemy fighter ships in hot pursuit! After I lost consciousness on the ship that the aliens had let me use, I found out later that disobeying normal Reptiloid military rules, and endangering his "Egg Line"; the alien Red Stinger personally rescued me before my ship exploded and carried me to safety! I woke up several days later literally floating pain-free in their version of a hospital; which apparently contains medical technology far in advance of Bomar Hospital where I was fitted with my cyborg parts! With their technology centuries in advance of ours, because I was able to successfully retrieve what they wanted me to get from their enemy's planet; since the aliens could not order new ones from Earth, they totally replaced my ruined body parts; both the 'original factor equipment' that was injured, and also the artificial limbs that I had been fitted with; that had been melted by the alien energy field! The amazing fact was that the Reptiloids somehow repaired my body with living Humanoid limbs; with arms and legs just as good as or better than my replacement parts from Earth; apparently using my own DNA to grow new ones; since there are no scars and they have some characteristics that were on my 'original factory equipment'! In addition, they somehow completely healed the interior of my eye sockets and replaced my cyborg eyes; enabling my new Humanoid eyes to be able to perform as good as, or better, than my original artificial lenses and sensors! They also completely healed my ear canals! In addition, now I can lift more weight that I could with the cyborg equipment, and with my normal-looking eyes I can still see as far into the spectrum as I could with my electronic eyes, and I can also still see in total darkness!!"

Sarge had seen and heard many amazing true stories while he had served his country as a military training drill instructor, working at the Pentagon; working as a trusted Presidential advisor, and as a black covert opts commander in ultra-secret missions on the moon, on Mars; and now as he was being given daily intelligence briefings and about to transfer to the White House; but the actual events that his young protégé had been telling him about for the last few hours was extremely hard to believe! But the sergeant knew this young MAN! He had been in deadly combat with him; when "all the chips were on the table", and their lives were at stake! Every time this young man had come through every tough battle and would never quit; even several times when severely wounded! In combat he had literally trusted Slate with his life and the young man had completely trusted him and had always instantly followed his orders; with absolutely no reservations or hesitations! All these facts combined enable Sarge to know deep down in his Heart that the young man before him had been relating **true facts**; even though they literally sounded like fantasy out of a sci-fi episode on television or at a "Star Conflict" movie! He knew down deep in his Soul that the young man sitting before him was telling the absolute; total; and honest truth! Sarge knew because he had secretly helped to train Slate to use his cyborg limbs and the lenses that had been implanted in his head to give him amazing visual powers! He knew all the telltale signs of the hidden mechanical parts that had been implanted in Slate's body to save his life, restore his eyesight, and give him amazing physical powers! But now, he could see and literally feel that the artificial limbs and the glass lenses in what he considered his "adopted son" were gone; all of them! The young man's arms did not slightly jerk as they moved; the surfaces of his eyes did not reflect light like camera lenses; and the corneas looked like the ordinary eyes that they were!

The "hardware" was gone; **BUT SLATE STILL APPARENTLY HAD HIS AMAZING PHYSICAL AND VISUAL POWERS! AS A TEST, DURING SLATE'S EXPLANATION HE HAD TURNED OFF THE LIGHTS AND HELD UP HIS MORNING NEWSPAPER IN FRONT OF THE YOUNG MAN! SLATE WAS STILL ABLE TO READ THE NEWSPAPER IN FRONT OF HIM IN TOTAL DARKNESS!! THEN THE YOUNG VETERAN HAD THEN TURNED THE PAGE AND READ THE ARTICLES ON THE EDITORIAL PAGE; AMAZINGLY WHILE IN TOTAL DARKNESS!!** Because of those amazing facts which were literally staring him in the face, **HE HAD TO BELIEVE THE YOUNG MAN'S FANTASTIC STORY; NO MATTER HOW IMPOSSIBLE IT SOUNDED! THE PROOF WAS LITERALLY IN FRONT OF HIM: THE YOUNG MAN NO LONGER HAD CYBORG PARTS; YET AMAZINGLY HE STILL HAD THE SAME PHYSICAL POWERS WITHOUT THEM AS HE DID WITH THEM!!**

"So now, Dad, I have what appears to be a normal body again; with what seems to be ordinary limbs and eyes! But somehow, the aliens rewarded me for saving them from a civil war by repairing my wounds that I received while doing their important mission and using their ultra-advanced medical technology to somehow pack tremendous energy in my limbs and spectrum-spanning vision in my eyes! So what do I do now, Sarge? You know that my former outfit has been tailing me for the last month or so; 24/7 while I rode my old cycle; and just like in the movies, eventually; they probably will want to dissect me to try to find out the medical secrets of the aliens if they catch me!?"

Sarge thought for an instant; then replied, "Right now, I don't know what you need to do, Son; but I'll figure it out and do what I have to do to solve your problem if you give me enough time to 'cod-ja-tate'! Just stand down; relax; and finish reading the newspaper you started reading in the darkness! Try working the crossword or work on the 'Number Box" to pass the time if you finish the other parts of the newspaper! I need a few minutes to 'cot-u-tate' the facts and then I will come up with a super plan for action; just like we did on those black opts missions on the mares of the moon when the game plan went sour and we had to think fast or we were literally dead! Let's order supper from Corinne; relax; and give me some time to think!"

"OK, Sarge! **YOU KNOW THAT MY LIFE IS LITERALLY IN YOUR HANDS!** I will trust you explicitly and I will do what you tell me to do; although I sure don't want to be captured by U.S. forces and taken apart! I don't think that our medical technology is advanced enough to 'reverse engineer' all the improvements that Red Stinger's Imperial medical technology was able to turn on down deep in what he said was my 'NA's'! I guess he was talking about my DNA and the RNA data down in my Double Helixes, in every one of my cells!!"

When the veteran soldier heard those words, Sarge turned his head to hide a small tear as it slowly made its way down the side of his grizzled face! **SLATE WAS LITERALLY HIS ADOPTED SON, A SON THAT AFTER MANY YEARS IN BOTH WAR AND PEACE; HAD GROWN DOWN DEEP IN HIS HEART! THE BOY WAS IN TERRIBLE TROUBLE BUT WHAT COULD AN OLD FORMER DI DO; EVEN IF HE WAS ABOUT TO CHANGE HIS JOB TITLE?? HE FELT SO HELPLESS!! HE WOULD LITERALLY GIVE HIS LIFE TO PROTECT SLATE; EVEN USING THE OLD "SPINGFIELD M1 GARAND" IN HIS DESK IF THE ARMED SOLDIERS TRAILING HIM BURST INTO THE ROOM! BUT THAT WOULD NOT DO ANY GOOD!! IT WOULD NOT SOLVE THE BOY'S BASIC PROBLEM THAT THE MILITARY WANTED HIM LITERALLY DEAD OR ALIVE BECAUSE OF HIS NEW UNEARTHLY POWERS!**

When the tear had quickly evaporated, he turned around and replied, "Don't worry about something like that happening, Son! I would literally die by putting my old body in front of you before I would allow that to happen! After I contact them to ask for a confab, if they break down the back door to get you dead or alive, I promise you that I will get in front of you and then stop the attack with the power of my new authority, or my dead body; to allow you to escape!!! Now, like I said, relax; let me 'cogitate' and sip my Sada Juice for a while over in the corner to figure out exactly what to do; while you sip your bottled lemonade, look at the latest news on my table screen, take a bathroom break, or play one of the combat games to sharpen your aim!"

Sarge sounded confident when he spoke to his young friend, but deep in his heart he did not know what exactly to do! **The odds seemed impossible!** How could he protect Slate from the military capturing him and wanting to literally dissect him to learn alien secrets, even there was no way they could learn anything by analyzing his DNA or his new genuine Humanoid body parts? What could he do? **What could he do!?!?**

Not knowing exactly what to do, Sarge decided to use a technique to obtain help and guidance that had stood him in good stead many a time while in tough spots and while in deadly to-the-death combat! While on this spot, h**e would pray;** and ask for guidance like many U.S. commanders did during World War II when they were in deadly circumstances; then he would get up and use his decades of military experience to do something to solve the situation!

As many impossible and improbable scenarios passed through the military veteran as he prayed and sought an answer to his dilemma, the Winds of Destiny continued to surge unseen; unheard; and detectable around him and Slate! The alternate Time Lines continued to appear and disappear as the Imperial Seers, on Empire Prime and around the Empire, continued to try to do their job! But the old adage: "More things are wrought by prayer than this world dreams!", still proved to be true!

Then abruptly, as solutions to problems sometimes tend to do in the minds of ordinary Humanoids, **SARGE SUDDENLY KNEW, ABSOLUTELY BEYOND THE SHADOW OF A DOUBT; WHAT HE HAD TO DO IN ORDER TO SOLVE THEIR PROBLEM! HE KNEW**

WHAT HAD TO BE DONE TO HELP HIS HEART-ADOPTED SON, EVEN IF IT MEANT THAT HE WAS DESTROYING OLD FRIENDSHIPS; LITERALY BURNING HIS BRIDGES BEHIND HIMSELF; RUINING HIS REPUTATION FOREVER; AND MAYBE CAUSING HIM TO BE COURTMARSHALED, REMOVED FROM OFFICE, OR SOMETHING WORSE! FOR HIS SON THAT HE HAD ADOPTED IN HIS HEART, THE OLD MILITARY VETERAN KNEW THAT HE HAD TO ACT; FIGURATIVELY "PUSHING ALL THE CHIPS THAT HE HAD TO THE CENTER OF THE TABLE"; BY PROBABLY SACRIFICING EVERYTHING THAT HE HAD; AND USING THE ONLY MILITARY MANEUVER AND TECHNIQUE THAT HAD ANY CHANCE OF SUCCESS!!

Out of the hundreds of military manuals and books that Sarge had every read, he had suddenly calculated the only technique for solving Slate's problem that had a chance of working! The old DI suddenly remembered reading in a biography about a unique military method that a famous American General had used quite successfully many times in the past, during battles when his forces were greatly outnumbered, and he had very little hope of winning against the superior enemy forces that surrounded his forces! It was very illogical and dangerous, but it had always worked for the general! Even though it had been successful on the battlefields of World War II, because of its uncommon and hazardous characteristics; it was a maneuver that had never been taught in the dozens of military manuals that he had studied in his long military service! The old military man thought deeply about the pros and cons of such a plan! He finally decided that even though it was not "logical", **AND WOULD NOT BE POPULAR WITH THE "BRASS" OR HIS OLD MILITARY BUDDIES THAT HE WOULD HAVE TO CONFRONT;** what he had come up with sure beat sitting around and worrying what to do! **LET THEM WORRY; NOT HIM AND SLATE! HE WOULD SHOVE ALL THE CHIPS WERE AT THE CENTER OF THE TABLE AND THE RESULTS WOULD BE EITHER ALL OR NOTHING AT ALL!** And so, as the Winds of Destiny swirled unfelt and unseen around Sarge, and alternate Time Lines kept popping in and out like popcorn; he put his **BOLD** plan into action **. . . . literally!**

At this point on the Time Stream his "Future" did not mean anything to him; even after the events of the past few months; only the well-being of one young military veteran; who had just successfully gone through an unofficial black ops operation that probably the "Stranger Still Zone" science fiction television program would not accept as a story line--the producers would call it too "far out"!! To solve the "Gordian Knot", he would emulate the tactics employed by Admiral "31-Knot Burke" and General Patton; such as go "all ahead flank toward the enemy ships!"; and "all available units move toward, and fire at will at the enemy tanks; until you are out of ammo; or dead; whichever one comes first!!"; and not worry about what would happen as a result! When this whole "shebang" was over; he might be "busted" or impeached; but **HE DID NOT CARE! A MAN HAD TO DO WHAT A MAN HAD TO DO; NO MATTER WHAT THE COST!** The old DI knew that if he quit and let his young friend down, he would not be able to look at himself in the mirror every morning when he shaved, for the rest of his life!! But by following this plan, he would be doing the right thing and he would have a clear conscious about what he was about to do; up to the absolute last second of his life!

As Sarge wheeled around to start his plan, he thought: **#OK, ADMIRAL BURKE; IT'S ALL AHEAD FLANK! GENERAL PATTON; ALL UNITS PROCEED TOWARD THE ENEMY AND FIRE AT WILL, UNTIL OUT OF AMMO AND EITHER YOU, OR THE ENEMY ARE DEAD!#**

While the loud words reverberated around the basement room, unseen and unheard by the two veteran soldiers, the Winds of Destiny continued at gale force!

CHAPTER 19

While Sarge was contemplating many minutes about just what to do, Slate did not feel like staring at a computer screen; either to watch the usually violent local or national news broadcasts or to play the very intricate "Combat Zone Sniper"; so he just quietly sat and walked around the room blankly staring into space, while for many minutes his friend and former DI sat quietly in the corner; pondering how he could help the young man out of his "Gordian Knot". The whole situation was a "Hobson's Choice", i.e., all his possible options were bad! How could supposedly a lowly Sergeant DI protect his young friend from the military probably wanting to medically find out how the alien reptiles healed and replaced Slate's cyborg parts with genuine Humanoid limbs; yet he was able to keep his cyborg powers, without the hardware?!?!

As his young friend also deliberated about the situation, Sarge had come to the conclusion that he would need all his military experience of the last few decades to solve his young friend's amazing problem! He mentally went over literally hundreds of scenarios of things he could do and the probable result of each tactic; with nothing that he could possibly do that would save the young man's reputation and his life! What could he do? What could he possibly do to help his adopted son!!! He then mentally went over the tried and true tactics of American generals; seeking something in the Past that would help the Future. But alas! Nothing that he rehashed in his keen military mind had any possible chance of success!!!

After many minutes of literally mentally groping for an answer, Sarge finally realized what he had to do in order to solve the "unsolvable". Slate's problem was such that a solution had to be "all or nothing at all"! But nothing he carefully pondered over the span of many minutes had any chance of success until he remembered similar military tactics of an extremely successful American General, who commanded troops in World War II; and a heavily-decorated American naval commander, who was known for winning naval battles by doing literally the impossible; hence his nickname! Their common unconventional tactic had always worked very, very well; for both of them!

Coming to a strong conclusion of what he should do and using his talent of total concentration, Sarge worked out the details of the ploy in his mind! During his long service to his country, he had done some "dirty jobs" for some people who were now in "high places". He had also saved a few lives of the people who had been with him on covert missions. It boiled down to the fact that to solve Slate's problem, he simply had have the nerve and the chutzpa to call in a few favors from some of the "Big Boys" that he had helped over the decades that he had served his country; then literally attack the problem at its roots--the commanding generals who were trying to capture Slate because they were searching for the boy in order to "reverse engineer" technology to make a "super soldier" so they could further their own careers; even though there was no way that Earth's relatively primitive medical technology could unravel the tiny mysteries in Slate's "'NAs"!! **PUT SLATE UNDER THE KNIFE? IN A PIG'S EYE!! LITERALLY OVER HIS DEAD BODY!!**

After many minutes of sitting quietly and reaching a final conclusion of what to do, Sarge suddenly got up with no warning; walked quickly over to the far wall of the room and opened a shiny sliding panel by pressing his right thumb on the locking mechanism! He had to first press his thumb on what appeared to be an ordinary opening latch button, without putting a key in the ordinary looking keyhole beside it first, or an explosive charge would have been detonated! Pushing the latch inward until it clicked allowed the cabinet to be opened without using the dummy lock mechanism. Sarge slid the panel to the right which revealed a recessed area containing what appeared to be an advanced military "com suite"; on top of a metal desk which had several locked drawers. On top of the desk there were several different colored telephones, including a conspicuous red one; which reminded him of one that was in the White House! (As he looked on to what Sarge was doing, Slate thought that the place sure contained a lot of advanced military communication equipment for being in the basement of a dilapidated country café over two hundred years old!!)

Sitting down in front of the desk, the graying military veteran once again tried to think of any other possible solution to his protégé's problem other than the one he had decided to follow, but he could not think of any other possible way to help his young friend; so he started to pick up the red phone before him on the desk!

#I hate sitting around and doing nothing to solve Slate's problem! But after all this exercising my rear posterior and after all this 'cod-u-tation', the best modus operandi that I believe will solve our problem is one that "31" and my ol' buddy George Patton employed successfully many times in battle when the odds were heavily against them! I think the admiral and the general had the right idea when it comes to dealing with a problem, maneuvering military forces, or fighting a WAR!!! During a war, a successful general or a commanding officer can't 'pussyfoot around', waiting for the enemy to make a mistake or strike first; EVEN IF YOU ARE HEAVILY OUTNUMBERED, YOU MUST QUICKLY MANEUVER ALL YOUR AVAILABLE FORCES AND ATTACK!!!# Sarge thought in his mind.

#Attack! Attack!! Attack! ALWAYS ATTACK; NEVER RETREAT OR SURRENDER! We need to forget thinking about surrendering and asking for mercy for Slate; attack is the best tactic; using every possible weapon at your command, including calling in favors from friends and enemies alike! During a crisis like this, I need to forget friendships and being 'nice'! That technique does not work very often because your opposition thinks you are weak if you act nice! If nice guys always finish last like a famous major league baseball manager named Leo said many decades ago; then in this particular and extremely unique case, nasty is the only way to go! SO THAT'S WHAT I AM GOING TO DO! AFTER I GET THOUGH WITH HIM, BECAUSE I KNOW PAX AND I KNOW THAT I WILL HAVE TO TALK ROUGH

TO GET HIM TO SHUT UP AND PUT ME THROUGH TO THE PRESIDENT, I HOPE MY OLD MILITARY PAL FORGIVES ME! Well, if he doesn't, considering the situation, if he doesn't, it means that after all these years of me helping him, he's actually been a fair-weather friend, and losing such a fair weather friend for Slate and Dixie's sake is worth it!!#

The military veteran reached down and grasped the wireless red phone in its cradle; lifted the receiver to his ear; and immediately replied, "Is this the White House? Good! Listen carefully! This is unidentified operator Lambda Omega Wilco Seven! Oh, yes, I recognize your voice! Good day, Major General Paxton! I am glad that you know my voice from past experience; although I know that your voice recognition circuits are now identifying me, but if you have to, in your card file by your right hand, look up my security clearance and read the fact that using this security clearance means that I outrank you! **Now then, get me President Blair, immediately; even if you have to wake him up, interrupt a state dinner, or one of his frequent golf games!** If he's in Air Force one, or somewhere in D.C., tell the switch board to patch me through to him, ASAP! This is a matter of National Safety and Security!. . . . . What is the authorization for my interruption? Operational Orders Blue, Foxtrot, Casey Stengel! What?? You want an explanation before you connect me?!?! I am not here to talk to you; I need to talk ASAP to the President! **I GAVE YOU THE RIGHT CODE; SO YOU KNOW THAT LIKE EVERY CALLER THAT YOU TALK TO ON THAT PHONE THAT GIVES THE RIGHT CODE, I DON'T HAVE TO EXPLAIN TO YOU WHAT IS GOING ON! STOP INTERUPTING ME; ZIP YOUR LIP AND MOVE IT,**

MISTER; JUST LIKE YOU DID IN THE DESERT SO LONG AGO WHEN YOU WERE UNDER MY COMMAND! As your long-time friend during both war and peace, I hated to say that, but I had to stop you from 'hem-hawing around' because at this second I am in an extreme hurry! Contacting the President is literally **a matter of life and death**; as the important lives of two of the people that I love the most in this world at this very moment hang in the balance, young people I love as if they were my own children; not to mention at this very second, my life is also in jeopardy!! I need to talk to the President **ASAP**; and I don't want to waste my time talking to that fool that passes for a Vice President, what's his name; Joe Blakley, while you are finding the Commander-in-Chief! I am literally sick of listening to his mindless yakking day after day after day on all the national media! The reporters listen to his drivel day after day and never call him on his so-called facts that are wrong, since he is good copy. **SO CONNECT ME DIRECTLY WITH THE PRESIDENT NOW AND DON'T PUT ME ON HOLD WITH THAT STUPID ELEVATOR MUSIC! THIS IS NOT A CALL TO PAY A UTILITY BILL; THIS CALL IS OF NATIONAL IMPORTANCE!**"

The incredible events of the past few seconds literally put Slate in a daze as he listened to the rough and tough talk of Sarge to one of his friends; supposedly wanting to talk to the President!! Just exactly who was the man he had known for many years as Sergeant Snyder? He thought that he knew him; but the way the veteran military man was acting, it was apparent that he did not know all the facts!! The commanding way his friend had talked to one of the top army generals, he appeared to feel that he outranked one of the top army officers! But from the way Sarge reacted to what the general said back to him; General Paxton accepted the fact that his old Sergeant Snyder, who originally trained him as a DI several decades ago, **APPARENTLY DID OUTRANK A MAJOR GENERAL, EVEN THOUGH HE ALWAYS WORE THE RANK OF SERGEANT ON HIS UNIFORMS AND HIS CIVILIAN CLOTHES!** Just what was going on?!? Was his old friend some sort of a spy?!? How in the world did he possibly outrank General Paxton?!?!? Just what was going on? These happenings seemed like an episode out of the "Strange Zone"!! No, the present situation was beyond that! It was weird and eerie enough to make a "Stranger Still Zone" episode!

As he continued to listen in a stupor, Slate found out that amazingly, his old DI Sergeant Snyder was still able to "pull a few strings" for the young man that he considered to be like his own son; ever since their mutual combat missions during which "off the record" they had both saved the other's life several times! For Sarge Snyder had been around long enough and was wise enough to know that one's family does not just consist of those so-called relatives who share part of their DNA and RNA on the Double Helix and, (as Imperial scientists know), also their XNA, YNA, and ZNA deeper in each Humanoid cell on the Triple Helix! He knew that **"Family is OF the Heart, and IN the Heart!"**

After pondering and researching the facts in the distant future for decades, Slate finally found out exactly how Sarge, (and secretly Dr. Wagstaff), solved his problem! At that time on the Galactic Time Line, he could not figure out how supposedly just a "lowly" veteran sergeant have enough rank and authority to just pick up what looked like just a red telephone, in the basement of a dilapidated café over two hundred years old, and immediately talk directly with the President of the United States; just to tell him to stop the military from harassing one of his former trainees, who was now a very wanted man!! (The secret lies buried in the forever covert files of the small; ultra-secret military group known as "The Unit"; a part of larger group called "The Force"; whose ultra-secret motto was, and is: **"On the sea, on the land, in the air, on the Moon, and/or on Mars!"**)

But perhaps the ultimate answer is found by examining unofficial military and political history! Perhaps the reason lies in the wholly American term: "President Elect"! But perhaps it was because the veteran warrior knew "where the skeletons were buried"; he had saved a few lives in combat, and was respected enough by Generals Paxton and Hartford, and President Blair; who had all been under his able training and command in the past, to be able to quickly intercede for the young man "off, and on the official record"! Because of all these facts, Sarge was able to pull enough strings to get the military command to "call off the dogs"; i.e., tell the armed combat patrols that were following Slate 24/7, literally on all fours sides when he traveled, to stand down!!

A few minutes later, after a short, but very important conversation over the "Red Hotline Phone" with President Blair, who, along with what was probably his former best military friend, "Pax"; had been two of his trainees in the desert a long time ago; the old DI carefully put the red phone back into its cradle; then he came over to Slate; put his hand lightly on his shoulder, and said, **"Relax, Soldier; stand down because the President has declared a Condition Green!** We can both stand down and relax! Everything is under control because, after being in this business for so long, I have a few connections that I decided to finally use, and a few favors that I could call in! I went to bat for you, using the Casey Stengel code word, which is only for extreme emergencies; and by the force's protocol, is only good today!! So they wouldn't go to waste when I retire in a few decades, I simply called in a few hard-won favors to help the cause! Tomorrow another code word will take Casey's place!! Using the day's emergency code word, I was able to talk directly to President Blair, which I actually had in basic training in the ultra-secret "Lion Battalion" quite a few years ago before he became a professional politician by successfully running for the governorship of his state when he retired from the military! After several very successful terms in which he greatly lowered personal and corporate taxes; reduced the budget for his state; and greatly increased the standard of living in his state by increasing the number of high-paying jobs, 'ol Gene successfully ran for the Senate! After being elected to the Senate and serving for several productive terms, Gene then sought and was elected to the Presidency! It also helped that I had trained both General Bill Paxton and General Hartford a few years before I had President Gene Blair!" (Imperial Editor's note: **NO KIN TO THE "TIME MARSHAL" SAMSON BLAIR!**) "The President listened to me and, over the telephone I heard him use the world-wide military communications equipment in his White House room to directly order the combat teams that are circled around us to immediately stand down and leave us alone! He also agreed to do what I requested to bring this whole amazing situation to a peaceful conclusion! Apparently the continuing mission of placing teams around you to observe you actions and report back to General Paxton is so important that the President has been continuously informed about what is going on in real time! So as the new Commander-in-Chief-Elect, when I asked him to have the combat teams stand down; he was able to 'call off the dogs'!" The President agreed to a suggestion that I put forth of a "peace conference" at a certain buried command post in Arizona; in the desert in the area of the Grand Canyon, that used to be a secret training base for all the branches of the U.S. military! 'Genie' Blair and Pax both should both remember its location well! It's the same one you trained at many years later; the one that tends to literally fry your brain! I always had my trainees march at least 100 miles on cold rations across the hot, sunny desert; with 100 pound packs of food and plenty of water in 110° weather; to get to the buried bunker so I could start their 'advanced' training! This very hot training tended to separate the 'sheep from the goats'! At this point, the dropout rate was always about 50%! When a man or a woman said they wanted to quit, I would immediately radio headquarters and choppers would come to pick up the ones who suddenly figured that they wanted easy military desk jobs instead of tough covert operations in hot deserts! Then, do you remember what we did next for the ones who were still left?"

Slate nodded and Sarge continued, "Yep! Both you and they did strength and stamina building exercises for another week; the trainees usually losing every ounce of fat on their bodies; before taking up the much lighter packs and marching back to civilization to continue their training in the nearby river!! At the river we immediately weight-trained enough to be able to swim for ten to fifteen miles with full combat gear without drowning! That's what weight-training in a desert does for you! It does separate the weak from the strong when a trainee quits; or if they don't quit; it makes the weak into strong soldiers!!"

Slate injected, "I remember that at the time it bothered some of the guys that a much older man like you could have more physical endurance than they could; especially swimming very fast with a loaded pack! I remember your training routine well! When that 'drowning exercise' was over; with more trainees dropping out; we trained in hand-to-hand combat, with sticks, and with, and without knives! When that was over . . . . ."

"OK, Slate! That's enough military history, which you remember amazingly well after being a survivor of the very famous and much-dreaded 'Sweat Zone'!" Sarge took a breath and then continued, "We are to wait in the area for at least two hours; then meet at the old buried training bunker at 09:00 AM in two days, to allow the President to make sure all the combat teams around us get the word to stand down! Hey! After all that thinking I am hungry! Finish up your lemonade and since it's been long enough for a young man like you to be hungry again, let's go get a steak at Joe's new steak place in the nearby town! This whole episode shows that it's not just your rank in this man's armed forces that matters; it's who you know; the location of skeletons in certain closets that you know; the favors you can call in; and the politicians and generals in 'High Places' you have trained!!! Come on Slate, let's get crackin' to the rendezvous so that we can get some steaks to eat!"

The Winds of Destiny remained at gale force around the two soldiers as they covertly left the "Rusty Bullet Casing" after telling Corinne that they had eaten all of their steaks, and walked to their cycles. As they traveled on their motorcycles to the scheduled meeting, Slate did not see Sarge covertly talking into a hidden throat mike; which made the tablet on his handlebars light up; and allowed him to send a message to parts unknown! (Actually it was to his Secret Service agents still at the café to tell them to covertly follow them!)

Slate's "dazed" condition remained in effect until he tasted his pink center; medium well-done steak at Joe K. Daniel's newly opened "Five Winds Steak House", a few miles down the road from Carson National Forest, on the main drag in Santa Fe, New Mexico; almost an exact duplicate of his two very popular restaurants, one in east Fort Worth, Texas, the "Four Winds Restaurant", and the "Five Winds Restaurant", (north, south, east, west, and up!), in downtown 'Panther City'; (as documented in <u>One Time Winner!</u>)

Then finally, as Slate literally 'came to'; when he tasted the first bite of the delicious steak, he still could not figure out exactly what had happened to break the "Gordian Knot" and cause the "powers that be" to start to solve his dilemma!

But deep down in his Heart, even though he did not know exactly what the Future held; Slate was at peace with himself and was not even a little bit worried about the seemingly impossible situation! Again, the cause for his inner peace was because many times in the past on black covert missions he and his buddies had literally put their lives in the hands of **THE MAN** known to them simply as "Sarge Snyder"! When the going got **TOUGH**; they had always followed his commands and directions and the tough old DI had never let them down; and over the years, their group had always come through with little or no casualties; (except for his one exception when he was under the command of a different person!) So for this reason, against all the odds, one more time he would put his life in the hands of the MAN he considered his "Step Dad" and he knew in his heart that the supposed DI would not let him down!

After a long meal of steak, bake potatoes, salads, and apple pie a-la-mode, Slate and Sarge headed out along the narrow highway and into the desert to bed down for the night among the stars, prairie dogs, wolves, and coyotes; with a black SUV trailing covertly far behind; using satellite infrared sensors to keep track of the two bikers. As the two soldiers slept soundly, with electronic sentries on guard on their motorcycles and the Secret Service agents "roughing it" several miles away in the forest; neither of them could not feel the presence of something else that was always present when important historical Anchor Events were happening in one of the Galaxies containing members of the Interstellar Condominium of Planets and Empires—**the Winds of Destiny were still swirling around their bed rolls at gale force as they slept on the hard rocky ground!**

As they both quickly dropped off to sleep with the intruder devices operating on both their motorcycles, and Sarge's tablet on his handlebars silently operating; the only sounds were the coyotes and the wolves serenading the moon, the crickets chirping, and the light whisper of the wind going though the tumble weeds; while above the stars twinkled and the very faint reflection of the hundreds of Earth satellites as they crisscrossed the sky. Before he dropped off, Slate scanned the immediate vicinity with his heightened regular eyesight and his infrared vision, but did not see anything "out of place" or threatening. He also looked around the heavens with his ocular infrared senses for contrails or any evidence that they were still being scanned from near-space, but his scans indicated that the U-4s were gone!

The black 4-wheel drive SUV, was parked so far away that his senses did not detect either it or the multiple Secret Service agents shivering in the cold in the area around it;

who had not been prepared for camping out on the prairie; since they had not gotten used to the unusual schedule of President-elect! (In the future they would always be properly outfitted and ready to go "any place; any time; anywhere" 24/7; with the new President!!) In addition to infrared sensors, a "bug" in Sarge's motorcycle, and a signal from the tablet on its handlebars, allowed the Secret Service Agents in the trailing black SUV to keep tabs on the location of the important person they were sworn to protect! In all the history of the United States, no winner of the Presidential Election had ever gone against "protocol" and wanted his Secret Service guards to follow him "incognito"; so that he could help a friend! But Sarge Snyder had never failed to help a soldier in need; so tradition was forgotten and the wishes of the man who would be sworn as President of the United States in a few days was accepted! So after Sarge received Slate's call for help, it immediately became the job of the men and women assigned to guard the "President Elect" to covertly follow him; no matter what; braving the very crisp cold desert air at night, and high speeds on narrow country roads during the day! Following the orders of their Boss, they stayed close to him in order to protect him; but not be obvious about it. They protected the area where Sarge was riding or sleeping; using all the electronic technology available to the nation; including NORAD scans; satellite tracking; ground infrared detectors; police scanners; and hot "Sterno packs"! (It also helped that the Secret Service always knew exactly where Sarge and Slate were headed, since the President Elect could sent them verbal coded messages from his tablet that was permanently attached to his handlebars and protected by alarms at night!)

CHAPTER 20

arge and Slate arrived around 08:00 AM at the rendezvous point far out in the arid Arizona desert, many miles from the nearest dirt road; with the same black SUV still tracking them. As they were nearing their objective they saw a thick, white contrail streaking across the sky; then curving downward; apparently landing in the desert several miles ahead over the horizon of the rugged terrain. Seeing the white streak, they looked each other in the eyes; nodded in agreement, and continued on across the dusty desert ground on their bikes. A few moments later, the white contrail rose up again and quickly disappeared into the sky. When they had seen the white contrails, the veteran soldiers had immediately known that someone just been dropped off by a U-4; since they both had heard that the high-energy fuel used in the U-4's landing jets sometimes tended to make dense contrails in dry; desert air at low altitudes.

Their objective was what looked like a very tall pile of large boulders covering several acres in the desert;

southwest from the Grand Canyon. They parked their motorcycles behind a large slab of lava and walked into the maze of jumbled rocks; which both of them knew quite well; having trained long and hard in the hot desert location many times during the period Slate had been in the covert military group known by several different names, including "The Unit", a part of "The Force"; "Lambda Force 13", and "Omega 3". They continued to travel deeper into the interior of the very tall stack of what looked like lava rocks. Finally, at the edge of a small dusty clearing in the middle of the heap of tall stones; they came to an old weather-beaten wooden and glass telephone booth that, from its appearance, had apparently been there for many decades. In the thick dry dust around the old-fashioned wooden telephone enclosure were many sets of footprints; some of them very old, and some new; all of which seemed to circle several times around the box and then lead toward an apparent solid granite stone wall. Stepping inside the phone booth, Sarge dialed a certain number on the antiquated telephone dial and in response, a large segment of the cliff facing soundlessly slid upward, exposing a well-lighted opening exactly where the trail of footprints led. Immediately walking into the bright interior of what was called the "Entrance Room", for the first time in several years, the two military men found a reception committee of only one person awaiting them—-General Paxton!

Never one to quit while he was ahead, Sarge's motto was to keep up the pressure on the opposition by being the first to speak. "Good morning, General Paxton, it's good to see you again. I'm glad you could make it to our meeting so quick on a U-4! Outside the pile of rocks; we observed your plane land and then take off again; probably leaving your famous aide, Lieutenant Crayton Danny, behind with what we hope are many aluminum food containers! But food aside, we need your help and we don't quite know where to begin! I'm sorry I had to speak so harshly to you yesterday, but as you found out, it was important! I was in a hurry for a very good reason! A good military friend of mine was in trouble and needed immediate help!"

In response to his apology, the dark-haired General Paxton came forward with a grin on his face and an extended hand. Sarge met him halfway and pumped his hand very vigorously, as his former trainee said, "That's OK, Sir! Your unusual words made me quickly realize that what you had to tell the President was extremely important and I needed to stop stalling and immediately contact the present Commander in Chief so he could help you! But that's in the past; this is now! Forget it! I realize that you had to do it! It's a very good morning, Sarge; although I won't be able to call you that much longer; I'll have to call you Mr. President! It's good to see the old place again where you trained me and I sweated so much; but it was for a good cause!! Like General MacArthur said, 'The more you sweat in peacetime, the less you bleed in war!' But I am still proud that I was one of the ones that did not quit during your very tough training! From looking at the many fresh tracks around the place, I think it is still used every now and then for 'advanced training' of perspective new members of our covert special operations groups! I know that I will never forget that hot march here; then the further training of our marching group that caused about half of our group to say they wanted out! You always immediately obliged them and the choppers quickly came to pick them up!"

"But that was then and this is now! I have been in daily contact with the Joint Chiefs of Staff and the President, and we have agreed on a three-point plan of action to solve our very vexing and very difficult problem! First, I believe that I need to have a recorded and televised conference with you and Slate to be sent in real time to the President; so that Slate can tell his side of this amazing story, and allow you to fill in any details that you wish to add! As soon as possible this needs to be followed by a second conference and physical with Dr. Martha Wagstaff, Slate's old unit's physician; to allow her to physically examine him so that we can know; for the record; that he is not a clone, and determine exactly what medical miracles have been done to the young man! Secondly, Slate needs to confab with his old unit commander, Colonel Carter, ASAP in order to hash things out about what he wants to do now that his cyborg parts have been replace with normal flesh and blood parts with no loss of efficiency! Third, we need a confab where we can discuss any foreseen problems with the mutually agreed upon plans!"

"Right now 'The Unit' is overseas on an extremely important covert mission! Using a com communications unit, its commander, Colonel Carter, has been kept in the loop about Slate, and when the mission is finished, he wants to hop a U-4 in order to meet with him ASAP at a certain spot off the old 'Mother Road', Route 66! The colonel said Slate would know exactly where to meet! If all three conferences are successful, I think we can solve young Slate's problem to everyone's satisfaction! From the looks of the details that I have been able to find out, this whole story line of what happened to Slate seems like a plot out of a new 'Stranger Still Zone' episode! This confab and the later ones will take a while; so I brought several types of liquid refreshments, 'soft' and otherwise, for our morning meal; along with a lot of very tasty ethnic food items fixed by the cooks at my base! For lunch, and possibly a very late supper, I also brought some very good 'Western-style meat' with all the 'fixins'! If we need more food, Lieutenant Danny can radio for more!"

"I had a comfortable sofa along with a conference table and chairs brought in for several meetings that have been scheduled in the inner conference room! Unfortunately, to solve this problem, following government rules and regulations, like all government procedures, we have to document everything in triplicate!"

Sarge interrupted to inject, "I know all about government requiring triplicate documents from every important meeting; so I understand! Your setup looks good, Bill! I'm glad that you brought me some Sada Juice because that rare beverage is hard to find in this neck of the woods; i.e., this tiny solar system that is in a very large galaxy, and often ignored by the so-called 'Empire' that Slate had dealing with! That percolating 'Mrs. Coffee's Latte Blender' that I hear and smell will help by providing stimulating refreshment drinks in case the pow-wows last a while; along with some lemonade for Slate in that clear plastic cooler! The ham; hog jowls; eggs; grits; chitterlings; biscuit and gravy, and the other ethnic breakfast fixings that I also smell, will also taste good about now; just before the first conference! Then, after the first conference for lunch, Lieutenant Danny can bring in some more eats; say, beef ribs, beef brisket; with no black edges; along with black coffee as corrosive as battery acid; along with some strong iced tea! All the caffeine-filled drinks will help us concentrate if the sessions last until midnight or after; so please have him also include the Sada Juice! We can let the lieutenant know what we want; after the second conference; when the time comes! I have observed that young man seems to have a very good talent for being able to get anything that is needed for 'high brass' conference meals!" exclaimed the old DI as, without an invitation, he picked up a paper plate and helped himself to some of all the breakfast items in the large aluminum containers being heated with Sterno packs, and filled a large cup with coffee "almost strong enough to walk"!

"Yea Sarge, Sada Juice is hard to get since it comes from so far away, but it should literally smooth the deliberations!" replied the general. "While you are eating, do you mind if I start round one and start video-tape them; while sending the video and the audio simultaneously to my superiors at the White House and also the Pentagon?"

"No, we don't mind! I want to testify before I eat breakfast!" said Sarge as he put down his breakfast items and took a last swig of the very black coffee that almost had to be eaten instead of being swallowed.

After everyone was ready in the conference room, Sarge started by saying: "First, Pax, turn that new-fangled camera around and tape me! I'll be the first one to testify; then you all can eat, and I can finish my breakfast!"

When the general complied with his request, Sarge faced the camera; and then continued, "I want to put certain facts on the official record, **BECAUSE NOW; WITH NO ROOM FOR ANY MISUNDERSTANDINGS, I MAKE THIS STATEMENT!** Slate has done nothing wrong, he has followed his orders to the letter, and he has nothing to hide! He has broken no laws and he is not a traitor! If you are viewing this tape, you should have already read the transcripts that I faxed to you, the President, and the Joint Chiefs! Like a science fiction novel, the boy just happened to be in the right place at the right time to do a job for those aliens called 'Reptiloids'; that he was capable of accomplishing with his cyborg parts that were made here on Earth! Those intelligent alligators or reptiles asked the boy to do a job they couldn't do because of enemy ECM would react with their DNA and kill them; and when he successfully accomplished the mission the reptiles sent him on; when he was wounded and his metal parts melted; as a reward for his successful mission, he got his hardware replaced with the real thing, using medical technology hundreds of thousands of years beyond our medical capability! Now back on Earth, Slate just wants to be left alone to do as he pleases and live out his life without being chased and hounded for information that he does not know; and we cannot possibly find out, even if he is killed and autopsied in the name of 'national security' and the advancement of medical knowledge!! I want it on the official record now that **I will literally fight to the death any attempt to operate on Slate to find out what the aliens did to him because there is no way with our low medical technology that we can find out how they replaced Slate's limbs!** So go ahead! Tape and transmit the whole thing; although I expect what the boy relates to you will be immediately classified as Above Top Secret!" (This prophesy of Sarge proved to be quite accurate! The tapes probably will be declassified and released in a few hundred years!)

"Thank you for your testimony, Mr. Pres. . ., er, Sarge! Let's eat; then Slate can start his testimony!" injected the general.

The conference room emptied rather quickly after his suggestion! When Sarge, General Paxton, Slate, and the lieutenant, had eaten and drunk their fill, they all went into the conference room; the bright lights were turned on; and the recording and transmitting equipment was again set in motion by Lieutenant Danny; who was sworn to secrecy about what he might hear as he was bringing food and drinks into the conference room! Hour after hour, as Sarge watched and very slowly sipped the Sada Juice, Slate was videotaped as he again recounted to General Paxton about his amazing exploits while among the so-called "Reptiloids from the Thunder Worlds"! The young veteran started from the moment he saw the light coming down on the mesa while he was bedded down for the night in his sleeping bag, and did not leave out any important happening; (except the important reason why he had been roaming aimlessly around the North American continent for the last few years)! Every few minutes as he listened to Slate's fantastic narration, the general would turn around to look at Sarge for conformation of the literally impossible facts he was hearing, and every time the old DI would just nod to back up the fantastic narration of what had happened; smile, and emphatically say every time, **"That's exactly what he told me!"**

Over the span of the very long conference, the Sada Juice supply ran quite low and it was several hours after the breakfast meal had been eaten when Slate finally finished his recounting of his fantastic adventure and General Paxton was convinced that he had enough video information to allow the plan to go to the next level.

As an experienced military interrogator, General Paxton was very impressed with young Steele's mannerisms and bearing all during what had to be a very stressful session of trying to tell what sounded like a narration of literally impossible happenings! Slate spoke very firmly and calmly; with his hands folded; always speaking slowly; and always looking the general directly in the face and appearing very confident as he related the amazing facts about his first encounter with the Reptiloids on the mesa! Slate coolly explained his impossible exploits while he was retrieving the important political icon for the alien known as Red Stinger; the enemy weapon melting his cyborg machinery; his rescue; and the fantastic and unbelievable replacement of his mechanical arms, legs, and his electronic eyes; with what looked like just normal Humanoid limbs and eyes; but which were much, much more! General Paxton noted that Slate did not rapidly blink his eyes, look down at the floor and all around the room all most of the time, or always be shifting around in his chair; he stayed still and spoke with conviction and clarity! He kept his hands folded and still the entire time of the tough interrogation! All these traits and characteristics indicated to the general that Slate was telling the honest, fantastic, unbelievable; and impossible—**TRUTH!**

When Paxton had listened to the complete story and had asked all the questions that he could imagine that his superiors would want to know and received the very satisfactory answers from Slate, he replied, "OK, round two may be coming up if the President and the Joints Chiefs of Staff have no further questions!! Just a second while I ask them!"

Taking a portable com unit out a front pocket of his camo uniform, the general clicked the transmit button on the #7 channel and said, "Mr. President, is there any other question that you need for me to ask Major Steele? No? Thank you for your time, Sir!"

Switching to #8 channel, General Paxton replied, "General Cleere, do you have anything else that you require for me to ask Major Steele?" After listening intently for a few seconds General Paxton turned his radio around and asked, "General Harmon Allen, the Chairman of the Joint Chiefs of Staff, wants to know if you think we can trust the particular group of Reptiloids that you fought with! What was the leader of the group, Red Stinger? Here's the phone, you tell him your answer!"

Calmly taking the phone, Slate had to think for only a moment and then replied, "Yes, sir, General Allen! Having communicated literally mind-to-mind with him, I think we can trust Red Stinger's government of the Thunder Worlds, unless there is an overthrow of the present regime! I talked to him directly using telepathy and I could not detect any deceit; and he could not detect any deception in my thoughts or speech! At the end of my mission as I was heavily wounded and fleeing from the enemy planet; even though the reptile did not have to endanger himself, he put his life on the line and endangered what they call his 'Egg Line', i.e., his whole present, past, and future, family in order to save me!" Slate then handed the phone back to General Paxton; who then spoke again to his superior; then hung up the phone when the general was satisfied with Slate's answer; and the video interview continued.

At the end of his video statement, General Paxton again asked the military leaders on the other end of the com if they had any other questions. As the speaker at the other end apparently said no, General Paxton switched the small communications device off; then cocked his head to one side to listen to a helicopter land nearby. Then he clicked his com to another channel and barked, **"To all teams; this is General Paxton! My caller ID should check out on your com units! Operational Code Montana, China, Potato Salad, Mustang! By my authority, attention**

teams Arapaho, Sargon, Calypso, and Music! Condition Green; Repeat! Condition Green! You are ordered to immediately stand down and return to base! Every one of you did a very good job! Well done, Arapaho, Sargon, Calypso, and Music! You will all be given a paid rest and relaxation leave of at least one month; with free transportation to any destination you want, and back to your assigned base! Payment for each of your expenses will be transferred out of my budget! Before going on leave, you must first be debriefed by your team commander; and then you will be released from your regular duty to go on your leave time; all at the discretion of your base commanders! Remember, each of you are sworn to secrecy, **FOR THE REST OF YOUR LIVES**, about all the events that you have seen, or heard about, in the past few weeks! This means you can't use anything that happened to you the past few days in your future biographies or memoirs; which should make them very dull! Each of you have a good relaxing trip; and expect a new covert assignment when you get back! **Out!**"

Clicking his com off, and suddenly hearing a noise outside, General Paxton said, "OK! There's been enough talk for the moment! Like somebody said in World War II or thereabouts, the military marches and moves on its stomach; or something like that; so let's get some food!! It's been a long time since breakfast! It's been at least four hours, and all that talking has made me hungry!"

Punching his com back on and turning the small LED indicator to another channel, the general commanded, "Lieutenant Danny, bring in some Bar-B-Q, bread, paper plates, Sada Juice, and lemonade from that fast chopper I just heard land; hopefully also bringing breakfast for in the morning!! We are getting dry and hungry after all the talking that was necessary to clear up this important matter! For this part of the agreed upon plan, and to finalize negotiations, Dr. Martha Wagstaff is also needed! We are lucky that she is available to do the vital examination for us! She just got back from a Miami Beach vacation with her husband, her daughter, and her three sons! I believe that one of her sons is in the military and actually wants to train in order to be in our unit! She should arrive here in a few minutes!"

After a few minutes there was a knock at the door as Lieutenant Danny, the general's extremely competent aide, brought the requested items. Behind him, Dr. Martha Wagstaff also entered. Her appearance, in sharp contrast to her usually pale completion, was tanned very dark after her recent vacation with her family on a sunny Florida beach. The very experienced military doctor was carrying a large black medical bag and pulling a large medical cart loaded with equipment. Without any prompting, she immediately set aside her medical equipment and joined them in enjoying a hearty late breakfast/early lunch; (although she did not like the smell of the chitterlings which still hung around; since her mother served them almost at every breakfast while the doctor was growing up; and she ate enough of the tasty intestines to last her a lifetime!)

After everyone was thorough with their meal, following orders from General Paxton, Dr. Martha Wagstaff stepped inside the conference room to examine Slate; so that they could compare his recorded physical condition before his cyborg operations; to what it was after his cyborg operations on Earth; to what it was now with the alien "physical upgrade", which used what looked like normal Humanoid tissue, but appeared to be superior to Earthly electronic creations! While the doctor was setting up her equipment,

Sarge and General Paxton left the conference room, opted for tea; then got plates for a second helping of ham, ribs, brisket, beans, and apple pie! With plates filled very high; they then walked over in the corner of the entrance room in order to quietly, and off the record, "talk shop" about their past secret military experiences; and Sarge's "new job" coming up very soon! The general made sure that there was enough food for the two military friends to much on while the medical tests were being performed on Slate.

But even as the two old soldiers rehashed their old military accomplishments; they each wondered deep in their minds about what Dr. Wagstaff would find as she tested Slate! Would he be a clone; somehow constructed by the nation's enemies to spy out military secrets; or would the young man test out to be a "new improved model" of the old Slate? Only the passage of TIME, and Dr. Wagstaff's medical expertise, would answer their unspoken questions! As they wondered about the results of the medical tests and "talked shop", the Winds of Destiny swirled unseen and undetectable around them!

CHAPTER 21

When everyone else had left the conference room, the competent doctor shut the door and started to prepare to give Slate a thorough examination on the conference table with the portable medical equipment that she had brought. Before she started, Dr. Wagstaff made a very private statement to the young veteran from the heart. "I asked General Paxton to be able to personally perform this exam; instead of letting one of the doctors under me in the unit, because years ago I examined you when you were a new recruit! Then a few years later when you were a combat veteran, I saw you the terrible day that you were brought in after you had been horribly wounded by the terrorist roadside bomb! As a doctor, I vividly remember your terrible wounds on literally every part of your body; most of which were then; and are now; still beyond our medical technology to heal with normal flesh and tissue transplants! All we could do was immediately freeze your heavily-injured body and send you to Bomar; so that those cutting-edge medical technicians could try to replace your totally destroyed limbs with ultra-advanced mechanical appliances to allow you to live a somewhat normal life!"

"Now, suddenly, you are now standing before me; literally a medical miracle because you suddenly have new normal, flesh and blood eyes, ears, and limbs; instead of electronic implants in your heavily damaged eye sockets; and steel rods used to brace plastic limbs as a replacement for your normal arms and legs! Now, as one of the doctors who first worked on you and saw the appalling wounds you received as a result of that bomb; I volunteered for this exam because I wanted to see for myself if you are actually the young man known to us as Slate Steele; and not some enemy agent cloned or surgically altered to look like him! I want to see with my own eyes if you are the young man that we knew and, because of a literal miracle, you have actually had your totally destroyed limbs and your ears and eyes replaced with living; breathing; pulsing absolutely normal arms and legs; with replaced ear tunnels and natural cornea eyes!"

With those impassioned words, the doctor began her examination of what was to her literally a living; breathing; medical miracle! Allowing time for both Slate and her to take frequent short breaks; it took Doctor Wagstaff a little over five hours to complete the required list of tests on her clipboard; aided by being able to use body sensors, portable X-rays, and testing equipment that were all electronically attached by encrypted microwave channels to her mainframe computer back in her office. A portable combination printer/fax allowed Dr. Wagstaff to immediately print out all the test results in real time, as soon as she completed each one; and also at the same time, the equipment faxed the data to the required military commands, the Joint Chiefs of Staff in Washington, D.C., the President, and the President-Elect.

The doctor tried to be professional and not say anything as she poked; prodded, X-rayed, and took blood samples from the seemingly uninjured young man; who the last time she had seen him; was a bloody quadriplegic with only one heavily damaged eye left and very little hope to be able to live a normal life or even just to survive beyond a few months! Having seen Slate when he was so terribly injured, while she performed the tests; what the doctor saw literally tore her nerves up inside as she remembered vividly Slate's condition the last time she saw him; which was absolutely the most horrendous and hideous military combat wounds she had ever seen in her long military career!

But Dr. Wagstaff was a very experienced and a very professional doctor; so she controlled herself and refused let the situation get to her and cause her to cry in Slate's presence while she was doing what needed to be done! (At least, she TRIED!) The X-ray films were normal, except for a very small spot deep in Slate's brain that appeared to be benign and harmless. Incredibly, her scans proved what a close inspection of his outward appearance and his "involuntary mannerisms" showed! Every MRI; X-ray; and sonogram indicated that virtually all of his cyborg metal limbs had somehow vanished; impossibly being replaced with what appeared to be normal flesh and blood arms and legs; with absolutely no scars at the junctions where they were replaced; exactly the same size as his original limbs; but with no loss in strength; and in fact; the young man was slightly stronger! The slight reflections that were always present in the young man's electronic eye lens were gone, replaced by what looked like ordinary corneas; as well as the very small jerks that Slate's cyborg limbs had exhibited as he moved about! Observing what was literally a medical miracle; the doctor still had trouble believing her eyes and the results of all the tests! With her instruments and her expertise, she found out that all of Slate's limbs were normal, and did not contain any metal or artificial substances! DNA she extracted from all his new limbs tested out exactly the same as in the tests performed before his accident! There were no scars on any of the new limbs; or any indications on any of the bone structures of the limbs which would indicate that the new section of the limb had somehow been grown and then transplanted to the injured stub! (#***It's as if the aliens simply caused his body to regrow new limbs, like starfish in the oceans of Earth can do! But how did they give him cyborg strength without metal parts?!?!?#*** Dr. Wagstaff thought to herself.) The only scars Slate had on his new limbs were exact duplicates of several small birthmarks that had been on his body before the bomb injury; hence they had been in his original old-fashioned DNA!

Both of his eyes appeared to be just normal corneas and the interior of each eye did not contain any plastic, glass, or metal which had previously been implanted to give him sight again after the blast! All of the "rods and cones" in the interior of his eyes appeared normal! But now, it had been reported that his new eyes had the same extra sensory powers as they had before with the electronic implants; only physically, under very close microscopic examination, they appeared totally normal, with no metal or plastic parts; or any clue how the aliens changed them to obtain a wider spectrum of vision! More than once out in the outer room, Sarge's keen hearing heard her exclaim **"This is impossible!**

Ooooooooooh... No way!", and similar outbursts! Every hour or so Dr. Wagstaff and Slate took breaks from the tests to relax and eat slight snacks to tide them over until the next heavy meal.

When Dr. Wagstaff was completely through with all of the required parts of her extensive physical exam, and her computer had printed out all the test results, she opened the door and called Sarge and General Paxton back into the conference room to talk about the amazing results of all the tests! Sarge brought along his laptop with a stack of papers perched on top. The doctor then passed out all the papers which listed all the results of the tests to Sarge, General Paxton, and Slate. Following written orders, she had already faxed all of this very secret information to the Joint Chiefs, all the required "top brass", the Central Intelligence Agency, and several other secret government agencies.

After controlling herself for such a long time, Dr. Wagstaff finally had to give in to her feelings! She turned around to speak to General Paxton with tears streaming down her face and said, "All of the testing showed that the young man before us is actually the person we knew as Samuel Eliot 'Slate' Steele! The secret tags that were put throughout the trunk of his body to guard against clones, while he was in training and throughout his military career, are all intact! He even has the four small birthmarks on his lower legs; which were originally destroyed by the roadside bomb! Although the last time I treated him he was literally shot to doll rags; with all of his limbs ruined, many wounds on his trunk; with one eye totally destroyed and the other heavily damaged, and many wounds on his head; now miraculously, he is perfectly whole! Slate has what looks like absolutely normal; flesh-and-blood arms and legs; perfect ear canals and excellent hearing;

and undamaged eye sockets and corneas! After a thorough physical I can state that at the present time this formerly heavily-wounded soldier is somehow now absolutely normal; as normal as any of my three sons; one of which is already in the military and has been home on leave! After performing many tests on him, I cannot find out any medical reason why even though Slate is medically absolutely 'normal', he still has all the physical attributes that he had when he was a cyborg; without having any of the mechanical hardware and plastic eye implants! Those aliens sure know a lot about the Humanoid DNA, and how to manipulate it, that we do not know and can't guess! There has to be something further down in the Humanoid genome that we do not know about that makes his powers possible! This ends my official verbal report!"

Then the doctor deviated from the normal protocol by then asking, **"Permission to speak and act freely, General Paxton; for a personal report, on or off the record; at your discretion!"**

"Yes, you may, Dr. Wagstaff! With your excellent work today testing Slate, you have more than earned the right to speak on or off the record!" The general replied. "Off the record it will be, unless you say otherwise!"

In response, the well-liked doctor, the military medical veteran of literally hundreds of bloody operations to repair combat wounds; calmly said, "Leave the camera on! What I have to say needs to be recorded!" Then Dr. Wagstaff turned around again to face Slate! She calmly walked up to him, and with tears still cascading down her face, gave him a motherly embrace; which was immediately answered by Slate! For only an instant the doctor hugged the young man; then she suddenly let him go as if she had touched something hot or something which gave her a shock; but at the same time still holding one of his hands! At that exact instant, the air conditioning in the subterranean bunker started affecting the eyes of Slate, Sarge, and General Paxton; and they had to turn around to wipe the condensation from their faces!

"I am so sorry for my unprofessional outburst of emotion! I have never done this before after I have done a medical examination with one of my former patients, and I hope I never lose control and do it again! But his case is an extremely unique; literally once-in-a-lifetime medical miracle!"

"Slate, when they brought you in on that U-4 after your body was almost total destroyed by that mine or bomb in the desert several years ago, more dead than alive, as a medical doctor I DID MY BEST FOR YOU, BUT IT LITERALLY BROKE MY HEART THAT MY BEST EFFORT WASN'T ENOUGH TO HEAL YOU; OR EVEN GIVE YOU A CHANCE TO LIVE A NORMAL LIFE! The fact that I could not help you literally tore me up inside and I could not sleep soundly, or have an appetite, for many weeks! It saddened me that with all the medical knowledge that I possessed, I could not heal or fix any of your terrible wounds to save your eyes; your legs; and your arms! When my team and I had done all we could do to help you; which was only to freeze your body in order to stabilize your critical condition; you were then flown out of my hospital on the same VTOL U-4 that brought you in, and flown to Bomar to try to save your life and replace your limbs with mechanical replicas, your ears, and both your eyes with computer chips and lenses!"

The doctor hesitated for an instant; then continued. "The cyborg transplants were very successful and you were able to function as an outwardly appearing normal young man, but secretly having super-human strength and new eye powers including infrared vision! Then after a few years of successful covert military service, you retired and for some reason, spent all your time aimlessly traveling on your motorcycle around the North American continent! Then you unexpectedly disappeared for a few months and amazingly you suddenly reappeared with normal limbs, as if you had never been severely injured; which is far beyond our medical technology and sounds like an episode of the 'Stranger Still Zone'!"

Martha started sobbing as she stood close to Slate; then continued, "I don't know who, or what, gave you normal limbs and an eye again, but what I have seen today is an answer to my daily prayers for you since that terrible day that I did my medical best, and yet; I could not help you!! I am glad for your sake that now you can lead a normal life! After reading the top secret reports that I was given, I don't know how the beings you describe as 'Reptiloid aliens' did it; and what they did to somehow give you back your normal arms, legs, and eyes is far beyond our medical technology to find out; so we don't even have to try; **IT WOULD BE IMPOSSIBLE!**"

The normally soft-spoken doctor suddenly wheeled around, pointed a finger at the video camera, and exclaimed, "Now let it be on the official video being filmed now and also on the official written record, that if anyone says different or wants to lock the young veteran known as Samuel Eliot Steele up and dissect him to find out how it was done, they will have to take it up with me first, and **GO THROUGH MY DEAD BODY!! I will state for the record that the politicos, bureaucrats, and/or military higher-ups will have to literally kill me first**

before they touch that young man!! I will state for the official record; and in front of any congressional committee; that the medical technology to find out the secrets that the aliens used to literally rebuild him, using the information in his cell structure, would literally take us at least a hundred thousand years of dedicated subatomic micro-biology research to duplicate! Because of this fact, there is absolutely no reason to harm Slate or kill him to perform an autopsy to unsuccessfully try to unlock their secrets, because we can't do it now, and for thousands of years of medical research!" The usually calm and composed doctor explained and firmly stated to the camera, as she turned around and looked General Paxton in the eye again.

Dr. Wagstaff reached over and grasped Slate's right hand; then released it; again acting almost as if it were hot! Then she explained, "I again apologize and state that I am sorry that I acted in such an unprofessional manner to hug one of my patients; but the cause for my outburst is the fact that my medical team did its best; but we could not help Slate! Now, I am very relieved that the young man that I saw so terribly wounded so many months ago is now totally healed, and again I state, we lack the medical technology to try to find out by killing Slate!"

The young soldier spoke up to say, "That's OK, Dr. Wagstaff, I understand; and I'm sure General Paxton and Sarge do also!! Like you stated, this is a very unique case!", also wiping the moisture from the air conditioning out of his eyes. "The long years I was with The Unit, you were the Chief Physician that took care of everyone that got injured; from broken bones to broken hearts when anyone got a "Dear John" letter from their sweethearts at home far across the seas! You always did your best under what were usually very trying circumstances! You were always there for us, when my buddies, or I needed you! You never let us down! You were always there 24/7, when needed at the MASH unit in the field or at the Lexington, when any of us needed help; rain or shine; day or night! You literally worked miracles, and we could tell that you cared! You were able to effectively treat everything from a broken finger to ruptured spleens, appendixes, and ear drums! If you could not help us while we were literally in the field, you quickly sent patients in our unit to the nearby fully-equipped hospital, or to Bomar, where they could . . . ." Slate had to stop talking because the air conditioning started making his eyes water; so General Paxton took up the slack!

"I don't think that your physical protection of Slate will be necessary, Dr. Wagstaff, and that last bit of your testimony will not be a part of your official medical recording!" General Paxton interjected. "Now that you can certify that Slate is totally normal, I will go to bat for him and take it to the next, and I hope, final level! For the last step, we need to have a conference with his former commanding officer, Colonel Carter, in a few days when he gets back from an extremely secret Black Opts."

General Paxton stopped to take a breath; then continued, "Now after all this talk, even though you had munchies to nibble on, I imagine that it's been too long since you and Slate had a meal! Out here while you were doing the tests, Sarge and I slowly foraged and we while we were 'talking shop'; we managed to eat all the Bar-B-Q ribs, chicken, and brisket; as well as drink up all the lemonade, and the Sada juice! So since we are out of food, what say we have a good late lunch or early supper down the road at the famous Four Winds Restaurant; which I will pay for on my departmental expense account? I can't believe that I am hungry again after two heavy meals of eggs; ham; bread; and Bar-B-Q ribs, chicken, and brisket!"

As they were walking out, General Paxton continued, "In a few hours when Colonel Carter gets back from his assigned mission, for the final necessary third step, after he goes over all the data on Steele and has a private conference with him at a certain nearby restaurant, the colonel gets to give the final clearance and the permission to allow Slate to rejoin his old outfit, join another group, or retire completely from the military! After that conference, what Slate does in the future is up to him!"

When he heard that statement, Slate felt relieved and started shaking hands of everyone in the room. Since Sarge and the general had literally eaten everything in the whole place, everyone agreed to the suggestion! Slate and Doctor Wagstaff were very hungry since they had only munched on a few granola bars and bottles of green tea during the whole time the medical exam was in progress. So everyone worked together to pack up all the reports; carry out all the garbage bags full of trash; and take Dr. Wagstaff's medical equipment out to her SUV. They also cleaned up the place for the next military group to use the facilities. When everything was cleaned up as well as when they entered the place; the group walked out of the large pile of jumbled boulders, and headed toward their vehicles to follow General Paxton's suggestion to eat at the famed restaurant a few miles down the road.

Sarge packed up his laptop; (along with the tall stack of papers that had printed out from Dr. Wagstaff's printer); and roared away on his cycle; while General Paxton hitched a ride with the black SUV which had come up to where the other vehicles were parked. Slate and Dr. Wagstaff were the last to leave the area and could not feel the Winds of Destiny swirling around them at gale force! But what "Anchor Event" was causing the Winds to blow?

CHAPTER 22

s Dr. Wagstaff was walking out of the conference room entrance just behind Slate, carrying the last of her reports and medical equipment out to her SUV which was parked outside the circle of rocks, the doctor called to him and said, "Slate I need to tell you something else about your tests in private! You can travel with me in my SUV to the restaurant so I can fill you in on a few details you should know! Your motorcycle can fit in the back of my extremely large 'Tonto' Western SUV!"

On the way to the restaurant, while they were alone together in her SUV, Dr. Wagstaff, because of a certain type of "feeling" that she got when she had hugged Slate and had also felt when she let go of his hand, told the young man a few fantastic facts. "Slate", she said, "Because of your recent adventures beyond our planet; which allowed you to see the wonders of the galaxy far beyond Earth; I am about to tell you certain things officially 'off the record' because for some reason I feel that it will be important information that you need to know in the near future, and I know that I can completely trust you! What I am about to tell you must remain confidential, and you must never tell anyone, for both my sake and you and your family's future well-being and destiny! This information will sound like a plot line from the new 'Stranger Still Zone', but the information that I am about to share with you is totally true! I don't know the exact reason why I feel the need to relate to you certain secret information about conditions beyond Earth and to tell you about my past, because it is entirely different from your amazing background with the alien beings known as Reptiloids, and if what I am about to tell you leaks out to certain authorities, I will be in serious trouble! So, for better or for worse, here goes!"

The doctor hesitated to take a very deep breath; then she said, "What happened to you was fantastic but what I am about to tell you will also seem more unbelievable than your recent exploits! I need to give you information and use terms that you are totally unfamiliar with, but it will be data that I feel that you need to know for your own safety as you literally travel to the stars in your military service! I will answer any questions that you have when I am finished! When I hugged you a few minutes ago, I suddenly felt that my Ultimate Destiny was somehow intertwined with your Present and Future Life Path and that you needed to know certain things! Although I am not what is called an 'Imperial Seer' out in the galaxies; for some reason I can sometimes sense certain things about someone else when I touch them! When I hugged you in front of everybody, I sensed that your Ultimate Destiny lies far beyond the stars among planets united by the intergalactic government called the 'ICOPE', or Interstellar Condominium of Planets and Empires' that the

Reptiloid Red Stinger told you about!! My maiden name was 'Blair', and my great-grandfather's name was 'Samson Blair'! Originally, over a hundred years ago, he was a United States Marshal back in the Old West, and amazingly, he is still alive today! (Documented in <u>Seth and Samson Blair</u>) When I first heard your story, to ordinary Earthlings it would seem like an episode from the old Hi-Def science fiction television show called 'The Stranger Zone', and merely a fable or something you made up! I believed your story of fierce alien beings that looked like walking alligators because in the distant past, my daddy's grandfather was actually a shape-shifting alien out beyond the stars and looking at him, you could not tell that he wasn't just an ordinary Humanoid! Amazingly, all of his descendants, including me and my sons, have the same unbelievable ability to somehow change the shape of our bodies at will! My father was trained to change the shape of his body by his daddy; and he trained me when I came of age! As each of my sons, and my daughter-to-be, comes of age, I will also train them!" (As documented in <u>Space, Time, and the Empire</u>!- "The Sheriff and the Spaceman")

Dr. Wagstaff stopped to take an deep breath and continued, "In the future, I will support you all I can and try to continue to protect you to keep the government from trying to dissect you to find out how to regrow limbs because my father, Samson Blair IV, told me that such advanced medical treatment was available out in the ICOPE to treat severely injured military personnel, but that the medical technology that was needed to accomplish such a miracle had taken several hundred thousand years of medical research of the Humanoid Double Helix; and what he called the ultra-deep Triple Helix,; that are embedded in every Humanoid cell; to successfully accomplish it with no side-affects! I am also telling you this; and absolutely trusting you not to tell anything that I have just told you; because I feel that sometime in the Future, I will possibly need an ally in 'The Unit' that I can call on for help!"

Slate listened to the doctor's amazing account in silence and when she finished, he calmly asked, "Let me see if I have the information that you gave me straight! After serving as my unit's physician all these years, and after hearing your description, which like you said, is like something out of the new 'Stranger Still Zone' television show; am I correct to state that you are telling me that instead of being a normal Human being you are actually a so-called 'shape shifter' and not a normal Humanoid?"

In response to his question Doctor Wagstaff took her right hand off the steering wheel of her SUV, extended her dark suntanned arm toward Slate, and suddenly, the entire arm turned bright green for an instant; then it returned to her normal Humanoid suntan-brown skin color!

"My family's original ancestors came from a solar system in the ICOPE's sphere of influence that joined the Empire a few thousand years ago! As a requirement for membership, the species of Humanoids that inhabited the system had to undergo detailed medical tests so that the Imperial scientists could find out, and gauge our mental and physical strength and powers! They originally thought that we were just of the basic Humanoid stock, but they found out different when the final results of their tests were examined! The DNA, RNA, XNA, YNA, and ZNA of my great-grandfather's species of Humanoid has been rated by Imperial medical scientist to be 99.99% the same as the species of Humanoids on Earth! It's that .01% difference that is very important! The thing that sets my people apart is one extremely tiny; extra organ deep in our brains! The only difference between your body and my body is that I have a very tiny organ in my brain that somehow; some unknown way, can almost instantaneously change my body structure to that of any being known to Imperial Species scientists; who have tried to classify every type of sentient being in the entire Cosmic All!" (As she spoke the last sentence, the usually astute doctor suddenly got the feeling that she was forgetting something very important! But the moment passed, and she continued with her explanation.)

"The only being I can't change to is the eerie 'Colloid Cloud' being; which looks like a small cloud of floating LED lights! Like I said previously, I am telling you all this unbelievable information to help you be successful at what you will have to accomplish out beyond the stars in the Future! Because of your enhanced physical and vision abilities, I have sensed that Destiny will seek you out and you will have to be ready when you are called upon! I also feel that somehow; someway, our destinies are closely intertwined; and I will need you as an ally in the future!!"

Slate had listened the whole time almost in total silence, except for grimacing and softly whistling a few times at certain points in the doctor's almost unbelievable account! But after seeing the physical proof by her hand demonstration, he thoroughly believed her amazing story; perhaps because of the amazing and unbelievable adventure he had just gone through in which he had encountered the bizarre intelligent Reptiloid Red Stinger and his battle group here on Earth, and they had taken him far beyond the solar system to strange worlds literally hundreds of thousands of light years away! So because of his previous experience with eerie beings on distant worlds, Slate was able to listen to her unbelievable story silently, and try to absorb what she was trying to tell him, instead of dismissing it as being impossible!

As the sound of her final words faded away, Slate hesitated for an instant and replied, "Dr. Wagstaff, what you have told me and shown me would be beyond belief for an ordinary citizen of the planet Earth! But because of the things I have seen and accomplished here on Earth and many light years away from our small planet, I totally and completely believe your account! I also appreciate your trying to keep the government from trying to dissect me to find out alien secrets, because you are right, they would be unable to find out anything useful without at least one or two hundred thousand years of intensive medical research! I will keep all of your secrets and maybe in the future we can work together on some preliminary mission plans! If I ever need help in solving a problem, I will call you on my coded line!"

Just as he spoke these words, the doctor pulled up into the restaurant's parking lot. As they both exited the vehicle, Slate extended his hand to shake Dr. Wagstaff's right hand. As their hands started toward each other, although they could not feel it, the Winds of Destiny continued to swirl at gale force around the SUV! When their hands touched to shake on their agreement to work together and keep what had been spoken secret, both Slate and the doctor suddenly felt a strange tingling sensation start in their hands and travel briefly up their arms!

Slate immediately thought that he had somehow hit his "funny bone" on his elbow in the last few moments and was just feeling it at that moment. But the doctor knew different! She knew exactly what had caused the sensation! ***#No way! He can't be a shape-shifter!!#*** Dr. Wagstaff thought to herself.

Then, a split-second later, everything fell into place for the doctor and she "put the pieces together as she thought! *#Wait a minute! Wait a minute! That's what I was trying to remember a few minutes ago! For the past few hours I have been in such a hurry to finish Slate's medical exam and tell "the brass" about it, that I did not stop to realize just exactly what a very small detail in the medical exam meant! Slate's X-ray of his head showed a very small lump deep in his brain; exactly where the strange organ resides that gives my particular species of Humanoids the ability to change their shape! I saw that very tiny dot on the X-ray, and I foolishly dismissed it as being impossible for it to be anything but a very small benign tumor, since it was so deep in his brain! There was no way in the world that I could think that Slate, supposedly a Humanoid born on Earth, was a shapeshifter!! Shapeshifters and Reptiloids come from outer space; not from Earth! So that's why I felt that his Destiny paralleled mine! No wonder my Fate is intertwined with his Karma! I have felt that unique tingling feeling before, and I know what it means! Apparently, according to that unique tingle that I just felt, and when I dropped his hand after my speech to the camera; that distinctive feeling only occurs when two shape-shifters shake hands or touch each other's bare skin, and one of them does not 'turn off the effect'! That tingling that we both felt means that Slate is a shape-shifter, and he acts like he doesn't know it! If he is a shape-shifter, then his parents are shape-shifters; and they should have told him* *when he was very young; and should have already trained him to change his shape! WOW! Apparently they did not tell their son about his lineage, and his heritage!! Why did they not tell him in order to protect him? Oh, me; oh my! Now that I have told him about myself, what do I do now? I can't believe it!! Slate is an untrained shape-shifter that doesn't know it! I wonder if, as an untrained shape shifter before 'The Change'; he has the usual hot flashes and high body temperature at irregular intervals? His body temperature seemed to be normal when I took it a few minutes ago! For Slate's own safety, sometime in the very near future I need to do the job that his parents should have done many years ago! Somehow; some way; I need to give an excuse to examine Slate once more so that I can secretly train him; just like my father trained me, for his own protection!#*

The doctor mentally paused; then continued making her plans. *#I must meet with Slate again; as soon as I can, perhaps on the excuse that some of his medical tests have come back and I need to ask him a few more questions! But for now, I will let the whole thing drop, stick with my original plan, and hope he doesn't make 'The Change' alone before I can train him! If I don't, Slate will have some very tough explaining to do when "the Change" starts! I hope he is not driving a car or doing something dangerous when it starts!!#*

It literally took only a millisecond for all of these thoughts to dart through Dr. Wagstaff's thought processes as she continued to stand before Slate as he rubbed his elbow and exclaimed, "Boy, my elbow feels as if I hit my 'funny bone'; but I don't remember hitting it on anything!"

"Here" said the doctor, "I can fix that by pressing a certain pressure point!" Using a combined physical and mental technique that her father Samson Blair IV had taught her many decades before, Martha rubbed a certain spot on Slater's elbow, and at the same time she sent out a certain mental impulse; both of which combined to stop the tingling sensation which occurred when two shape-shifters touch!

As the doctor pondered what else she could do to protect both Slate and herself, the Winds of Destiny gradually faded away outside the restaurant; as the regular Humanoids, and the two shape-shifters; all exited their vehicles and entered the restaurant together after Slate got his cycle out of the back of Dr. Wagstaff's SUV. But the Winds of Destiny then started to gradually undetectably blow softly through the popular roadside restaurant; perhaps because Slate's important meeting with his old group and his former commanding officer was scheduled to begin in a few hours at another location; a meeting which would also help to determine the young soldier's Ultimate Destiny!

The outcome of the extremely rare, and important "Galactic Anchor Event", would determine if Slate would rejoin his old group, enter another combat group, retire from the military for good, or. . . .? In other words, Slate's ultimate future would be decided by the final decision made after a private conference between him, and Colonel Carter! But to avoid trouble down the road of his Life Path, or even Death, all the young veteran had to do was simply choose all the options on his Life Journey very, very wisely! (Which sometimes can be very, very tricky and very, very hard!)

So as the Winds of Destiny swirled undetectably around them, the regular Humanoids and the two shape shifters entered the popular restaurant to enjoy a good steak dinner; with General Paxton picking up the tab on his expense account! Slate was looking forward to meeting his old leader of 'The Unit' as soon as possible; either before, during, or after the meal! He did not care; he just wanted to get the important meeting over with, and get on with his life; especially since he hopefully would not be dissected; since Dr. Wagstaff and Sarge had both said they would literally defend him with their lives!

After Slate and Sarge Snyder finished their steak dinner with all the trimmings, they excused themselves from the large table and, after shaking hands with General Paxton and Dr. Wagstaff; they exited the café, mounted their motorcycles, and headed out for the agreed upon rendezvous point for the scheduled meeting; hopefully only an hour or two in the future; and with the black SUV still tagging far behind.

Slate had been told that this meeting with his former commander was only happening because his experienced instructor, (i.e., Sarge Snyder), also had used his influence, supposedly with the nation's present "Commander in Chief"; to somehow set up a private conference between them and the "top brass", i.e., the top generals at the Pentagon, and comrades of his old combat unit. The projected plan was that they would all meet, privately and securely, in another very small out-of-the-way café on old Route 66; originally the first interstate highway from Chicago to California. The conference was at the famous Corral Café and it would be held with the tightest security that any portion of the old and legendary "Mother Road", AKA "Route 66", had ever seen;

even when it had in the distant past been used by a President of the United States!

And so it came to pass that in an unprecedented and very unusual act; when the location of the meeting was relayed to the Joint Chiefs of Staff and the "high brass" in Washington D.C.; a very strange thing happened; that never got in the so-called "national news"! By order of Homeland Security; the Federal Bureau of Investigation and the state highway patrol; instead of just protecting the area around the meeting place; coordinated their efforts to throw up very secure roadblocks in both directions from the café where the very important conference would be held! In addition; by orders from the Pentagon; the law enforcement officers manning the roadblocks, stopped all vehicles to allow identification of all occupants! The drivers of the dozen or so vehicles which happened to travel down the obsolete highway, had to show an up-to-date driver's license and vehicle registration papers from the particular state shown on the vehicle's license plate! Also, all adults in each vehicle also had to produce some form of identification, before the van, car, or truck could proceed! Following the orders from Homeland Security; the officers manning the checkpoints also obtained a visual identification of all persons traveling down the "Mother Road"! Using a portable video camera, a picture of each car's occupants were taken to be used for almost instant identification! All the information that was gathered was immediately inserted into a high-speed satellite data link which was connected to numerous state; local; and national; police data bases in order to swiftly check out the identities of each vehicle's occupants! Amazingly, all occupants of all of the vehicles who traveled down old Route 66 were "clean" and were allowed to pass through; although they were told not to stop at the café where the important meeting was to take place!

In addition to this surface protection, the United States Aerospace Force also sent four U-4s, and changed the orbits of several ultra-secret "Com-Air" satellites; in order to secure the atmospheric and the areas in space above the meeting place!

And so, as the Winds of Destiny watched, all the "players" that would play a part in the "Anchor Happening" on the Galactic Time Line were slowly, but surely moving into place! But would this Event turn out to be "good" or "bad" for one military combat veteran by the name of Samuel Eliot Steele; otherwise known to his friends as "Slate"? Only the passage of "time" would reveal the answer to this perplexing question! As the "pawns" on the Galactic Chessboard gradually shifted into the same Life Path; from the depths of their permanent home; which was deep, deep down among the atoms of the entire Universe; the Winds of Destiny also watched and waited!

CHAPTER 23

A few hours after the meeting with General Paxton and the physical examination by Dr. Wagstaff, the extremely important "third step" took place; only because Sarge Snyder had literally "stuck his neck out", and "called in a few favors", to try to help his protégé escape death by autopsy! But the old DI was experienced enough; in the ways of the military and Washington politics; to know that there were a few more very important 'loose ends' that had to be taken care of---**ASAP**!! After he rode with Slate to the designated meeting spot for the 3rd conference, a very famous café on Route 66; instead of entering the meeting area with the young man, the veteran soldier stayed on his motorcycle and told Slate that he had a very important meeting that he had to attend!

After shaking hands with the young man and wishing him good luck with his meeting with Colonel Carter, Snyder roared off on his battered 'hog' to make a few coded calls on his cell phone and take a certain "oath of office" that was scheduled very soon in Washington, D.C.; with his extremely faithful wife; Mary Pearl; by his side! As the DI left the old café, the familiar black SUV pulled out from behind the café and literally roared after him; the skilled veteran driver trying to keep up with was supposed to be just a very old motorcycle! As Slate watched the dark SUV follow his friend, he glanced at the position where the license plate should have been; but just like the other black SUV that was outside the first rendezvous point, the vehicle did not have one; it only had large black numbers where the license plate should have been! He almost used his cellphone to warn Sarge that he was being tailed by unknown agents; but he took another moment to try to jog his memory to recall the numbers on the first SUV! An instant later Slate concentrated and used his photographic memory to literally picture in his mind the first string of numbers on the first SUV that he saw! Mentally comparing the two strange sets of numbers; he realized that they were the same! If this was the same SUV that was parked outside the "Rusty Bullet Casing"; he wondered if they were friend or foe! He had to warn Sarge! Slate immediately texted Sarge's cellphone about the unknown vehicle; even as the old DI was speeding down the highway to some unknown meeting; with the unidentified black SUV trying to stay close! Immediately Sarge used his voice-to-text app to send back a cryptic message: "Don't worry! They are on my side! Condition Green! Out!"

Far down the highway, as Sarge was finishing his conversation with Slate; he pulled over to the side of the highway to allow black-suited Secret Service agents to load both him and the "Gena Mae" into the vehicle! (Sarge had left the café before the rendezvous because he did not want Slate to see him being picked up by what were his Secret Service agents; to prevent the young veteran from thinking he was being kidnapped and trying to save him!)

But at the same time, back at the café, Slate had something else to hold his attention; something that no one on the old highway had ever witnessed! What he was observing was an event unprecedented in both the history of the old café and the first "interstate highway" in the United States; also known as "Route 66"!

CHAPTER 24

The first green vehicles of a long convoy of olive green military trucks and Lorries started arriving. As they arrived; unseen by the participants; as the Anchor Event unfolded on the Time Stream/Time Cloud, the Winds of Destiny; unseen and unheard; increased in velocity through the famed eating place on the famous "Route 66" highway of yesteryear; the first "super highway" in the United State; that had been nicknamed "The Mother Road"!

Many military vehicles, large SUVs with dark tinted windows, "camo colored" jeeps, and large olive green U.S. Army supply trucks; (all bearing the men and women and the supplies of the covert military group called "The Unit"); rumbled down the narrow two-lane highway and surrounded the old Corral Café that fateful day; just before Slate was to have a reunion with Colonel Robert "Rusty" Carter and the veterans and new men in his old group. The meeting was to "clear the air" about just what was going on, and allow Colonel Carter to decide just how he would handle this unique situation! The soldiers put up signs all around the café indicating that the café had been rented out for the evening and was closed to the normal clientele of the business.

His old commander, red-haired, and starting to slightly grow bald, came in the front door of the restaurant with a big grin on his face and his right hand extended toward Slate; who was sitting on a stool at the bar; sipping a glass of cold Sada Juice after Sarge had recommended it to him. (His old DI had also told Slate to be careful with the very potent drink, always taking small sips, and never drinking more than one glass; until he had figured out just how the strong alcoholic drink affected his senses and his metabolism!)

After shaking hands with Slate and slapping him on the back, Colonel Carter led him to a back table; while the rest of his combat group followed orders; fanning out, and sitting at all the surrounding tables to shield the colonel and Slate from any "local interference" while they had their preliminary "confab" before the planned evening meal. At their private table, Colonel Carter started out the private conference by telling Slate that he had orders to listen to all the facts; take all the time he wanted in order to make his decision about how the very unique situation should be handled; and then input to Washington his recommendation as to just exactly how the United States military should treat him! He did not tell Slate that he had been told by the President-Elect that his recommendation or recommendations would probably be followed to the letter; (as long as the young man would not be medically autopsied!)

Not being an officer who liked filling out forms, when Colonel Carter had finished up interviewing Slate after the meal; he planned to write a few sentences down on a piece of paper indicating all of his recommendations; then he would order "The Unit's" com officer to use his portable communications box to fax the hand-written letter to Washington using a triple-coded line. Slate listened to what Colonel Carter planned to do; then told him that procedure was fine with him! The two soldiers then got up and shook hands, as Colonel Carter loudly said, "Group confab!", and used one of the group's command gestures to signal for military group to conference together.

So before the planned meal officially started, everyone mingled with all the other members of the "black opts" group for a few minutes to let everyone reacquaint themselves with Slate; to allow the new members to meet him, and afterwards for Colonel Carter to tell his combat group several more important facts. The "old hands" in the combat team who had been around when Slate was injured, were quite surprised when Colonel Carter told all of them, during a private conference at the back of the restaurant, the startling fact that he was no longer a cyborg; yet he still had the same fantastic physical abilities! They were not told how Slate's limbs were replaced; they were just told that one very important fact; and then ordered not to tell that information to anyone not presently in the room; for the rest of their lives; on penalty of 99 years of hard labor at Leavenworth!! After that order was given, everyone in the room one-by-one came up to Colonel Carter; saluted him; and stated to him that they understood the order, and would obey it until the day they died, or they were told by a superior officer that they were no longer bound by their oath, and given a notarized legal paper signed by the President of the United States stating the same fact!

When every soldier had made the pledge, Colonel Carter announced that military decorum was suspended for the duration of the party to follow! At the colonel's command, chests of soft drinks and hot foods were brought in from the supply trucks outside; as the close-knit combat group celebrated the safe return of one of their own! Slate was a member of their military unit who had been literally forged into their close brotherhood after long years of toil, combat, sweat, and blood! Over long years of covert combat missions; each of the members of the group had literally saved the lives of almost everyone else! Slate was also a "Blood Member" of the Unit; having also saved many lives! Now, when he returned to their group, it was as if he had never left! (Good; <u>solid friends</u>; especially those rapports literally forged in combat; and are closer than brotherhood; tend to be that way, and <u>stay</u> that way! The bonds of friendship among combat veterans are very durable and last virtually the lifetimes of all the members of the Unit!)

After a large part of the food had been eaten, to pass the time; most of the combat brigade started playing cards, the café's colorful video games, shuffleboard, and darts. The Unit had rented out the café for the evening and following in The Unit's tradition, all the waiters and waitresses would be given very good tips by the servicemen, that would more than make up not having regular customers for several hours; and would also be well paid for the evening by the owner of the café! So finally; amid the hubbub and after all the preliminary happenings and the meal; Slate and his former commanding officer went to a quiet corner in the back of the café and settled back in comfortable easy chairs for a top-secret conference about Slate's future; a future that would be still vague and invisible to all of the visions of the Imperial Seers for many decades to come!

So as the Destinies of trillions of sentient beings on the Galactic Time Line were at stake; the extremely important meeting started!

CHAPTER 25

Before the important meeting started, Colonel Carter also employed several electronic devices around their table to prevent eavesdropping by anyone in the café; outside the café; or by extreme altitude spy craft; (such as the Soviet spy plane called "the electronic vacuum cleaner"); or by eavesdropping satellites. The colonel used a classified device to set up a curtain of "white sound"; which literally "corralled" the sounds they made during the conference by preventing their voices from echoing off the nearby walls. Security was also helped by the fact that both Slate and Colonel Carter made sure they were facing the back walls at all times to prevent what they were saying from being glimpsed by possible "lip readers"; hacking into and using any electronic device in the café to learn exactly what was going on! A heavily-shielded video camera was used to officially record the meeting. The recorder was totally encased in thick lead sheathing; which prevented any electronic tampering with its video record.

Colonel Carter started the meeting off by stating, "Your close friends and I are extremely elated that somehow your cyborg limbs and your electronic eyes were somehow replaced and completely healed as good as new! I am so awed to see you whole again, that you will have to excuse me if my mind tends to wander at times during this interview! I have read many reports about the situation! Everyone appreciates the fact that you have been completely honest about the incredible events that have happened to you in the last few weeks, Slate! You have cooperated fully with everyone who has interviewed you about the incredible incidents surrounding your fantastic replacement of your limbs and eyes! I carefully read all the incredible medical and intelligence reports after the President and the top generals had finished going over them! After hearing and viewing all the evidence; both the politicos, and the top military generals; are totally on your side about the situation! They also believe that you have been totally honest with telling us about the fantastic adventures that you recently went through, far out in space beyond our solar system, and the amazing physical transformation and impossible healing of your limbs by some fantastically medically advanced technique that you now show the evidence of! Perhaps the only explanations possible; in order to explain the impossible; is that the aliens somehow stimulated your body to grow your limbs and your eyes back; or perhaps the aliens could have analyzed your DNA on the Double Helix to grow new ones in their laboratories and somehow splice them onto your stubs and your eye sockets!"

"After much discussion among the top politicians and military leaders, They have realized certain additional facts! The replacing of your cyborg parts by the Reptiloids was something that you had no control of because you were unconscious because of enemy action! Even though you were severely wounded, you successfully completed your assignment given to you by the alien reptile called Red Stinger! We also believe what you said that the Reptiloids somehow replaced your limbs and your eyes as a reward because they were extremely grateful that you successfully retrieved their political symbol and saved the Thunder Worlds from a civil war! This fact will be top secret forever, since it would cause trouble if the Thunder Worlds found out that their symbolic claw had been replaced with a forgery!"

"Dr. Wagstaff examined you; determined several interesting facts; and then made several recommendations! She first stated that all the secret markers that had been placed in your body, to guard against a clone spy taking your place, were all in their previous positions; so you were the genuine article! While she tested you, the doctor found that sample DNA that she extracted from each of your new limbs is exactly the same as your original military medical records indicated when you joined my group!"

"She could find no evidence that the replacement limbs were grafted back onto your body because there are no needle marks, scars, or scar lines on any of the bones; which would indicate that they were somehow attached back onto your body! Apparently with medical technology that is literally half a million years in our future, the Reptiloids simply grew new legs and arms from your stubs, and eyes from your damaged eye sockets!" (#*I wonder if they can regrow hair!*# Colonel Carter thought to himself.)

With our present level of medical knowledge, we can't tell that anything is different in your present DNA; it matches exactly with your DNA that was extracted when you joined my combat group! This means that there has to be something else deeper in the Humanoid Cell that determines the physical characteristics of a person's body; such as greater strength and the ability to see the infrared wavelength; qualities and traits that you now apparently possess!"

"Dr. Wagstaff found that while your replaced limbs are exactly the same physically as your original ones, there are a few differences! All your scars you got while in childhood and while playing football are gone! The small birthmark that was on your old right forearm is somehow on your new limb; and your little toe on your replaced left foot is still missing the toenail that was off the toe when you were born! Apparently these two small defects were in your original DNA! The doctor also warned that any medical experiments on any part of your body to determine just how the replacement of your limbs and your eyes was done would not be feasible, would be totally fruitless, and would in all probability result in your ultimate useless death! **Dr. Wagstaff also warned everyone again, on the unofficial video, and a very 'emphatic' signed and sworn medical memo; that anyone wanting to put you under the knife and mutilate your body, or ultimately kill you in order to try to find out how the aliens replaced your limbs; would literally have to go through her dead body first! The doctor stated that she would actually use physical violence on literally anyone to defend you from what would be medical malpractice! She use very emphatic language on the secret part of the unofficial video; and extremely explicit "Anglo-Saxon terms" on the medical memo! Because of her use of very explicit terms; everyone who sees the video and reads the medical memo believes her when the Doctor states that she will use violence to**

protect her former patient from medical procedures that would be absolutely useless and cause your death!"

"The medical technology needed to perform such fantastic replacements of your limbs is beyond our present medical capability, and will be for probably literally hundreds of thousands of years! So, after many conferences and a total review of all the medical evidence, the present President, the President Elect, and the commanding Generals are in total agreement!"

"I was told that after hearing and reading all the medical reports, all the Pentagon generals and the President came to several important decisions! One, they voted to 'physically and medically leave you alone'; since you were unconscious when they were replaced and there is no way that we could ever find out how the aliens regrew your limbs!"

"Second, they agreed to allow you to decide for yourself what you want to do with your impressive new limbs and eyes! Which means, Son, you can again become a member of the United States military in my group or another one; or you can retire with full benefits; the choice is up to you! The entire group wants you back; but again; the choice is totally up to you! I think it would be a good idea not to rush your decision as what to do!"

"Third, I hereby officially give you as many days of leave as you need to make your decision, and when you decide what you want to do; to immediately get back to me on my private coded number! At this moment, I will immediately send the required paperwork over the computer link to Washington, D.C., indicating that I am giving you such an 'open leave'! Good luck; and God bless you; your family; and your final decision! This meeting is officially ended!"

Slate saluted as he stood up to leave; and then extended his hand to shake his former commanding officer's hand, and said, "Thank you, Colonel Carter! I appreciate your total support and your thoughtful recommendations! So many incredible things have happened to me in the last few months that I think what you have suggested is an extremely good idea! Like you advised, I am not going to make a final decision about my future until I have a chance to slow down and relax for a few days, and maybe visit my home town, now that I don't have to worry about armed combat teams both in the air and also on my 12, 3, 6, and 9; literally 24/7! I will do what you have suggested and contact you in a few days on your coded channel to let you know about my decision! I appreciate your wisdom advising me how to handle this matter!"

"Take your time, son, at least a month, or more! It's your life and you are the only one who can live it! Call me at any time if you need any information or you just need to talk!" Colonel Carter replied. "You have my com number, so when you decide, text or call me 24/7! We would love to have you back in our group! 'Off the record', we have a very difficult assignment coming up on Mars and we will need your expertise about the Red Planet in order to successfully complete it! Oh, by the way! Snuffy, Greenie, and Binko send their regards! They are on special assignment on the far side of the moon, investigating several unidentified surface contacts found by NASA's photo interpreters on several new Lunar Surveyor photos they were examining! They said the photos appeared to show evidence of an early Soviet manned moon landing that failed; and they are highly interested in excavating the site! Because their orders to investigate the situation took, (what some people call the 'Terrible Three'), 'off planet'; they could not make this important meeting!"

"Thank you, Sir! Send them back my thanks, and tell them that we will more than make up the time we lost today at the next meeting! Again, I appreciate your support, your backing, and your wisdom during this difficult time! I will make my decision and get back to you as soon as I can!" Slate returned as he again shook his former commanding officer's hand; then said, "I think I need to go around the room once more for old times' sake!"

Colonel Carter returned, "Take as long as you need; the place is ours until 10 o'clock tomorrow morning! But before you leave; see me for some orders that you have to do before you take your indefinite leave!"

"Yes, Sir!" Slate said as he saluted; did an about face; and left the sound-protected conference area.

Slate again took the time go around the room in order to renew and making new acquaintances and cement old friendships; since he probably would not see anybody in the group for several months. When he had rendezvoused with literally everyone in the room; Slate made sure that he texted "audios" again to Sarge Snyder over his cell phone; then finally; as ordered; he met once more with Colonel Carter; and received certain orders he had to follow before he took his leave. After taking the time to read and ponder the two unusual orders in a quiet corner of the room; he immediately set out to obey the first order and headed his motorcycle in the direction of Texas for a rendezvous with a certain supply store on a certain military base, in order to pick up a new uniform and a new military ID to reflect his new rank; which he had earned by his heroic actions during the last few months! After following this part of the set of orders and getting the required equipment; in order to obey the second order; Slate traveled on his motorcycle to meet with a certain very important person in Washington, D.C.! He hoped that when he had ultimately finished what was required of the second set of orders, he could meet up ASAP with a certain young woman, one more time; for "old time's sake"; and to again ask her a certain very important question!

At this point on the Galactic Time Stream, the young military veteran did not know that, while traveling down the Time Line, sometime in the Future; he also had another required meeting with **DESTINY!** The <u>Probable</u> Past; Present; and Future Time Line visualizations; by the mental powers of the Imperial Magi as they pondered on Empire Prime; of his future important meeting with FATE; indicated that "The New Anchor Event"; like the one that just happened; would also have the capability to either prove beneficial, or totally destructive to the young veteran! This meant that there were many possible outcomes of this happening; some "good"; some "bad" and some still blank or dark!

But one Slate Eliot Steele was oblivious to all of this information as he happily looked forward to the unknown Future; free from being tailed 24/7 from in the air and on the ground; and he was looking forward to meeting a "certain someone" again! Just like the many times that type of "event" happened before; Slate's "mental equipment" could not feel the tremendous surge of the Winds of Destiny as the powerful "Daisy Mae" streaked toward Washington, D.C. for a very important meeting; with a certain familiar "VIP"; and then, hopefully, quickly on to another important meeting in Texas!

The required conference in America's Capital City went quite well for Slate! In the "political arena" consisting of our

Nation's Judicial; Executive; and Legislative branches; if you have the Head of the Joint Chiefs of Staff, 5-Star Brigadier General Ron Cleere "in your corner"; you will have no problems; so Slate "was in the green"!

A week or so after the "Meeting of Destiny" that settled Slate's path in Earth's military history and hastened his passage out to the stars, another "Anchor Event"; which would either hasten or hinder his present course; was about to happen! The many visualizations by the Imperial Magi that were dark, very dim, or fuzzy, indicated that since the Event had not happened yet; it could not be ascertained just what would happen; and all the parties who were involved trying to find out where Slate's Destiny was headed; i.e.; the Imperial Magi and even the Winds of Destiny, would have to WAIT! So; all parties concerned patiently waited! Then finally; when things finally settled down; for some reason, important events started happening fast; **VERY FAST!**

CHAPTER 26

It was an extremely hot Monday morning on the main street in Cleburne, Texas; even when it showed 8 'o clock on the hands of the Johnson County Courthouse clock; as the local citizens sitting in the shade of the large Pecan tree in front of the local "Corral Café"; watched a black SUV having very dark windshields; with several numbers permanently printed on the back and front of the car instead of license plates, cruise past the nationally famous "Western Cuisine" restaurant, and continue down the main street of the fast-growing historic town. To the onlookers, the failure of the large vehicle to stop at the historic and renowned café was extremely unusual, because the eating place was nationally famed for all of its breakfast, lunch, and dinner specials. Even most of the Texas members of both the National House of Representatives and Senate frequented the restaurant many times when they came back from Washington to visit with their constituents.

As "Lady Luck" would have it, a few minutes before the locals spotted the strange black SUV, Police Corporal Barney Drum, a veteran member of the local police force, was on routine patrol on the highways outside the town. As always, he was very alert; always looking around for anything that was unusual and out of the ordinary, which could spell "trouble" for the town he was sworn to protect. As he was just entering the town's city limits after having just got on state highway 174 from U.S. highway 67 east, behind his patrol car in his rear view mirror; Barney had observed a very large and unusual black vehicle exit from U.S. highway 67 east and get on state highway 174 to apparently travel through the town on Main Street. An instant after the black SUV got on highway 174, three other similar vehicles exited highway 67 and also turned on 174. After a few blocks, the three black vehicles each turned in a different direction from that taken by the first black SUV. To Barney it was as if they were covertly following the first vehicle, or protecting its 3, 6, and 9; just like in the spy movies!

Barney had been traveling faster than the very large SUV, (as usual, a few mph over the speed limit); and used a shortcut to get ahead of the unknown vehicle. He stopped his patrol car in the town at his usual spot behind a very large advertising sign that he always chose to observe the happenings in the town; (and catch speeders). Behind the patrolman the unknown driver chose the Main Street exit from U.S. highway 174, and passed by his patrol car on the "main drag" of the town. He then watched as it passed the nationally famous Corral Café without stopping; and that fact aroused his curiosity; along with what he saw when he closely examined the strange vehicle! The very large black SUV looked unusual because it had what looked like literally dozens of telephoto television and camera lenses, short wave radio antennas, television antennas, small rods, parabolic antennas, and open-ended rods sticking out in all directions from its dark surfaces; some even spouting from the front and back windshields and the side surfaces! To Barney, it looked exactly like one of those spy vehicles out of one of the "rough and tumble; everything blows up" adventure movies, featuring "Spy X"; that he loved to go see with his wife Thelma Jo! To the veteran lawman, so many antennas on the SUV also meant that the occupants of the vehicle were in continuous contact with many different locations at once, and following most of the scripts of the same type of movie, it probably meant that at least one person in the vehicle was <u>very important</u>! Maybe he was looking at the SUV of a top general; an important foreign diplomat; or . . . . even the just sworn-in President of the United States!?!?!

Out of habit Barney looked at the vehicle's normal license plate location to help identify the unusual visitor to the town it was his duty to protect; but he found that there were no license plates either in front or in back! Where each license plate was supposed to be attached, there was only a long string of large black numbers! Out of curiosity, since he could not observe who or what was inside because of the vehicle's extremely dark glass, Barney quickly took his laptop, which was always strapped down, open and ready for use, on the front seat of his patrol car beside him, and entered the I.D. number of the mystery vehicle to find out who or what government agency or bureau was passing through the growing town. It took thirty seconds for the normally fast identification system of the Cleburne, Texas, police force to get an ID for the unusual vehicle, because the computer program apparently had to access many civilian and military files to find the answer! After the short wait which seemed very long as he continued to observe the mysterious SUV from long range at his parking spot with his binoculars, Barney was astonished as a very loud authoritative voice started speaking the following message that appeared in very bold and large letters on his laptop computer screen:

"ALERT! ALL LOCAL, STATE, AND FEDERAL LAW ENFORCEMENT AGENCIES! The Vehicle with this Numbered Plate is a United States Department of Defense vehicle THAT IS ON OFFICIAL BUSINESS REGARDING A VERY IMPORTANT NATIONAL SECURITY ISSUE!! - DO NOT FOLLOW OR OBSTRUCT THE VEHICLE IN ANY WAY; DO NOT USE ELECTRONIC DEVICES TO RECORD ANY CONVERSATIONS OF THE OCCUPANTS FROM LONG RANGE; AND DO NOT DIRECTLY OBSERVE FROM CLOSE RANGE OR TALK WITH ANY OF THE OCCUPANTS OF THE VEHICLE UNLESS FIRST SPOKEN TO BY THEM!! FAILURE TO FOLLOW THIS DIRECTIVE WILL RESULT IN YOUR MUNICIPALITY, STATE AGENCY, OR FEDERAL AGENCY BEING GIVEN A VERY HEAVY FINE BY THE DEPARTMENT OF HOMELAND SECURITY AND/OR IMPRISONMENT OF THE PERSON OR PERSONS VIOLATING THIS DIRECTIVE AND/OR LOSS OF EMPLOYMENT OF THE PERSON OR PERSONS VIOLATING THIS DIRECTIVE! THERE ARE NO EXCEPTIONS TO THIS DIRECTIVE! (NOT EVEN FOR FOREIGN DIGNITARIES OR AMBASSADORS; MEMBERS OF THE EXECUTIVE BRANCH OR THEIR

SPOUSES, CONGRESSIONAL MEMBERS OF CONGRESS; THEIR AIDES; OR ANY OF THEIR SPOUSES!) THERE WILL BE NO EXCEPTIONS OR ANY POSSIBLE EXCUSES TO DISOBEY THIS DIRECTIVE BY ORDER OF THE HEAD OF HOMELAND SECURITY! ANY FOREIGN AGENT OR FOREIGN DIGNITARY POSESSING DIPLOMATIC IMMUNITY DISOBEYING THIS DIRECTIVE WILL BE IMMEDATELY DECLARED 'PERSONA NON GRATA', AND EXPELLED FROM THE COUNTRY BY BEING ESCORTED BY FEDERAL AGENTS TO THE NEAREST BORDER FOR EXPULSION! How the foreign agent or dignitary gets to their home country from the point of their expulsion, (including deserts and lake areas), will be their problem!"

After just rescuing kittens out of trees, writing parking tickets and a few speeding tickets for his entire police career in the sleepy town of Cleburne, Texas; where the most serious offense was failure to pay a parking or a speeding ticket; Officer Drum was impressed by the warning! He quickly mentally formulated a plan of action! *#I won't obstruct that black vehicle, but I sure am going to follow it from a distance with my binoculars and keep it under close surveillance! In the movies things happen around those big bulky cars because of the important people inside them and the secret things they are doing; so I want to be around if there is any trouble so that I can protect my town! That's a good enough excuse to follow it; and if something happens and my police superior, Police Chief Joe*

Monday, asks me what I was doing following that DOD vehicle when the strict instructions from the Department of Homeland Security posted on the internet said not to; I will tell him exactly the reason why I followed the unknown vehicle! I was protecting my town!!# Barney thought to himself as he slowly eased his cruiser out from his parking place and tried to covertly follow the black vehicle from several blocks back; hopefully far back enough to avoid getting videotaped by the many lenses sticking out of the sides of the target vehicle, which in the movies, large black SUVs would always employ real-time cameras in all directions for security purposes!

Patiently, Barney continued to watch from several blocks back as the black SUV cruised down Main Street until it reached Elm Street and turned left. Stopping his patrol car as soon as he turned right onto Elm Street, he used his binoculars out the back window to continue his tailing of the enigmatic secret government vehicle as it cruised down the familiar street that he had grown up on as a boy. The mystery car went at a moderate speed until it came to the house that he knew belonged to the family of Dixie Davis; where it immediately stopped next to the curb. (He knew Dixie's family lived there because he had dated her several times in high school, until she started going steady with a close friend of his; Samuel "Slate" Steele, the local high school star quarterback for the town's "Yellowjackets" football team.)

After the vehicle parked in front of the Davis house; the Cleburne policeman watched through binoculars as a medium tall grey-haired man with five stars and five rows of metals on his impressive military uniform, (which had a very tight collar and he was unaccustomed to wearing), emerged from the back of the vehicle and slowly approached the house carrying a large black briefcase! The military man somehow looked familiar to Barney as he observed the situation from a block away; using his high-tech binoculars. Then a split-second later Barney excitedly thought: ***#I know that I have seen that imposing man somewhere before! Was it on the national news or. . . . . No! WOW! I saw him on Hi-Def television several weeks ago! He looks like the newly sworn in President Snyder, or his twin brother! But what's the very new President of the United States doing in the sleepy town of Cleburne, Texas; dressed up like a general?!?! He's not a 5-star general, he's the President and the commander-in-chief of the whole U.S. military! What is he doing in Cleburne covertly dressed just as a general; instead of being totally surrounded by the Secret Service, and dressed in a business suit? Well, since he is the newly sworn-in President; probably that black SUV he is riding in, and the other three vehicles following him, have his Secret Service and his armed guards inside!* WOW! TO THINK THAT THIS IS HAPPENING IN GOOD OLD CLEBURNE, TEXAS!! TO THINK THAT THE PRESIDENT OF THE UNITED STATES IS VISITING SOMEONE IN OUR TOWN! I WONDER WHO IT COULD BE?!?!?#***

As the impressive military man wearing the uniform of a general in order to perform one last service for the best soldier he had every trained as a DI; (and probably also wearing the uniform of his previous military rank for the last time after becoming President of the United States a few days ago, after winning the national election on the second Tuesday of November), neared the house he heard somebody softly crying; with the noise apparently coming out of a partially opened side window and echoing off the side of the house next door.

After he politely rang the doorbell, a short grey-haired woman came to the door. Taking off his military hat, the general said, "Good morning, Gena Mae! I hope you remember me when I was growing up here in Cleburne! You have to remember that I named my old motorcycle after you, way back when we were 'an item' in the local society scene! That old 'hog' still works, and I still call it that, for 'old time's sake'! That was a long time ago and you know, (because you observed me leaving that day), that I left town rather hurriedly that fateful day when you turned down my marriage proposal! I never did know why you turned me down! But I did return here to Cleburne briefly about a decade later when I was a recruiting officer for a year or two. But if you don't recognize me in this uniform, here is my identification! I hate to bring up old memories that are best forgotten; but this is important and I need your help! Just like my uniform attests, for just this visit to Cleburne, I am called General Snyder; and recently I was elected President; although back then, you knew me just as Larry, the son of your next door neighbors! But enough talk! I am here on a very important mission! It's very critical that I speak with your daughter, Dixie! It is a matter of utmost importance!"

After hearing his words about the past, the woman grimaced, and said, "Well, looking at your uniform I see that you made good and you became a general and now, President; so I guess now that I see you were elected President; I can finally know for sure that I made the right choice when I chose not marry you! I don't think I could stand to live in Washington, D.C., it's too formal and proper! Even while we were dating, and we were so much in love; I could sense that you were 'married to the military', and would be more loyal to it than me if we were married! Back then, I wanted to marry a normal man; not a 'rising star' in the military or politics; then settle down peacefully in Cleburne to raise kids; and live here forever with my kinfolks and trusted friends!"

"For these reasons; even though I was madly in love with you; I ultimately followed my rational feminine reasoning; instead of my Heart; and said 'no' to your marriage proposal! I cried for days afterwards!! So finally, after all these years I see that I was right in thinking that you were totally loyal to the U.S. Army; and still would be; even after you married me! From the looks of your very high rank, you still are; after all these years! I also turned your marriage proposal down, even though I loved you, because I did not want to raise our children by having to move continuously from base to base; all over the world; as you were reassigned literally every few months! Quite a few years ago I heard that you had been married; and then over the years I heard on the local gossip grapevine when you had children born to your family; some up north and some overseas! Through the years at the local 'chat society' bridge games and social gatherings; I also heard that they are all grown up and now they all have families of their own! I am glad for your sake that you were able to have a family; be a good father to them, and still be loyal to the army and serve our country! Since you have been so successful in the U.S. Army and in politics, I imagine you don't regret my decision to turn down your marriage proposal, and I sure don't! I have had a wonderful life with my adorable husband Buddy, who I came to love very much while we were dating; and I will love him till death do us part; along with our sweet daughter Dixie! Oh, yes! I'm sorry to have rambled so much! You need to talk to Dixie!"

Then without saying another word, Gena Mae abruptly turned around and went back into the house. A moment later the sound of crying coming out of the open side window stopped and a good-looking young woman with extremely swollen and red eyes walked slowly to the door.

"Dixie, I hope you remember me from long ago because I need to speak to you in private about an important matter. May I please come in?" the tall military man asked.

"Yes! General...? Please come in! Oh, now I recognize your face, Larry. ., no, I see now that it's not Sergeant, it is General Snyder! At first I did not recognize you in your formal uniform with apparently your new rank! I don't listen to the news much and I don't even know who was elected president a month or so ago! Congratulations! It has been quite a few years since I saw you last! I was just a preteen when one day Mama introduced me to you as we were walking to the grocery store! You were working at the front desk of the U.S. Army recruiting office as we walked past the front door of your office. At first, Mama led me past the front door of your recruiting office; she hesitated; then had us retrace our steps and go inside to say hello because she apparently knew you even though I had never seen you before!" Dixie explained as she led him down the hall to a back room.

Behind locked doors; in a cozy den at the back of the house, Dixie and the high-ranking military man she had met once quite a few years ago, started a very important conversation, even as the Winds of Destiny swirled unseen around them! The meeting was so important that before they started talking, General Snyder turned on several top-secret devices in his black briefcase; (exactly like the ones Colonel

Carter used during his conference with Slate); to make sure no one could eavesdrop on their conversation! One device took care of listening devices which measured vibrations from the windows of the house to listen in; while another prevented electronic hacking of any electronic devices in the room; such as the television or any cell phones, whose electronic circuits could be altered by spy devices from several blocks away to become listening devices. The device set up an electronic field of static to stop all ordinary electronic devices from being turned on; such as televisions, radios, and cell phones that were in the entire house! A third device projected "white noise" to baffle any passive listening device, (or listening ears), anywhere in the house! As they talked, unknown to their normal Humanoid senses, the Winds of Destiny still swirled around them, indicating something of Galactic Importance was happening!

"Dix, I'll cut to the chase and immediately lay all my cards on the table, so you can make the most important decision of your young life!!! Time is important and we don't have any time to dilly dally! From my 'intelligence' sources, I know that you had an important job in a large bank in New York City for a few years; then for some reason the job did not work out; and so you then returned home here in Cleburne instead of trying to find another job in the Big City! You have known Samuel, whom all his military nicknamed 'Slate', for quite a few years! You know him better than I do; since you have known him since you both were attending the town's Robert E. Lee Elementary School and Jefferson Davis Middle School; while I have only known him since I was his commanding officer for basic training in the U.S. Army! So because of these facts, I need to give you some vital information and say a few personal things in order to help you make an important decision that you must decide on very; very quickly! The ultra-top-secret information that I am going to tell you must remain in this room; and in your Heart forever! I have been in the service of our country's military for many years as a drill instructor and several other military jobs; finally culminating in the top commander of 'Black Opps' in the United States, which is the very highest ranking military office; over all the generals in the military and only following orders of the President! Several years ago, I trained the young man that I know you love deep down in your Heart; first as a very raw recruit, and after he finished basic training and advanced training; I served with him on many covert missions overseas, domestically, and 'otherwise'! I kept up with him when I was assigned to the White House as a Presidential Military Advisor, and also when I returned to supposedly being just a DI; and finally when I resigned from my highest military job; ran for President as a military veteran like Dwight Eisenhower did; and won!"

"For months I have wearing my old uniform; riding my old 'hog'; and being covertly tailed by the Secret Service so that they could protect me! Originally I escaped in the unregistered Homeland Security SUV parked out front; so that I could get out of the White House without the paparazzi, the normal local and national news reporters, and all the foreign and domestic spies around DC from seeing me leave; following me; and preventing me from secretly talking to you! The numbers on the SUV simply gave a warning; they did not give a specific identity!"

"Slate was; and is; a fantastic soldier, literally the very best I have ever trained! I was with him before; during; and after he got severely injured; and I know him as well as I know my own children, and my beloved wife, Mary Pearl;

now living in the White House in Washington, D.C.! In my own heart I have adopted him; and I consider him like one of my own sons; and he treats me like he does his own Daddy! Family is of the Heart; and that brave young man and I are family! I have served with Slate for many years; in good times and in tough times! When he was injured, our military medical technology was able to save his life, his arms and legs, and his sight! Then because he loved you with all his Heart, with absolutely no reservations, when Slate was home on leave for the first time after his severe injuries were repaired, he disobeyed top-secret orders and told you certain extremely secret and sensitive facts! After you heard what he said, because you were afraid after hearing horror stories from some other military wives, you refused his serious marriage proposal! When you did that, it literally tore him up inside his mind, and from listening to your sobs when I came up to your house, I believe that your spur-of-the-moment refusal hit you hard deep down in your Heart, and you still regret turning down his proposal to become his wife! I think your covert display of emotion in the back of your house as I walked up, shows that you are still grieving about your decision to turn him down! You know the Heart of that young man because you grew up and went to school with Slate in this town since both of you attended Robert E. Lee Elementary School! I know and you know the fact that Slate is a good person and he would never hurt you; either awake or asleep!! He still loves you with all of his Heart, which is why after he was honorable discharged from the military, he has been roaming all over the country for years on his cycle trying to forget you, instead of settling down somewhere; going back to school free on the GI Bill, and building a new civilian career! From hearing you weeping as

I came up your sidewalk, I think you still love that boy too! Oh, oh! Your tissue is wet! Here! Use my clean handkerchief; you can have it! Stop crying; and swallow your pride! Forget your huge mistake of the past and put your Heart into the future! Take my cell phone, punch speed dial 1 to contact the young man who loves you with all of his Heart, and talk to the MAN who wants to cherish you and spend the rest of his life with you; because having listened to your mourning, I think that feeling is mutual!"

Dixie took the phone and pondered the extremely important decision for an instant! Did she want to take a chance on "old-fashioned love" to spend the rest of her life with the Man she loved with all of her heart, and wanted to vow "in sickness and in health till death do us part!"? But conversely, did she want to take the chance of getting killed in bed one night, like her bridge club friends had warned her? **OH. . . . Fiddlesticks!** Deep down in her Heart and Soul she knew that Slate would never hurt her-asleep or awake! Dixie swiftly weighed the situation! Deep; deep down in her psyche she quickly decided to follow President Snyder's advice to forget the horror stories she had heard from the other women during the regular bridge games and follow her Heart, since she knew that Slate also loved her with all of his Heart! After pondering the situation for a few seconds more; **SHE KNEW WHAT THE ANSWER HAD TO BE FOR HER TO FIND HAPPINESS IN HER LIFETIME; BECAUSE THIS WAS ONE OF THOSE "ALL OR NOTHING AT ALL" REAL-LIFE SITUATIONS!** Then she quickly obeyed her throbbing Heart and punched speed dial 1!

During the moments that Dixie was thinking deeply about the situation, her very, very important visitor had covertly left the room, moved quickly down the hall, and had quietly unlocked the front door! As he was opening the door, Dixie was pressing speed dial 1; then she heard the phone ring for only an instant. Outside, at literally the same nanosecond, the passenger's side door to the black SUV parked in front of the Davis home flew open! A split-second later, a tall veteran soldier with the ID tag marked "Steele"; in the dress uniform of a full colonel with four rows of medals; some of the "Secret" variety; emerged and proceeded to literally smash the world record speed in the 100-yard dash getting to the front door of the house; with the objective of finding one young woman named Dixie inside the house **ASAP!!** Before the cyclone came in the front door, the supposedly Five Star General "Sarge" Snyder, (and actually the newly sworn-in President of the United States), had unlocked the front door, and held it open as a blur whizzed past! The tall President had previously made sure that he and everyone else in the house was safely out of the way as Slate came speeding down the hallway!

But amid all the "hubbub", Dixie's folks did not seem to mind the interruption; and amazingly; Gena Mae Davis was no longer frowning! She was standing arm-in-arm with her husband, Buddy, in one of the doorways leading out of the main hallway, and grinning like a "Cheshire Cat" as Slate made his move and passed them traveling at breakneck speed down the hall!

#I would say that this is going to be a marriage made, and bonded in Heaven after being literally tempered and forged for years in that other place!!# The President-Elect happily thought as he shut the bedroom door to give Dixie and Slate some privacy, after he retrieved his cell phone! (At that instant on the Time Stream, the

Imperial Magi could again visualize the entire Main Galactic Time Stream! Also at the moment of that Anchor Happening, Sarge did not know just how close to the absolute truth his statement was, but it the coming centuries, **HE WOULD FIND OUT!!!**)

"Have a good day, Gena Mae and Buddy! I hope that I will see you again at the wedding!" the tall greying man said as he passed them in the hall on the way back to the black Presidential SUV. He didn't know how long this very important "conference" would last; so he decided to go get a bite to eat until its conclusion and Slate followed the orders he had given the young man in the SUV and signaled him on his wrist communicator at the successful conclusion of his "objective" to get Dixie to at least talk to Slate!

As the President walked to the black SUV he was thinking to himself. Let's see. He and his driver, and his Secret Service guards hidden in the vehicle; and the other three vehicles that were covertly ringing the house from several blocks away; could get food at McKenzie's Bar-BQ, the Corral Café, the Mexican restaurant on the town square, or several dozen locations at the edge of town. *#Choices, choices, so many GOOD choices!#* He thought to himself as he entered the SUV and the driver headed away from the house. Sarge knew all the good choices because he had grown up in what was then the small town of Cleburne, Texas!

As the large vehicle left the curbside, as the couple watched from the porch, Buddy said, "Gena Mae, I thought that guy had resigned from the military and had been elected President of the United States! We saw him being sworn in on television several days ago! What's he doing in our sleepy town dressed as a 5-star general?!?!"

"I don't know, Buddy, but it appears to have something very important and having to do with Dixie and Slate! It sure must be very important for the President of the United States to covertly come to our town seemingly without his Secret Service guards! Perhaps he did so to avoid unwanted publicity when he left the White House without all of his Secret Service guards and traveled to our town hidden in that SUV with heavily tinted windows!"

"Maybe so, Gena May! Maybe so!" Buddy answered diplomatically.

As the Winds of Destiny swirled unseen and unfelt around them, Gena Mae and Buddy would never know just how important that meeting was! It was literally a "Galactic Anchor Event", that would forever change the future history of the Cosmic All! As such it was an event that was unique in the Annals of the Imperial Magi! It was unique because as the Event started progressing; it had caused the Magi's visions to "come back online"; and also it was one of the few events ever recorded by the Seers in their almost five-hundred thousand year history that would literally affect the Time Lines of virtually all the galaxies in the Cosmic All!

But as this was happening, how would this Very Important Event ultimately affect the United States military? **Would they let Slate back in his old outfit; or do the unthinkable?**

CHAPTER 27

The low-level generals which commanded the covert combat organization at various times called "The Force" or "The Unit" and nicknamed "The Area 51½ Team"; were extremely confused by the events of the past few months! To add to their puzzlement, when they received Colonel Carter's faxed recommendations, what he said added to their bewilderment!

A few weeks ago, during a total video briefing by General Paxton; authenticated by a complete medical report filled out by the unit's doctor, they found out that one of their top-notch soldiers, who had been given ultra-advanced cyborg equipment several years ago to literally save his life and give him sight and the ability to walk again; had suddenly and impossibly been transformed into a "regular" Human again with normal-looking bones and tissue; and the "hardware" which had greatly expanded his physical powers and enhanced his vision was impossibly missing! But that was not the only "riddle" within the unique situation!

Slate's cyborg parts were gone, but according to the reports they had received from the combat teams that had followed him continuously for many days several weeks ago; **HE STILL EXHIBITED MOST, IF NOT ALL OF THE POWERS THE CYBORG EQUIPMENT HAD GIVEN HIM AND PROBABLY SEVERAL MORE NEW ONES, SUCH AS APPARENTLY BEING ABLE TO MENTALLY DETECT THE BRAIN WAVES OF ANY LIVING CREATURE OR HUMAN CLOSE TO HIM, INCLUDING MEMBERS OF THE GROUP ORDERED TO TAIL HIM 24/7; BOTH ON THE GROUND AND SEVERAL MILES ABOVE HIM IN THE AIR!** (They still did not know that Slate could not just detect the brain waves of any living creature or Humanoid around him, he was also telepathic as a result of his numerous mind-to-mind contacts with Red Stinger! But in the coming decades, they would find out this amazing fact!)

The commanding officers of The Unit had realized that their physicians did not have the technology to medically find out what had incredibly been done to Slate; even if they somehow did the unthinkable and ordered the execution of the live young man in order to perform a total autopsy! They also knew that they did not have the capability to physically examine and "reverse engineer" all of the literally undetectable Nano machines and other subatomic devices that had originally been fitted to Slate in order for the cyborg machines to work; (although they had been able to "reverse engineer" the many alien artifacts after the Roswell UFO crash; like the secret antigravity systems used in the amazing VTOL hypersonic U-4)! The fact that they were unable to find out all the medical secrets of Slate's miracle replacement of his damaged cyborg limbs with seemingly ordinary Humanoid limbs was a good thing for the commanding generals of the U.S. Army to realize, because unknown to them, it had taken the Empire almost five hundred thousand years of constant research on hundreds of Humanoid planets in order to gain that incredible medical knowledge! So how could medically backward Earth attempt do the impossible; order the execution of Steele in order to perform a total autopsy; and try to somehow successfully "reverse engineer" that medical information that was buried deep in the Humanoid genome below the Double Helix in the Triple Helix? (**THE EARTHIANS COULDN'T HAVE FOUND THE SECRET IN THREE HUNDRED THOUSAND YEARS OF EARTHLY RESEARCH USING ITS PRIMITIVE MEDICAL TECHNOLOGY AS A STARTING POINT FOR ITS RESEARCH!!**)

The top military "brass", after many hours of heated debate in the secret conference rooms under the Pentagon, finally agreed that medical secrets which transformed Steele's melted artificial limbs and his ruined eye lenses into regular living Humanoid limbs and eyes probably were not on the "Double Helix"; they had to be buried extremely deep in the cells of his body besides on the Double Helix, and were beyond the capability of Earthian medical science to retrieve for an impossible time span! (They did know anything about the "Triple Helix" yet, which is buried ultra-deep in every Humanoid cell, far "below" the "Double Helix"!) But they also realized that if they used the normal, or the brutal, or even the chemical hypnotic interrogation techniques on the young military veteran known as "The Man"; they probably still could not find out from Slate "who" performed the medical miracle! But perhaps a better question would be: "**What**" had the advanced medical knowledge to somehow give an ordinary Humanoid at least the equivalent strength; the all-spectrum eyesight; and the energy level of his former mechanical "cyborg self"!! But knowing "who" or "what" had performed the medical reconstruction of Slate's body would not help the Earthian medical researchers find out **"HOW"** it was done! So this meant that anything beyond normal interrogation of Slate would not be used because it would be useless and it might do physical or psychological damage to the young man!

So instead of irrationally dissecting Slate like an episode out of the old "Stranger Zone"; (or the new really far out spin-off program entitled the "Stranger Still Zone", or on another network, the rival bizarre "Future Zone"); to somehow discover ultra-advanced knowledge that was literally beyond their scientific capability to fathom and find out with the present level of their medical technology; a group of top, "Top Brass" had a "confab" to decide exactly what to do with literally "no-win" situation! General Hartford, the covert group's commanding officer; several other lower commanding officers from Slate's old Opts group; along with President Snyder's representative, General Paxton; were in attendance. After the meetings under the Pentagon were inconclusive, further meetings had to be held; so finally it was decided after several extremely heated conferences in the subterranean conference rooms below the White House in Washington, D.C., and also nearby in West Virginia, built during the Cold War; to follow Colonel Carter's endorsements to the letter!

They would use an indirect approach to find out exactly what had happened to their former "super soldier"; who, despite losing his cyborg limbs and eyes, **WAS STILL "SUPER"**! It was also decided by the generals to be conservative about the situation; follow Colonel Carter's and the President's recommendations to let Slate decide what he wanted to do; and then they would back his decision 100%! They would allow Steele to reenter his old ultra-secret black opps military unit or some other group if he wanted to reenlist; or he could opt to continue to retired; get married, and settle down in his hometown of Cleburne, Texas! If Slate wanted to; he could decide to continue to roam the North American continent on his motorcycle for as long as he wished; or he could use the G.I. Bill to go to college to become anything he wanted. The young man could literally choose to do anything he wanted, as long as he cooperated and communicated with the military as agreed.

The "Plan Zero" that finally they adopted was the use of mild interrogations spread over many months if Slate returned to duty; or the normal medical procedures used during his regular yearly medical exams if he remained retired; and to start a secret medical bureau; which would coordinate what would probably be a long, long, eons long, medical study in order to find out at least the preliminary path to learn the answers to the medical riddle of Slate's new physical and visual powers which did not depend on "machinery or computers"!

The military generals, the commanding officer of his old unit, and his longtime friend, President Snyder; who all unanimously agreed on the final strategy and came up with that plan; never regretted their decision! Because he was given a choice of options, instead of being ordered what to do, Slate decided to reenter the military and his old black opts outfit and to ultimately follow in the footsteps of Sergeant Snyder; supposedly as a lowly DI! But the "History of the Galaxy", as recorded in the Annals of the Imperial

Seers, records the fact that ultimately he would not be just a DI; he would actually follow in the footsteps of the person who had been covertly the highest ranking soldier in the U.S. military, and now was actually the President of the United States, Larry Snyder!

But at that position on the Time Line, the young man called Slate Steele could not imagine the impressive string of his Final Destinies; all of which literally lay far beyond the North Star and even beyond the Capital Planet of Empire Prime! He could not realize that the path of his future military career would start on Earth and would ultimately branch out into the huge area controlled by the mighty ICOPE, i.e., the Interstellar Condominium of Planets and Empires! At that moment he could not imagine the large family that Dixie and he would raise over many years on Earth and far beyond Earth's solar system; and he could not envision his ultimate career as a military attaché to the Empire, and later, his further career as a General and ultimately, an Admiral in the Imperial Armed Forces far beyond the familiar stars and constellations around Earth! All these events are documented in many other historical volumes in your local Earthian library, any large library on any planet in ICOPE's sphere-of-influence, and also in the huge Emperor's Imperial Library on Empire Prime!

So as a very important "Anchor Event Person" named Slate Steele was living his life to the fullest on the Time Line, other important and pivotal events were also happening; which would affect his future life; events such as . . . . **but wait!** The narration is getting ahead of the Magi visualization, which as previously stated; telling the outcome before the Event happened, could affect the "Future" and cause "Time Disruptions", "Time Paradoxes", and several other bad effects!

So, as this record proceeds at the correct pace and the Galactic Time Stream flows on, many years in the future, we observe. . . . . . (or you WILL observe; depending on your position on the Main Galactic Time Line!)

And so, it came to pass . . . . Many light years from Earth on a planet called Empire Prime; a very important event was about to happen!

CHAPTER 28

One day on Empire Prime, several years after the effects of a certain Anchor Event on the distant minor planet called Earth were totally finished, and the Galactic Time Line had become stable and smooth again; while hurrying to an important meeting, Seer Rondoe Kanne happened to glance down the boulevard and noticed an extremely tall Reptiloid walking down the street toward him; wearing an ornate military uniform with many rows of combat metals; many of which the Imperial Seer knew were very, very hard to earn! The veteran Magi somehow sensed, with one of his latent mental powers that seemed to work involuntarily at odd times, that the gigantic Reptiloid gliding toward him on the public streets of Empire Prime had the secret Battle Pack Warrior Name of "Red Stinger". Immediately the instant Kanne sensed that fact, the experienced Magi felt the Winds of Destiny; which had been totally calm; pick up to moderate force; necessitating him to raise his mental shields!

#What is going on? Why is my meeting a Reptiloid on the street, who I have never formally met before, so important that one of my involuntary Magi powers immediately tells me his secret combat name; which only his blooded battle comrades should ever know? But why, when I realize what my powers are telling me, and I mentally think that Reptiloid's secret combat name; do the Winds of Destiny pick up; which always indicates that an important Anchor Event is happening! What is going on?!?! Why is my meeting this Reptiloid so important? I remember seeing him several times before, in years past, on the streets of Empire Prime, and also seeing him at a diplomatic conference just last year; and each time before, the Winds did not pay any attention to the situation, and this did not happen! Why now? Why is this chance meeting so extremely important? I must find out!# The Seer thought to himself under his strongest mental screens.

His question was almost immediately answered; because at that instant, on the Galactic Time Line; he sensed that for some reason at that position on Empire Prime, a very unusual Extra-Sensory Event was happening as the Karma of both Reptiloid and Human became tightly intertwined! This rare phenomenon caused the mental "logic-illogic center" of the Imperial Magi to feel a mental attraction to talk with the other dissimilar being! The Seer sensed that the Reptile had not perceived anything; so he had to make an excuse for a meeting with the tall being so that he could find out the reason for the unusual Galactic Time Stream Phenomenon!

Verbally addressing the extremely tall Reptiloid from a distance in the standard language of the Empire, as they continued to walk toward each other, the Seer lowered his mental shields to allow a mental conversation, and said, *#Hello, there, Sir! I am Imperial Seer Rondoe Kanne and I have important business to discuss with you; although I have a very important scheduled meeting with the Emperor in five minutes! First, can you understand me; and secondly, can we meet as soon as possible after my meeting with the Emperor at a nearby location to talk over important matters?#*

#Yes, I can, Most Honorable Imperial Seer! I am deeply honored that you address me! My legal Reptiloid and family name is "Karkanza"; and I am also known on my planet, by members of the battle group that I command, as "Red Stinger"!# The Reptiloid telepathically stated very loudly in Standard Galactic; and then continued. *#I, too; am hurrying to an important meeting with a long-time military friend of mine, who is a high-ranking Imperial Naval Official; in order to discuss some important business about my planet's confederation along with the Imperial Ambassador to our worlds! I doubt if you know the naval officer, because his transfer to the Imperial Navy was an unprecedented event; since previously he had absolutely no Empire Navy training! Just last month, the Humanoid was promoted to a very high Imperial Navy Officer position after he transferred from an obscure planet that had just become a member of the Empire; after many years of being far outside ICOPE's sphere of influence! The insignificant planet never had any official contact with the Empire; and it never*

received Imperial Ambassadors prior to being accepted by the Empire and getting on the official list to become a member; yet somehow it had enough contact with the Empire so that the small, yet important planet eventually became a member without going through any of the official steps to becoming a member planet! Apparently that insignificant planet had very significant contacts and friends in the Empire for such a unique; first-time event to occur! I have known my Humanoid Battle Friend for many years! My trusted friend of several decades is also an experienced combat veteran; having literally shed some of his blood for my Thunder World, and now I need his military expertise to quickly train a combat team for an important mission ASAP! Can we rendezvous in an hour at the very popular Jarcon Dozer Restaurant down the block in order to talk over certain important matters?#

Rondoe Kanne immediately replied telepathically. *#Yes! That would be convenient for me also! Very good! I haven't tasted Sada Juice in many a moon phase, because I don't go to Jarcon's very often since the cafes in my office building are much closer and I am always in a hurry! I will meet you in exactly one hour from this instant, unless my supposedly short meeting with the Emperor delays me! In which case I will temporarily excuse myself from the meeting in order to send you a telepathic message on one on your Omni-phone, whichever would be more convenient for you!*

#After conversing at short range with me, you now know my telepathic wavelength; so just contacting me telepathically after your meeting is fine!# Red Stinger replied.

After the ceremonial handshake between Reptiloid and Humanoid, which consisted of a Humanoid fist briefly touching the right top principal claw of the Reptiloid, which had been lowered so that the much shorter Humanoid could reach it, the two very dissimilar beings each traveled on to their appointments and the further molding of their Ultimate Destinies! Red Stinger walked to his scheduled meeting with his friend, and the ambassador from his three Thunder World confederation planets of Reptilus, Reptilon, and Reptilee to Empire Prime; while the Seer, by means of his wrist communicator, electronically transposed up to the Emperor's Royal Meeting Room using the only transposer wavelength; out of several quadrillions possible; that could penetrate the dense Neutronium-enhanced walls of the palace.

After each of their important meetings, at the agreed-upon time, both the Humanoid and the Reptiloid met in front of the famous restaurant. As the meeting started, Imperial Magi Rondoe Kanne needed to find out exactly why at that Fated Moment, a little over an hour previously; he felt his Karma somehow meld with the Reptiloid's! Red Stinger, lacking the mental powers of the Imperial Seers, did not know exactly what had happened at that moment, but while he was walking toward Rondoe Kanne the first time on the street; because he was a very experienced combat veteran who could control his emotions; his Battle Reflex suddenly "came online"; yet, his outward facial expressions did not indicate the fact that he had also felt that something important was happening! At the exact same instant that Red Stinger first observed the Imperial Seer, his trusted Reptiloid "Battle Sense"; i.e., a sense of "foreboding"; had alerted him that something important was about to happen; maybe good or maybe bad! But Red Stinger had also noticed that his "Battle Hackles" on the back of his long neck; had not reared up, which always indicated imminent danger; so he thought at the time that maybe the event that was about to happen would be good!

In the past several hundred years he had felt that particular feeling in his psyche many times; sometimes with, and sometimes without the back scales on his neck rearing up! One time was just before the battle force that he was commanding was about to be ambushed by a rogue Hunan battle force! Trusting his battle sense that indicated that something bad was about to happen, he took a chance and acted to save his combat force from ambush! The admiral's daring action of immediately calling his task force to battle stations several seconds before a rival Hunan war fleet from another far off star federation dropped out of hyperspace; literally saved the lives of all the Reptiloids under his command! Instead of finding a fleet totally unprepared for battle and with their energy and kinetic protection screens down, the Hunan raiders unexpectedly were met with a withering fire from the Reptiloid fleet who was unexpectedly at total combat readiness; ready to fire the instant the enemy fleet dropped into normal space! His battle leaders in his fleet could not figure out how he was able to alert them in time; and also the survivors of the utterly defeated Hunan fleet; never figured out how their rival fleet knew that the enemy was about to unexpectedly strike!

At the present position on the Time Line and at that particular moment, carefully analyzing what he felt at that instant, all he could fathom was that "something" important had happened at that past moment; although he did not know exactly what had occurred! So literally another instant later, when the Imperial Seer walking toward him unexpectedly asked him for a conference, the Battle Leader accepted; knowing the reputation of the Imperial Magi as being experts in "mental matters", and hoping to find out exactly what was going on! As a good faith gesture, he even told the Seer his legal name Karkanza; along with his Battle Group name "Red Stinger".

Originally, the restaurant had been called "Trader Kank-Ker's Sada Juice Bar" for almost a thousand years, but the name had been changed two years ago when the restaurant had changed owners and, for some unknown reason, they had the name changed to "Jarcon Dozer's Restaurant and Bar". In the course of their meeting which was held at a very private table at the back of the very extremely popular "refreshment" restaurant, the Imperial Seer and the Reptiloid Commander found out the very important fact that they had a mutual acquaintance and friend: one Imperial Colonel General Samuel Eliot Steele, the Empire naval officer that Red Stinger had been going to see!

And so it was that over the course of the afternoon, so that each of them could perform their jobs better, and also find out the reason that their meeting was of Galactic Importance, the Seer and the Reptiloid commander each shared facts about the relatively young Humanoid male! The Reptiloid told of Slate's second ultra-secret mission for the Thunder Worlds several years after the first; having accepted the dangerous assignment at that time with the complete and full permission of the Earthian military!

Ultimately they exchanged facts that were very interesting to both Imperial and Reptiloid Naval Officials after; with an agreement between the Seer and his new acquaintance Red Stinger to be under a binding oath not to ever tell the information they were to be told to anyone else; unless given written permission by the other! During the course of their important meeting, Seer Rondoe Kanne and the Reptiloid Admiral Karkanza, each related some amazing stories about the unusual Humanoid called Steele that provided each of them with vital information about the combat veteran Earthman that would help each of them make important decisions in the future! The tall reptile and the Imperial Magi were each provided with vital information that they would find extremely valuable in the coming centuries as Samuel Eliot Steele rose higher and higher in the Empire's Imperial Navy, with his superior intellect, and his unusual Humanoid physical and vision powers!

At the end of the very useful conference, each important officer thanked the other for the very important information, and promised to communicate often in the future via either telepathy or electronic means. Then, after another ceremonial touching of Reptiloid claw and Humanoid hand, each of the two sentient beings continued down their own Path of Destiny on the Eternal Stream of Time; with each destined to make important wise decisions for both the Imperial Seers and the Thunder Worlds! Unfortunately, although Seer Rondoe Kanne and Red Stinger conversed many times over the centuries with telepathy or using the FTL Imperial messaging system; they were never to physically meet again this side of Eternity! Meanwhile, as the two new friends parted, on the Galactic Time Stream other important events were happening, each of which would affect each of their home planets and Empires!

Because elsewhere in the gigantic Universe: Under the watchful eyes of the local proxies, and at times, the mental senses of the Royal Seer specifically assigned to the planet for some unknown reason by the Supreme Seer, the Auxiliary Time Streams for the vicinity of the planet Earth and the entire Cosmic All moved swiftly forward, as they had from Time Immemorial. From the position on the Galactic Time Stream during which the Reptiloid and the Magi met, months; then years swiftly passed by; then one local day on the small, but important planet Earth; at one particular point, another Anchor Event was about to happen, and the Winds of Destiny rose to swirl about the participants; who were at that point moving into position for another very important Pivotal Happening which, just like the previous one, would literally change the course of the Galactic Timeline!

CHAPTER 29

I t was extremely hot in a desert on the planet Earth, in the state of Arizona, in the United States of America, on the North American Continent, as the perspective "Black Opts" trainees for the newly-formed "Team #116" of the "off-the-record" military force, which was still unofficially called "The Unit"; trudged double-time through deep burning sand under a blistering sun; protected only by the standard sun hats, lightweight canvas pants to shield their legs, and temporary canvas sleeves snapped to their standard issue shirts. As they marched along, morale was high, although the trek had been tough, because of certain events that had occurred before they started out early this morning before sunup. The reason for the optimism was the fact that, going against all standard military protocol, all of the so-called trainees had been handpicked by their new DI from the entire group of over one thousand soldiers in training! The outstanding recruits thus picked officially became members of a new "Team #116", and immediately headed out into the heat of the desert; marching double-time; with their new DI in front of the long column; leading them at a very fast pace; even though the military "rumor mill" said that he was apparently many decades older than any of them!

Several team commanders that had been instructing the trainees assigned to their team around the desert base for several weeks, suddenly found that their best warrior recruits were taken out by a well-known veteran soldier; a new One Star General, named Steele! He had been directly appointed over dozens of candidates with more seniority and rating, by United Nations President Snyder; who formerly had been the senior DI in their combat section! Rumors were also flying up and down the base's "Scuttlebutt Information System" because the general had personally interviewed all of the trainees very quickly, and had somehow picked the ones that were mentally and physically the best; without looking on any of their information sheets! Also adding fuel to the rumors was the fact that before the members of the new Team #116 started out on the so-called "training mission", which would be situated far across the arid desert; their commander had sworn every one of them to secrecy about anything they would see on this trip!

So leaving all the rumors behind, Team 116 headed out across the barren landscape; supposedly in order to start their "special training" required to become a member of a "Black Ops" team for "The Unit". As the trainees walked, their extremely heavy packs, composed of just field rations, water, and whatever else they chose to pack, seemed heavier and heavier, and the straps of the packs dug in deeper and deeper into their shoulders as the hours wore on; as they tried to reach their training site before dark. But alas, their goal of reaching their objective was not accomplished; since their commander's GPS said they were about fifty miles short of the training site; therefore the new trainees had to make a cold camp out under the stars and eventually reach their objective sometime tomorrow.

After the new soldiers ate their self-heating food packets, then cleaned up the campsite, and settled back to sleep on the still warm desert surface under the dark Arizona sky, a few of the more observant trainees who were familiar with astronomy, noticed that one particular bright point of light did not seem like a star because it was moving! The point of light was not moving like a satellite or a meteor in an arc, it seemed to be zigzagging; and it seemed to be getting larger as it moved here and there across the dark western sky; as if searching for something!

Suddenly the soft, muted sounds of the desert were broken by a sharp, unfamiliar detonation! As one, the members of the team looked up and all around to see what had made the noise that sounded louder than a rifle being fired, but less than any hand-fired ordinance! Before their startled eyes, an arc of light rose up from their very senior DI and ascended high up into the heavens! Colonel General Steele had suddenly fired off a very fast moving flare; seemingly aimed in the direction of the radically-moving bright unknown object! After a few seconds, the flare snuffed out and the desert night sky became dark again! But in response to the signal; without any arc of light to disclose its source, at the edge of their campsite there suddenly appeared an extremely large bright flare; which immediately faded to blackness; leaving a very large dark object on the ground!

Out of the night's gloom a gruff; guttural voice spoke in a language unknown to all but one of their troop! In response, from among their group's midst, for an instant, a similar gruff-sounding language was immediately spoken by their commander, Colonel General Steele; then he switched over to English so that they could understand what was happening!

"Moneaco keblon seniele!...Welcome back, Red Stinger! I hope you still remember the dominant language spoken on this planet! It has been too long since I was an honored warrior guest at your fire when our situations were reversed! Now I can return the favor you gave me, and give you a Warrior's Welcome to our fire! These fellow Humanoids are not physically enhanced, like your Reptiloid science did to my Double Helix and my Triple Helix, but they all are combat ready and want to learn to be superior warriors! They each have the physical talents necessary, and all they lack is a few weeks of intensive training to hone their combat skills!" Slate replied in English to Red Stinger's talking in Standard Galactic.

At the sound of Slate's voice, the dark, extremely large dark shape beyond the edge of the ring of light cast by the fire came forward; coalescing in the light of the flickering campfire into an impossible sight! To the young trainees it was a shape literally out of a nightmare! The form before their startled eyes was like the shape of a space alien out of a "Stranger Still Zone" episode; as before their startled eyes what looked like an extremely tall reptile, with a shape similar to a slim, very large alligator with a small slim tail; literally erupted out of the darkness! At their first glimpse of the fearsome sight, which also seemed like something out of a childhood dream or one of the popular "Star Conflict" movies, the trainees tried to open their nearby packs and obtain weapons to try to defend against this unknown alien being! But for some reason, the weapons that they each had placed inside their back packs that morning following the orders of their commanding officer, were missing; and they had no protection against this scaled monstrous being! Amazingly, as they fruitlessly searched; virtually all of the weapons the trainees had inserted in their packs before they left the base were also missing!

Instantly, as their searches were futile, the commander of their training exercise spoke orders to calm the situation! "Relax, trainees! **Stand down! At ease! Condition Green!!** This fierce-looking being is what is called an Imperial Citizen; literally from beyond the stars, and believe it or not; also a good friend of mine, for many years! I have known him for well over fifteen years; so stand down and put down your packs and quit looking for your firearms! That's an order!! For your protection, I covertly tried to make sure before our march that all of your pistols and knives were left behind, so that this veteran warrior by the combat name of Red Stinger would not have to hurt any of you! If I missed one or two weapons, immediately put them down! Even if you tried, you could not hurt him, since knives and ordinary bullets would simply bounce off his thick Reptiloid hide and tend to make him mad!!"

"Quite a few years ago; on top of a certain steep mesa, our first meeting together was a little different! That time, our positions were reversed; when Admiral Red Stinger was around a fire on the top of a mesa; and I was the one to come out of the darkness into his group of blooded warriors that were around his campfire a few dozen miles from here! I hope before our military training exercise is over each of you can personally meet this veteran warrior from beyond the stars and get to know him, as I did some years ago! So relax, stand down and put away your weapons if you were able to find one in your pack, and sit down for an important briefing!"

Slate stopped speaking to look into the eyes of all the trainees; then continued, "First off, you need to know that, just like the authors say in the science fiction novels, it's a rough Universe out there and you have to be ready! You will have to learn that fearsome and unfamiliar beings such as this large Reptiloid are the rule; and not the exception out in the far-flung galaxies! Beings like us are called Humanoids, and we are almost the weakest sentient creatures in the Cosmic All, but we make up for it with our brains! Some of the beings that you will meet will look even more fierce and uglier than Red Stinger! But enough talk! **Welcome to our fire, Honored Warrior Red Stinger!**"

"Thank you, Honored Warrior Steele! You honor me by allowing me to enter your campfire's glow, returning my favor of quite a few years ago!" the tall Reptiloid replied verbally in flawless English to all the trainees; instead of projecting mentally so that only Slate could receive his message. "After all these years, I am glad that I am now finally able return the favor and to unexpectedly meet you at one of your warrior campfires! History has now repeated itself, and you had to call off your warriors under your command, just as I had to do at our first fateful meeting! The last time we parted with the traditional Reptiloid Warrior's Parting Ceremony, as I touched your hand with my claw, I told you that I sensed that we would meet again, and here we are!" Carefully touching his Reptiloid claw-like hand with Slate's Humanoid hand, Red Stinger produced a loud roar, his reptile version of a laugh, and without thinking; treated him like a Reptiloid comrade; slapping him on the back with his other major claw hand; which should have severely injured the much weaker Humanoid's shoulder! But amazingly, that was not the case! For an instant, Red Stinger thought that he was hitting a

Tytano Steel wall; instead of a weak, soft Humanoid shoulder! Incredibly, Slate's back and shoulder were not injured by the powerful blow and did not give a millimeter; only producing a loud "THUMP" when the blow landed! This amazing result was very different from the last time he had slapped his friend on the shoulder while celebrating the success of his first mission that had literally saved his worlds! That time the Humanoid had reacted entirely different--he had been knocked down!

This time, Slate was not harmed by the tremendous blow because this time his Human body had undergone "the Change" of his extremely rare Humanoid species! By birth, Colonel General Samuel Eliot Steele was a Humanoid genus described as a "shape shifter" who, since the last time he had been whacked on the shoulder, had successfully gone through what his particular Humanoid species called "the Change"! While on military leave several years ago, he had gone back to Cleburne just to visit his mom and dad. During that fateful trip to his hometown, his mom and dad had finally told him about his amazing "heritage" from beyond the stars, and covertly had been able to teach him a few "tricks of the shape shifter trade"!

Now, because his body had previously gone through the normal process of metamorphosing into that of a being able to convert his body into almost any other body shape and species; the wallop which should have knocked the supposedly weak Humanoid down; instead cracked the outer shell of the protective scales on Red Stinger's claw hand, and caused a small amount of Reptiloid body fluid to ooze out!

Ignoring the minor discomfort and pausing a moment without looking at the minor wound which swiftly closed up, because he did not have the time to privately ask his friend why his shoulder felt like a Tytano steel bar, instead of usual soft Humanoid flesh; the reptile admiral continued as if nothing had happened, "But this time, my warrior friend, instead of pursuing a single warrior in order to perform an important covert mission to prevent a civil war, you know that I am here, with the permission of your planetary and continental governments, for another reason! Let's go aside where we can talk privately!"

Traveling a few yards across the hot desert sand, the Reptiloid privately continued his important talk to Slate in a soft, guttural voice speaking in his native language! "The Thunder Worlds are in need of a specialized group with certain combat skills and the President of your Solar System; President Larry Snyder; personally recommended you, and your new combat team which is in training; to go on the important dangerous combat mission! The United Nations President wants you to lead Members of Team 116 on the mission; after you feel that your training is completed; hopefully in just a few of your planet's weeks or months!"

"Yea, Red, United Nations President Snyder, my old former Earthian military DI still likes to wear his official-looking 5-star general uniform in covert situations where the people he meets don't know that he is not a general anymore; but the newly appointed, top 'Commander in Chief' of the United Nations! The President briefed me last week about what you needed and gave me permission to form a high-talent combat group by taking the best trainees from the entire battalion and quickly training them to attempt the job! He even promoted me by ordering the 'powers that be' to skip my rank up several levels from a lowly Sergeant DI to a one-star general for the mission! (He said if the mission goes well, the ranking is permanent!) The other DIs did not like the idea of either my skipping ranks, or my raiding their trainee groups and somehow picking out the best men! But 'Sarge', er, President Snyder, the 'head honcho' of the entire planet's military, gave them their orders directly for them to allow me to pick my men from their best trainees; he told them it was for a classified mission that had to be accomplished ASAP, so they all agreed to follow such unusual orders without complaining, and they cheerfully allowed me to pick and choose my team!"

#All right, Warrior Steele! It is a good plan! I will do my best to cooperate fully with you and the Earthian authorities!# Red Stinger projected privately to Slate. *#By the way, I have casually scanned your trainees and the auras on some of them became instantly brighter in response to my sudden appearance, which means they have a fierce drive to succeed as a warrior! For some reason, one of them has a very bright aura, whose shape; size, and coloring, for some unknown reason, are all very similar to yours! I did not take the time to scan his name, but he is the tallest one in your group, next to you! Also, when I lightly scanned the group, a few of them exhibited better than average Humanoid mental powers; like you did the night you approached our campfire up on what we call "Mesa One"! I thought you would like to know this information about your trainees, (although, with your past mental training, you probably already know the facts that I just told you!) Good luck on your training! When I train my Reptiloid soldiers, I always try to take my time and make the novice soldiers sweat and bleed a lot in order to forge*

them, like Tytano Steel is purified, into superior warriors! But as a blooded combat veteran, you already know these facts; having sweated and bled when you were trained and forged into an exceptional warrior; and also, because in years past, you have trained several very successful combat teams in this region since then!#

Red Stinger stopped for a moment; then continued, #When you are satisfied with the combat efficiency of your team, send me a telepathic message on the band that we have used all these years for communication! Your telepathic messages always come in strong on the Thunder Worlds, even though they are many hundreds of thousands of light years away! After you call, after a certain amount of time, I will meet you and your team where you will be training them, at the old mesa where we first met; although after all these years, I'm afraid that the facilities are a little run down! I'm sorry that I can't stay longer to meet each of your combat patrol separately, like we originally planned, but, like you say: "Duty Calls! A job that as the Pro Tem President of the Thunder Worlds, I must immediately take care of; beckons!#

#Yes, Red#, Slate projected back, *#It's too bad you can't stay! We still haven't gone on that hunting trip we promised ourselves over five years ago! It also would be interesting to see if any of the group's mental powers would become greater if you tried to telepathically talk with them; especially the tallest trainee with the aura you said is similar to mine! I believe I just now successfully read in*

his mind that his name is Wagstaff! I remember that he is the son of the doctor assigned to my old unit, which suddenly answers a lot of questions! As you suggested, I will telepathically contact you in a week or two when we are ready to roll! It is amazing how telepathy between two warriors such as you and myself can quickly span galactic and intergalactic distances! Until we meet again, hopefully sometime in the future, as the Reptiloid Warrior's Greeting and Exit Credo each state: "True steel weapons, superior ships, and a true warrior's ending be your fate!#.

The reply from Red Stinger was not long in coming. *#I wish for you what the motto of the Thunder Worlds Navy states: "A fast ship on the ocean and the chance for a true warrior's honorable death in battle against thousands!!" Farewell, Kif Warrior Steele; until we meet again!#*

An instant later, as the Winds of Destiny swirled around the area, the Reptiloid Commander was englobed in a brilliant aura of light as his "Battle Ball" battleship, in orbit around Earth with the permission of the Solar System Defense system, transposed him up. Only one of the Humanoid soldier trainees felt a slight shiver as the reptile's body was reduced to energy to allow him to instantaneously travel back to his ship, where it would be converted back to his Reptiloid body again on the ship's Battle Bridge!

(As Slate remembered, the apprentice soldier named Elijah "Eli" Wagstaff happened to be great-grandson of Old West Sheriff and Marshal, Samson Blair; who had been nicknamed the "Time Marshal"; and the son of Dr. Martha Wagstaff; and so he knew why Elijah's aura was bright! The good doctor had not told her son that his commanding officer was also a shape-shifter, she would let him find out that fact on his own; probably while he was home on leave after the present training or after a combat mission in the future!)

Several years ago, after his visit with his parents, Dr. Wagstaff had taken time from her busy military physician's schedule to make an appointment with Slate, supposedly to go over some medical tests with him; so that she could secretly further train his shape-shifting powers! Her additional coaching of Slate in the use of his natural powers, (after his first shape-shifting training from his mom and dad); had gone very quickly and his power to shape-shift was very strong, and would prove very useful in the future!

As soon as Red Stinger's transpose flash vanished, Slate seized the moment to teach the beginning special opts soldiers a few things about the "Galactic Facts of Life" when it came to how things were out in the galaxies beyond Earth's solar system! "Men and women, most of you, after you satisfactorily complete your training; are about to embark on a mission that will be exciting beyond your wildest dreams, and I have to prepare you so that you can withstand what you are about to witness! This information is also top-secret; just like what you just witnessed when Red Stinger suddenly appeared right before your eyes; and you have previously sworn not to tell anything about this training or the mission to follow at any time in the future, or face the consequence of incarceration for the rest of your life!"

"Like I told you before, that large being that looked like a walking alligator was Red Stinger; and appearances can be deceiving! That fearsome-looking being is actually a very excellent Admiral commanding a fleet of vessels in the "Thunder Worlds"; whose citizens are one of the 4 or 5 major species in the galaxies called 'Reptiloids'! The other major kinds of sentient beings recognized by the scientists of the Interstellar Condominium of Planets and Empires; i.e.; 'ICOPE'; are 'Insectoids', 'Snakoids', 'Humanoids', and sometime, 'Colloid Cloud' beings! Red Stinger's species is very strong physically and has several mental powers including telepathy, a 'battle sense', and so-called 'battle hackles' on the back of their necks, which can warn them of impending danger!"

"A few years ago I very satisfactorily performed an ultra-secret combat mission for him that Red Stinger and his warriors were unable to accomplish because of their particular physical characteristics; which shows you that strength is not everything! Now, what does this mean to you? Because of certain missions that I have gone on and successfully accomplished; and because of certain combat skills that I possess, I was promoted to a new ranking, 'Colonel General' by United Nations President Snyder, and given a job to train new soldiers for a new ultra-secret mission; a mission that is so involved and dangerous that even the fearsome Reptiloids from the Thunder Worlds will not attempt to accomplish it!!"

"For those of you who finish the very hard training and don't 'wash out'; if you measure up and are chosen; you will go on your first so-called 'Black Ops' mission, perhaps here on Earth; perhaps on Mars, on Venus with protective gear, or maybe it will be beyond our solar system searching for the legendary hidden "Planet Nine"!! This will start an exciting period in your life and the amazing adventures you will accomplish will be beyond your wildest dreams; and ultra-top-secret that you cannot mention to anyone for the rest of your life-----**OR ELSE!!!** The United Earth Military Command wants our top soldiers to be given special training so they will not experience 'culture shock' when they travel from Earth; and will be prepared to cooperate and work with all the physically different and exotic beings that inhabit every galaxy that you can see above your heads! You will meet beings such as the tall, spindly Insectoids; the very slender Snakoids with very tiny legs; the fearsome Reptiloids; the Colloid Cloud beings who look like floating clouds of fireflies; and the many different sized and shaped Humanoids! As you will find out during your advanced training; with hand-held navigation equipment out in the desert under the stars, and in the classrooms that have been built up on the nearby mesa; some of the pin point motes of light you can see are not the light from an individual sun, they are each the light from an entire galaxy where these many different types of sentient beings live!"

"Some of you will actually experience real adventures in your life that will rival or surpass plot lines in 'The Stranger Zone' or even the newer and eerier shows like the 'Stranger Still Zone' and the 'Future Zone'! Again I emphasize the fact that members of this group who pass the rigorous physical and mental tests which you will be given in the next few weeks, after you receive very mentally and physically tough specialized training; can expect to see and work with many bizarre alien beings; including other similar Reptiloids like Admiral Red Stinger, in the future; and possibly far out in the galaxies! You may also work with strange-looking Humanoids; and other similar-looking, but different species from the Reptiloids like the 'Hunans'! You will see beings that I mentioned called Snakoids, and Insectoids; and maybe even a few of the spooky 'Colloid Cloud beings, who each look like a small cloud of floating points of light!"

"The beings in the Empire that live all across the Cosmic All literally come in all shapes and sizes and the strange beings look different from us, but you must remember that they will be intelligent, sentient beings with likes and dislikes just like us! Some of these sentient beings have societies that have been in existence for over four or five hundred thousand years! As an Imperial Citizen of the Interstellar Condominium of Planets and Empires; you will have to treat them like any other civilized being; accept them as equals and try to become friends with them; even if they 'look down at you'; and work with them for the Common Good of all the cooperating Empires, Federations, and solar systems, that they represent!"

"Now that you have been briefed about what is to happen to you in the future as a result of this mission's specific training; anyone who is not sure they can measure up to perform such a mission as I have described; and who wishes to do so, may put in a request to transfer to another group training nearby for duty solely on Earth; with no questions asked and no indication on your permanent record to indicate what happened! **Anyone who chooses to transfer out will still be sworn to secrecy for the rest of your lives; until you are buried with a civilian or a military funeral; with no exceptions and no excuses for having leaked this important information!** Anyone who leaks information; either verbally to another person, by writing articles, or on either secret or social media at any time in the future, will be automatically be reinstated into the military; then court martialed, and imprisoned for the rest of your life; or depending on the consequences of your leak of top secret information; immediately executed; even if you have retired from the military and are a civilian! It applies even if you are stationed on the moon or other planets; other solar systems; or other galaxies! But I know that none of you loyal trainees would do this! Now, before we begin, are there any questions before we start your next phase of training?"

Slate paused a second to glance around; and then continued speaking with a wave of his hand in a large arc below the stars of the sky to emphasize his point, "But men and women, for emphasis, I need to repeat that what you have seen tonight is only a sample of the wonders out there! I remember how it affected me when I first saw the Reptiloids on top of the mesa a few miles from here! It literally blew my mind and I thought I was dreaming! When you get a chance to calmly think about it; your future will literally be like the plot lines of science-fiction novels come to life, or like the fictitious alien beings on the science fiction shows on ordinary television or satellite telecasts! You all must get used to seeing unexpected sights and strange beings that make the characters constructed by computer-aided-graphics shown on the first new 'Full Eclipse Zone'; that just came on last week; look like dull old cartoons! Literally, what you have seen is only a small part of the wonders and strange beings that exist out there! The galaxies are populated with many types of unusual beings, mostly controlled by multisystem governments, such as one I previously mentioned, called the 'ICOPE', or the 'Interstellar Condominium of Planets and Empires'!"

"For the sake of security and you own safety and wellbeing, again I command you not discuss any of the things that you have seen tonight with anyone else outside this specific group! Do not spread rumors or ask questions about what you **THINK** you saw tonight, even among this group of trainees! Starting from this instant, and in the future; just like in the past, my office door at the base is always open if anyone wants to talk about anything you have observed tonight and do not understand! In any open or secret conference with any of you, I will truthfully answer any legitimate question that you ask me, so you can ask me anything and not spread rumors! If I am not in my office when you come, simply tell my secretary, Mrs. Brenda Hill, that you need to talk with me, and she will schedule an appointment ASAP! When anyone meets with me, if I don't know the answer to any legitimate question that is posed to me, I will always research an accurate answer and get it to you! ASAP! Again, any questions?"

Pausing a moment to allow questions, when there were none, Slate said, "OK, let's hit the sack. When the sun rises in a few hours we have a long march of about fifty miles ahead of us in order to reach your training site far across the desert, so at 5 A.M. reveille will sound, we will breakfast on cold rations; then we will start marching early, and make the 50-mile journey in a little over six hours by marching double time!"

As the tired soldiers-in-training went to sleep on the hard and warm desert surface, the Winds of Destiny swirled very lightly around most of them; except it whirled a little heavier around Slate, and the other secret shape-shifter in the group whose name was Elijah "Eli" Wagstaff! (See Appendix I) The next morning the trainees were awakened at 5 A.M. sharp by the sharp notes of a bugler sounding reveille and quickly ate their cold ration breakfasts. As promised, as he had done for many years for many training sessions, their commander started the journey to their training site; leading the column of trainees using double time. After the distance was covered shortly before 12 noon, some of the trainees noticed that their commander, who was probably more than double or triple some of their ages; was not breathing hard when they entered the shadows formed by what looked to be a tall mesa. (The only other member of the group who was not physically tired was Elijah Wagstaff; for the same reason that their commander was not tired; a few months ago, he had secretly received the shape-shifter training from his mom and dad!) To explain why a much older man was in better physical shape than young men and women such as themselves, the observant trainees finally came to the conclusion that General Steele was not breathing hard because over the years, he had been constantly giving combat training to young men and women, and because of this, he was simply more physically fit than the much younger trainees that he was teaching to survive combat!

As recorded in the Annals of the Imperial Seers, on top of the tall mesa; in the renovated old secret military base of Red Stinger where he met Slate many years ago; the training of the group went swiftly and very well, with no "washouts", since the trainees under Slate were the "cream of the crop"; and hand-picked from the large number of new recruits undergoing training! After his orientation speech, and a good night's sleep, Slate had immediately put them into a crash strength-building course similar to how Sarge Snyder had trained his groups in the same area; i.e.; **it was tough!** It was tough for one very good reason! Like a famous United States Army general once said: "The more you sweat in peacetime; the less you bleed in war!")

After several weeks of strength training; every trainee was physically strong enough and sufficiently trained to quickly grapple up and down the mesa with grappling hooks and ropes; swim with a heavy pack for at least a mile; hand-climb up and down the mesa like a gecko on a wall; and be able to use camouflage infrared netting to sneak across a moonlit desert floor without being seen or detected by infrared sensors! When Slate was satisfied with the level of accomplishment, he contacted Red Stinger very quickly telepathically; even though the Reptiloid was back out in the Thunder Worlds, many light years away! When he instantly received the telepathic message, the Ruler of the Three Worlds dropped all of his normal business and came immediately as he could to the "Mesa of the First Meeting"; his favorite place on Earth!

With the help of several of his Reptiloid aides; while Slate was taking a short military leave; for about seven Earthly days, Red Stinger added his own tough reptile version of military teaching to see if all of the trainees could be compatible and successfully work with strange life forms! Everyone in the group passed the tough physical tests to the Reptiloid's satisfaction; which made him very impressed with Slate's training methods, and the strength level of Earth's species of Humanoids! While he was training the young Earthians, Red Stinger suddenly remembered the past moment when he slapped Slate on his soft back and the blow had hurt his scaled hand! At the time, he vowed someday to ask the Humanoid just how that had happened, but so far on the Galactic Time Line; he had not had the chance! The Reptiloid immediately forgot that line of thought again as one of the Humanoid trainees came hurtling by while trying to complete an obstacle course in the shortest amount of time! Would Red Stinger ever remember to ask Slate about his sudden strength? Only the Winds of Destiny knew for sure!

While the tough extra training of the group by Red Stinger and his aides was going on, Slate pulled a "few strings" to accomplish something else! He used the time to make a quick trip home for a very special meeting with his family! On top of the very familiar mesa, he was picked up by a very familiar hypersonic VTOL U-4 to visit Dixie in Cleburne Memorial Hospital! His beloved wife had just given birth to twins; and he also wanted to visit with his six other children of varying ages; who were being cared for by their grandparents in a nearby Cleburne suburb!

CHAPTER 30

And so it came to pass that while on patrol one hot Monday morning, Police Sergeant Barney Drum; while out in the town checking the performance of several new police officers while they were working in their assigned areas; was very surprised when Police Chief Monday personally radioed him and told him not to be surprised if he saw a jet plane flying extremely low over Cleburne; the Federal Aviation Agency and Homeland Security had both cleared the flight; and he had already relayed the information to the Cleburne Airport tower!

Chief Monday had been very surprised when literally minutes before, he had got an order directly from Homeland Security to allow a secret United States Aerospace Force VTOL to land in a few minutes at the local airport! The chief was also told that the Federal Aviation Agency had cleared the flight "on orders from above", and the airplane should ask the tower for permission to land in just a few minutes! In addition, all police officers were to give all required assistance to all passengers who would disembark; with no questions asked! The chief immediately gave Barney orders to go to the airport ASAP in order to meet the airplane and transport any of the embarking passengers anywhere they wanted to go; literally anywhere between Cleburne and the Moon! Drum was also ordered to stay with the passengers and be their taxi until they left Cleburne; probably within a week.

After looking both ways up and down the street, the policeman immediately accomplished one of his famous "two wheel" U-turns with his patrol car rising up on one side and got to the airport as fast as he could; with his red lights flashing and his siren on full! A few minutes after he reached the airport, Barney was very surprised when a strange-looking unfamiliar airplane, a design that he had never seen in any of the many aviation magazines that he avidly read; suddenly came down out of the sky vertically at very high speed! It looked like one of the "lifting body" research planes of the 1960s; with several major differences! The eerie wingless airplane, which looked like an ovaloid spacecraft out of the "Star Conflict" movies; stopped suddenly about five hundred feet up; directly over the Cleburne airport runway, and its pilot asked the airport tower for permission to land using the correct frequency; which was immediately granted! The craft looked like a jet or rocket lifting body with literally no protruding wings; and no air intakes for jet engines and no engine exhaust ports! The spooky craft then proceeded to very slowly vertically land next to the airport terminal; <u>without kicking up any clouds of debris from its jet or rocket exhaust; and all the while being totally silent!</u> With no noise or blowing dust when it landed, the patrolman could not figure out how the strange craft was propelled; except by remembering one of the plots of a "Stranger Still Zone" episode where an alien UFO using a so-called "antigravity drive" came down silently and kidnapped the hero of the story!

#IS THAT AN ALIEN SPACECRAFT?!?! NAH, NO WAY; I HOPE!! BUT THEN, MAYBE IT'S ONE OF OURS; USING 'ROSWELL CRASH SITE TECHNOLOGY'!!# Barney thought.

After contemplating for a moment, the patrolman started making a few educated guesses. *#Coming down vertically like it is, that unknown craft can only be using antigravity for propulsion, just like on the sci-fi television episodes; since it does not have any air intakes or exhaust ports for jet engines! That's literally the only way it could land vertically without stirring up any debris or producing any sound of downward jet thrust! A weak ion drive, like those used on spacecraft, would not produce enough thrust enable the craft to land! Mmmmmmmmmmm . . . . that craft looks so advanced; I wonder if an alien being will disembark?!?!? Naaah! Probably not!!#*

But the answer to that amazing question quickly exited from the side of the mystery craft! Barney was very surprised when a familiar person; that he had known quite well in the past and hadn't seen in seven or eight years; quickly exited from a doorway which suddenly opened in the side of the black aircraft; carrying only one small suitcase! The tall man dressed in a military uniform walked very fast from the craft's open hatch to Barney's police car. Slate shook hands with his old friend and immediately asked to be taken to the Cleburne Memorial Hospital! On the way to the hospital, the two former classmates of Cleburne High School reminisced; while Barney got him there as fast as he could; using the police technique that he loved to use; weaving in and out of traffic; with all his red lights flashing; his emergency "hooter" howling; and his regular siren blaring! Sergeant Drum got Slate to the hospital safely and following orders from the chief; waited outside to take him anywhere he wanted to go.

After Slate had a short, very personal, and tender meeting with his wife and the newborn twins; Barney dropped his friend off at his house; where his other six children and his parents were waiting. As the uniformed man left the police car, the two old friends again shook hands and vowed to meet again at the next Cleburne High School alumni meeting; if not sooner. Barney told Slate to call him on his cell phone, day or night; anytime he needed a ride; until his leave was over and he left Cleburne!

The veteran warrior made full use of his leave time; visiting Dixie and the twins every day; until they were dismissed from the hospital on Thursday afternoon. He also stayed up late every day; listening to; laughing with; and talking to each of his children; until it was so late that they had to go to bed; so that they would get enough rest to be able to go to school the next day.

The rest of the visit to Cleburne literally zipped by and it seemed only a few hours later that it was Friday evening and his leave was about over! Slate was dropped off at the airport by his parents; his dad was driving the family "bus", which could hold ten passengers; and Barney's police car held the rest! After hugging and kissing all his kids; his parents; and his beloved Dixie last; the entire "Steele Mob" cheered and waved as their Dad; their Son; and their beloved husband; was picked up at the airport's helipad; situated on top of the main building; by a "plain old" U-4, instead of the ultra-secret "U-5 Stardust" which had been made with the help of Imperial technology; and had immediately returned to military duty on the opposite side of the Earth after it had dropped Slate off at the Cleburne airport on Monday. Unknown to his loving family, their loved one was taken directly back to a certain mesa in the middle of a very hot and dry area in order for him to face his next Moment of Destiny!

After this brief period of leave from his men; the secret files of the Earth Aerospace Force record that General Samuel Steele returned to lead the men and women of "Team 116" to their historic first mission on Mars; (but not their last!); the ultra-secret details of which will be recorded forever in the permanent Annals of the Imperial Seers! After this historic secret mission, the members of "Team 116" felt that they needed a new; unique name; and so by a unanimous vote, they asked to be given the new title and be called "A+ Team"; a part of "The Unit"! The actual name given to this highly-talented group of commandos can be found by viewing secret file #336-274-219; at the Earthian Space Force building; (which is only available for viewing by personnel with the required very high security clearance, and also having the correct position on the Main Galactic Time Line!)

Following Imperial Regulations, this top-secret information will be protected from destruction well beyond the time the last sun flickers out in the Cosmic All; being stored several hundred miles below the surface of Empire Prime in bomb-proof and transpose-proof bunkers, and recorded on document material with an "Eternity Paper Rating". Any Imperial Seer with the necessary seniority and security rating, and residing on the proper position on the Main Galactic Time Line, may journey to Empire Prime to view the records of Eli Wagstaff at any time, using the standard Seer mental techniques to access the Magi files deep under the surface of the Capital Planet.

The Destinies of Red Stinger and Slate Steele, two very different life forms, (i.e., how they each lived their lives "Well", and in the future both would/will be designated as an official "Time Winner", and how, and when, or **IF;** they each died "Heroically" on a lonely battlefield; or somehow were missing during a mission to the far reaches of the Great Dark; or simply slipped away to the next level of existence peacefully with their loved ones gathered around them); can be researched at any library on Empire Prime or any well-equipped library on any of the planets and empires who are members of ICOPE! The future heroic accomplishments of these two amazing sentient beings; as each made their "mark" on the Galactic Time Line as warriors, statesmen, family men, and diplomats, are worth reading about! They each stand individually as a worthy example for young Humanoids, Snakoids, Insectoids, and Reptiloids; over the standard "Coming of Age" time of 200 years, to emulate! (Imperial Editor's Note: Admiral Red Stinger did eventually remember to ask General Steele the reason his shoulder was so hard that it caused damage to his scales when he slapped him on the back! He received a very satisfactory answer; as well as a demonstration of General Steele's new secret shapeshifting powers!)

For some Seers residing near or far from this present position on the "Time Line", each of the individual Time Lines on the Main Galactic Time Line of Red Stinger, Elijah Wagstaff, or Slate Steele, may be very faint or totally dark; for the simple reason that the warrior, diplomat, statesman, or family being; may not have accomplished certain heroic deeds or important accomplishments in relation to your position on the Main Galactic Time Line; yet. In other words, if the position of the seeker of knowledge on the Galactic Time Line is before the position on the Time Line where the deeds of the valiant person were accomplished, for all but the most powerful Magi; a vision of the time lines mentioned is impossible at that time, but may be visualized after the deeds are accomplished!

AFTERWORD

But as a permanent resident of a Time Position far, far in the "Future" from this instant in "Time", I, Seer Rondoe Kanne, have read the above Imperial document and I can attest and affirm that all of the amazing deeds written in the previous historical record, and all the information about them written in the official permanent documents of the Imperial Mage which are sealed in the vaults of the Seers deep under the surface of Empire Prime will; and/or have occurred; exactly as they are recorded!

= * = * = * = * = * = * = * = * = * =

THESE HEROIC FANTASTIC AND UNBELIEVABLE DEEDS WHICH HAVE BEEN RECORDED ON THE ABOVE IMPERIAL SEER DOCUMENT WILL OCCUR, IN "TIME", AND ON THE PROPER HISTORICAL SCHEDULE AND IF NOT YET VISIBLE TO ANY SEER OR GOVERNMENT OFFICIAL; ALL ANY SEEKER OF KNOWLEDGE HAS TO DO FOR THEIR REQUIRED INFORMATION IS – WAIT-WAIT AND BE VERY, VERY PATIENT UNTIL YOU REACH THE CORRECT POSTION ON THE MAIN GALACTIC TIME LINE TO ALLOW THEIR VIEWING!

WARNING!: SOME SEEKERS OF INFORMATION MAY HAVE TO WAIT UP TO SEVERAL THOUSAND YEARS FROM YOUR POSITION IN "TIME" UNTIL THE HEROIC DEEDS YOU ARE SEEKING INFORMATION ABOUT HAVE BEEN RECORDED ON THE MAIN GALACTIC TIME LINE! DO NOT ATTEMPT TO USE ANY MAGI OR "TRECIAN WITCH OR WARLOCK" TO FIND OUT THE INFORMATION ABOUT THE SPECIFIC HEROIC DEED YOU ARE SEEKING BEFORE IT HAS ACTUALLY BEEN ACCOMPLISHED!! THE BREAKING OF IMPERIAL TIME LAWS CAN CAUSE THE MAIN GALACTIC TIME STREAM OR ANY OTHER AUXILIARY TIME STREAM TO DOUBLE BACK, TO FRACTURE, TO PRODUCE TIME PARADOXES, OR TO SPLIT INTO TWO OR MORE PERMANENT ALMOST-IDENTICAL TIME LINES!

APPENDIX I

The Controversial Winds of Destiny!

The subject of the so-called "Winds of Destiny" tend to be quite controversial throughout the Empire to those members of the Reptiloid, Insectoid, Snakoid, and Humanoid species who only possess the normal common mental powers of their species and do not have the extremely rare ability to sense their powerful presence! But the mentally powerful beings from four of the five major species of beings making up the legally-constituted group of mentally trained counselors to the Emperor known as the "Imperial Seers", or the "Imperial Magi"; know that the fabled Winds of Destiny do exist because the Magi can sense their presence all over the Cosmic All! In fact, these eerie ultra-small; yet extremely powerful energy beings have secretly been a subject for intense study by the Empire's Imperial Magi for hundreds of thousands of years! (Only four of the five major sentient being species are members of the Imperial Seers because for some reason, no Colloid Cloud being, each of which are made up of thousands of "motes of energy" floating together; when they have been formally invited to join, has ever agreed to become a member of the elite Magi.)

Even after diligent research by an ordinary Citizen of the Empire, the low-level, ordinary, and non-secret archives and the research computers of the Mages accessible to them do not contain very much in the way of "concrete information" about the controversial "Winds of Destiny" for the "normal" Imperial population! The information accessible to "normal beings", and compiled and written by "ordinary beings"; without any extra mental or physical powers; apparently only contains lies, hearsay, fables, and second-hand quotes of other regular media sources! All accurate and "medium level and above" information about the Winds of Destiny can only be compiled and printed on the pages of the Official Annals of the Imperial Seers; which are eternally stored in the Archives of the Empire's Magi in an armored installation buried deep down under the surface of the Capital Planet! These top-secret records are only accessible by Royal Seers using their mental power to transpose for short to moderate distances directly into the headquarters of the Imperial Seers, which also exists far below the surface of Empire Prime! These documents are always labeled and stamped on every page with the following: "Ultra-Top Secret – **NOT TO BE DEVULGED TO ANYONE WITH A SECURITY RANKING OF LESS THAN FIVE STARS OR LESS THAN THREE HUNDRED IMPERIAL YEARS OF SENIORITY**"!

But to the Empire's Mages with the required seniority and Imperial Security Clearance; in these secret installations, which as previously mentioned, are buried several hundred miles below Empire Prime's surface; there is a lot of ultra-top-secret information only available to them about the strange and very important energy beings! To the mental facilities of the Imperial Seers, the Winds of Destiny are not a fable; they exist; and it can be proven that they exist; no matter what misinformation the Magi continue to tell to the rest of the Imperial Citizens, (for Ultra-Secret reasons of their own!)

To the powerful mind senses of the upper echelon of Imperial "Seers", the extremely tiny wisps of sub-atomic energy are very helpful in sensing literally "second-hand" when extremely important events are happening or about to happen anywhere in the physical Universe! From the very first instance in which they were detected by the first group of Seers investigating and training their mental powers over five hundred thousand years ago, it has always seemed that the Winds somehow and someway can detect "Galaxy Important Events" before and as they are happening; and then "surge" toward and around the Event as it is happening! Why? The Imperial Seers have never been able to find out!

The answer to the question of where the Winds go to after they have surged through the location of an important event is also not known! In addition, even though the answer to the question of how the legendary Winds can swiftly detect and instantly rate the importance of literally trillions of "events" that are happening across the entire Cosmic All has been researched for many millennia, the answer to that perplexing question is still unknown to the Imperial Magi even today! Why the ultra-tiny energy beings want to bring attention to such important "Anchor Events" by their streaming to the immediate area of each important event, and the effect the Winds have on the Important Events occurring is also unknown!

Perhaps someday, on some planet in the Universe, some sentient being besides the for-hire mercenary who goes by the name of "Condor Mac Murphy" will be able to somehow be persuaded to communicate with the Winds and find out the answer to these perplexing questions; documented in "The

SWAP Team"! (The previously mentioned Humanoid being, one of whose names is supposedly "Mac Murphy", absolutely refuses to discuss the Winds with anyone; even his Dad, who is still the Captain who commands a civilian passenger liner on routes in and out of Empire Prime!) When contacted several times through the centuries, the mercenary known as Condor Mac Murphy would not even talk to a group of Imperial Seers who tried to have a covert meeting with him "off the official and unofficial record" to obtain information about the Winds! (It is also very strange that the Imperial Seers will not disclose just how they learned of Mr. Mac Murphy's peculiar and unique power to communicate with the Winds of Destiny; and what he did actually tell them during the covert meeting!)

Until the instant that the mercenary leader, or some other sentient being with the peculiar power to communicate with the Winds, is willing to "come clean" and discuss what they know "on or off the record" with an Imperial Seer, the tedious and largely unproductive research on the eerie Winds of Destiny by the Empire's Magi will have to continue to be at a standstill or at the very most, at a very slow pace! (Since there has been absolutely no new information on the Winds for several hundred thousand years, it probably means there will be no new information for literally the "foreseeable future"!)

= * = * = * = * = * = * = * = * = * =

The previous document on the Winds of Destiny was added at the request of Seer Rondoe Kanne to help Imperial readers with the proper security clearance who are interested in the famed "Winds

of Destiny" and want to further understand and ponder just what they are; what they do; and WHY. Perhaps the previous documentary of several surging episodes of the Winds of Destiny will help the investigations of any Royal Seer with the proper credentials, mental standing, and seniority. Any Magi with new information on the Winds of Destiny may use telepathy or electronic means to contact the main headquarters of the Imperial Seers on Empire Prime 28/8, using the standard protocol.

Imperial Publisher's Note
for The Cy-Soldier

The following document is covered under the very strict Imperial Information Laws of the Interstellar Condominium of Planets and Empires, (ICOPE), concerning any stored or transmitted telepathic or oral; photographic; and/or written data in any language in the Imperial Sphere of Influence, that could be construed as being insulting and/or dangerous to any member of all the Commanding Officers and/or Enlisted Persons of the Imperial Royal Navy of the Interstellar Condominium of Planets and Empires; and/or any member or members up to being twice-removed from the Imperial Royal Line! Also covered is any previously-mentioned mental; printed out; and/or published data that contains sensitive scientific information that could be very dangerous and extremely disruptive to the Main Trunk of the Main Galactic Time Line; or another Auxiliary Time Line; that could influence Destiny of the Empire! Any such disruption could cause the Principal Trunk line of the Main Galactic Time Stream to split into two or more identical Main Galactic Time Streams; thereby creating havoc and total chaos! According to delicate scientific studies carefully researched through the long millennia of the Empire's existence by the Imperial Magi; it could also create "Time Paradoxes"; and/or "Alternate Realities"; and/or "Alternate Timelines"! The haphazard creation of any of these "rival realities" would eventually completely destroy or totally shred the Main Galactic Time Stream; thus totally destroying and making irrelevant the present Major Galactic Time stream that we live on; which is what we call "Reality"! The previously mentioned disastrous results of the publication or mental projection of such information listed above in the past is the reason for the Imperial Law; hence the very harsh punishments listed below!

To quote the Official Expert on proper document procedure, Seer Ronka Wad-Dee, appointed Galactic Time Stream Watcher for Empire Prime 563 Imperial years ago by the reigning Emperor of a Million-Million Worlds; and at the present time; the Seer that is the Ultimate Source for legal help and advice on the use and public transmitting of "dangerous" and/or "malicious" information about any Royal Line participant or any publication that could change any Time Line: **"Failure to follow the accepted legal protocol concerning articles extremely insulting to the Emperor; Empress; or any other member or "secondary member" of the Royal Line; and/or the publication in any form of material that could be very dangerous to the safety of the Empire; will result in immediate and severe prosecution to the fullest extent under such laws by a Compu-Judge or a duly constituted Imperial City Court Judge or any City Court Judge on Empire Prime; or on any planet in the Empire's Sphere of Influence! The findings of the presiding Compu-Judge or Court Judge will then immediately be simultaneously mentally or electronically transmitted to both the guilty defendant and the closest Imperial Police Officers or Interstellar Marshal; to allow immediate incarceration and/or punishment of the blameworthy perpetrator! Depending on the severity of the crime, punishment can consist of any or all of the following: Automatic loss of**

Imperial Citizenship and/or lifetime banishment to one of the Imperial Prison Planets or a primitive planet outside the Imperial Sphere-of-Influence; with all memories of the Empire erased! Lifetime incarceration of the convicted felon on one of the Imperial Prison Planets which requires working 20-hour days; and getting one meal a day; for the rest of each perpetrator's very short physical life! The sentence may also include total mental erasure and reprogramming for manual labor the rest of the being's short life span; depending on the severity of the crime!"

As always, in any Certified Imperial or private document or any mental projection that is allowed to be published and/or publically transmitted by the Imperial Ministry of Information, any allowing of the mention of the very controversial mythical "Winds of Destiny"; "Trecian Witches"; "Trecian Warlocks"; "Haf-Cott beings"; "Trankor Beings"; "Wer-Women", or "Wer-Men"; in any non-fiction or fiction manuscript; in any mental book; or in any media public broadcast; does not mean official acceptance of their possible existence by Imperial media authorities and/or Imperial scientists officially in charge of sentient being assessment and type placement! Searching of the Official Imperial List of Sentient Beings that are found on planets in the Cosmic All, will reveal the fact that "Trecian Witches"; "Trecian Warlocks"; "Trankor Beings"; or "Wer-Men" and "Wer-Women" are not on the <u>official list</u> of sentient beings that have been discovered and cataloged by Imperial scientists during the history of the entire Royal Empire; also known as the Interstellar Condominium of Planets and Empires, or ICOPE! Therefore such use of the fictitious terms mentioned above may merely indicate the author's own misguided and totally wrong opinion about their existence! Also; writing or projecting stories about such fabricated terms including the "Winds of Destiny"; (since they are supposed to be fantastic subatomic energy beings with extraordinary mental powers too small to see); is simply an example of the common technique of fiction, (out of several dozen taught at the Imperial Writing School on Empire Prime); which uses weird and bizarre terms to describe incredible creatures which are intended to hold the visual reader's or the oral listener's attention!

So any reader of visual or telepathic literature mentioning the fictitious terms listed above is cautioned by Imperial Information Officials; and the Imperial scientists whose job is to study "being types"; to not believe such fictional information and to merely read or telepathically absorb the mental projection of such literature and accept it as merely fiction to read and enjoy; and not actual fact!

If any reader of this document has any question concerning anything in its contents; you may sent your question to the Imperial Seers on Empire Prime using the manual printing; fax; mental; or any other communications equipment at your local Imperial Library; or the Emperor's Royal Library on Empire Prime.

Books, Novellas, and Stories

**by John R. Carden available for purchase,
now or in the future, either in
book stores or online:**

1. The Seasons of Space – Out of Print
2. Three Time Winners!
3. Space, Time, and the Empire!
4. Jeopardy in the Empire!
5. Samson Blair the Time Marshal
6. Two Time Winners (And a Seer)!
7. One Time Winner! The Empress Emeritus Zinabar!
8. Cleonardo the Trecian Witch
9. The Trecian Witch and the Imperial Admiral
10. The Trecian Witch and Warlock – In Preparation
11. The Cy-Soldier!
12. Two Warrior Time Winners!
13. The Adventures of Captain Gallant! - In Preparation
14. The Empa! - Not published yet
15. Rex and Regina! - In preparation
16. The Com Bats from Sand Dari! – In Preparation
17. The Filly from Sand Dari! - In preparation
18. The SWAP Team! (Special Weapons and Powers! IP
19. The Forest Foundling - In preparation
20. The Blue Road to Infinity - In preparation
21. The Invincible Fleet - Not published yet
22. The Four - In preparation
23. The 300 Earthians - In preparation
24. The Old Spaceship - Not published yet

25. **Tappan Sunset - In preparation**
26. **Strella McCoy - In preparation**
27. **The Prince from ICOPE - In preparation**
28. **The Reptiloid and the Child - In preparation**
29. **Joseph and Cleopatra - In preparation**
30. **The Visitor - In preparation**
31. **Old Blood - In preparation**
32. **Tales of Earth! – In preparation**
33. **Tales of the ICOPE! – In preparation**
34. **Tales of the Empire! – In preparation**

**Many other books, novellas,
and short stories are being worked on!**

So long for now, and as they say in the 50th:

"Be there! Aloha!!"

www.ingramcontent.com/pod-product-compliance
Lightning Source LLC
Chambersburg PA
CBHW030118010826
48973CB00002B/311